Teresa's Tale

Michael Wright

This is a work of fiction. All characters, events, organizations, and portrayed in this novel are products of the author's imagination or are used fictitiously.

All Bible quotes come from the KJV version of the Bible.

Acknowledgement

I thank Mrs. Dora Sorrel for the extensive interviews she granted to me about her experience as an undocumented migrant who rode the Mexican freight train, known as the beast, which brought her to the United States from the Republic of Honduras.

My thanks Reverend Ana Andújar Vélez. As a pastor, she gave me valuable advice on the translation of my novel into Spanish, a language which is not my mother tongue. Even more important, I received recommendations from a pastor who not only knows the importance of good writing, and how to write clearly, she also advised me on the theological validity of what certain characters express in the novel.

My thanks to Ms. Jill Braun who helped me brainstorm the initial outline for the novel, which became the basis for many chapter headings.

I am also grateful to Ms. Sandra Hall and Ms. Connie Lemon for their valuable feedback and suggestions to improve the novel's manuscript prior to publication.

I especially thank Mr. Tom Laputka, who read the manuscript four times and provided significantly more feedback and suggestions than anybody else. The novel is a much more compelling story because of his recommendations

Life in the Barrio

Señorita Teresa Amador sat barefooted in front of the shack she called home in one of the poorest *barrios* (neighborhoods) in Tegucigalpa, the capital city of Honduras. Many there lived on less than one dollar per day. One of the poorest countries in the Western Hemisphere, two-thirds of this Central American nation's citizens live in poverty. Honduras is also among the most violent countries in the world.

Teresa sat on a stool made from the top of a metal barrel with three cement blocks to support it. A teetering awning sheltered Teresa from the rain shower that was now ending. The rain increased the intense humidity and created very muggy conditions.

One of the many stray mongrel dogs in the neighborhood sat beside her. Teresa petted the hungry, skeletal animal, and the dog's wagging tail expressed happy exuberance. When Teresa stopped, the dog nudged her, begging for more of her tender touch. Because of the dog's frequent visits, Teresa named her Manchita, a Spanish word, which alluded to the dog's different patches of color. Manchita showed up to seek shelter during the almost daily rain showers. So, she was almost always wet when she came, which exacerbated the dog's foul, funky stink.

At 8:30 in the morning, the temperature was 85 degrees. The 100 percent humidity made it feel like the mid-90s. Cumulus clouds, like ice-cream castles, were already climbing higher into the sky, with the threat of more heavy downpours in the afternoon, typical of Honduran weather in September. As Teresa sat, she shaved the bark off some yuca, a potato-like root vegetable, which would be the day's only meal her family would eat later in the morning. Because of the hot and humid September weather, this minor physical labor bathed her in sweat, and she kept a rag beside her to wipe the sweat from her brow from time to time.

Teresa and her family tolerated, as did their neighbors, the putrid stench emanating from the garbage in the muddy dirt road, which crushed the combined pleasant scents of wood-burning fires and the enticing aroma of cheap cuts of roasting meats such as *chicharrones* (pork rinds), *mondongo* (tripe), and *patitas* (pigs' feet). However, on some occasions, these enticing aromas wafted above the usual stench to whet the appetites of the *barrio's* hungry, impoverished residents.

Teresa could hear salsa, merengue, and mariachi music that emanated from neighbors' competing radios, which also competed with the frequent blaring sounds of car horns. The loud rumble from the un-muffled exhaust of large second-hand school buses, used for public transportation, and which dwarfed the shack where Teresa and her family lived, contributed to a clashing orchestra of torment. This rumble intensified like a misplaced musical crescendo when the bus drivers revved their diesel engines to change gears. Occasional ear-splitting blasts from the bus' air horns drowned out all other sounds to interrupt this maddening orchestra with a rude, crass, solo performance. The bus' diesel fumes were only a minimal improvement over the stench from the garbage, but nasty nevertheless. Street vendors pushed their colorful but dilapidated carts up and down the road. Their strident voices added a raucous, bizarre choral element to the chaotic orchestra as they yelled out what they were selling: Plantains, yuca, bananas, watermelons, snow cones, brooms, fish.

Aside from the colorful street carts, the only color in the *barrio* came from the buses, painted in red, white, and blue and the vibrant green color of palm trees, citrus trees, and other tropical plants. Otherwise, the unpainted, dingy walls of the shacks contributed no color.

Teresa sang along with the mariachi music on one of the neighbor's radios, and all of a sudden, Manchita caught her attention when the dog's ears shot up. The dog raised her head and produced a low, guttural growl.

Enrique, a member of the *Mara Salvatrucha* gang, approached Teresa. She had known Enrique and his family for her whole life. Whereas before he was a well-liked young man, now, with his hands, arms, and face covered with tattoos, he had become a cruel, disdained gang member. *Mara Salvatrucha* was one of the two main gangs which dominated the area. The other rival gang, whose turf was down the street and visible from Teresa's shack, was *Barrio* 18. There was a strip of land, deemed to be neutral territory, which separated each gang's turf.

These gangs' violence and extortion produced widespread fear, which reigned throughout the *barrio*. The *Mara Salvatrucha* gang, infamous for its cruelty, is also known as MS-13. The gang originated in Los Angeles, California, among immigrants from El Salvador. After deportations from the United States back to El Salvador, gang membership spread out into Honduras and other Central American countries. The *Barrio* 18 gang has similar origins in Los Angeles.

Enrique said with a scowl on his face and a threatening voice, "I wanna see your brother."

The dog's growl grew more threatening, and she showed her fangs.

Teresa looked up from her work and tried to hide the disdain she felt for gang members as she replied, "My brother's not here."

Enrique demanded, "Tell me where he's at. I wanna talk to him."

"Why don't you leave him alone, Enrique? He doesn't want to join any gangs."

"Oh! Maybe you and I should go for a walk."

Teresa stuck her nose up, raised her upper lip as if she smelled a foul odor, and looked down at him. "And why would I wanna do that?"

"Because I want you to." And Enrique grabbed her arm.

The dog detonated a deep-throated, vicious growl and lunged to attack him. Enrique wrestled with the dog and fell to the ground. Manchita sunk her teeth into his arm. He shrieked with pain, and his eyes widened in alarm.

Enrique cried out, "¡*Carajo*! (Spanish cuss word) Get her off me! Get her off me!"

Teresa clapped her hands three times and shouted, "Manchita," and the dog freed Enrique's arm. But Manchita continued to show her vicious fangs, crouched in an attack position, and growled, ready to go after Enrique again.

Enrique, his arm bleeding, looked at Teresa and said with a snarly voice, "You'll be sorry for this."

Teresa looked down at him, sneered with contempt, and said, "You grabbed my arm, and the dog protected me. I got the dog to stop, and you now threaten me? What kind of animal are you?"

Enrique didn't reply to her question, but said with a threatening tone, "You tell your brother I'm looking for him."

"Why don't you leave us alone? Enrique, I know you. Do you even like being a part of your gang?"

Enrique looked at the ground. Her last question produced a look of hopelessness on his face. Teresa soaked the rag she had beside her in a puddle of water and offered it to him for his bleeding arm. Surprised by Teresa's act of kindness, Enrique looked up at her like an abused child. He wrapped the rag around his arm, said nothing more, got up, and walked away.

Shaken from this confrontation, it took some time before her trembling subsided. She feared the gang would continue to harass her brother, José. A happy-go-lucky teenager, José worked to help support his family, liked to play soccer, and was popular with the girls. Evil was as foreign to his nature as it is to a songbird. He had no desire whatsoever to join any gang.

Teresa went into the dark shack, which was her family's home. The home had no electricity and no running water. Kerosene lanterns were their only source of light. They owned a battery-operated transistor radio, which entertained them with music and news. On occasions, the radio station transmitted messages from relatives to their family members in the *barrio*.

The shack consisted of a wooden frame with cardboard walls, a few rough boards, and a corrugated tin roof. Water stains on the walls revealed that the roof leaked. The family had to replace the cardboard with some frequency. When possible, they acquired more boards to replace the cardboard walls.

Teresa lived in the shack with her parents and two brothers, José, age 18, and Pepe, age 6. Like most families in this *barrio*, they were malnourished, underweight, and somewhat stunted in their growth – making them shorter than average. Sheets, hanging from the ceiling, divided the shack's interior into three rooms. On one wall was a framed, black and white, water-stained photograph of Susana and Pedro, Teresa's parents, taken on their wedding day. A rickety table with four chairs was the only furniture. On the table, a glass contained wild crimson-colored flowers, which Teresa picked earlier in the morning – the single notable color in the room.

Hammocks hung from the shack's wooden frame, where Teresa's parents slept at night. Teresa and her two brothers slept on ragged rugs, which covered the dirt floor. The shack occupied a precarious location on the bank of a small stream, which flowed behind the shack and was their water source for bathing and washing clothes. The shack's floor was not level and slanted downward toward the stream. Drinking water came from a common well. They shared an outhouse with their two neighbors, and they cooked their meals on a wood-burning stove behind the shack.

A tea kettle whistled, and Teresa took it from the wood-burning stove and proceeded to make a pitcher of lemonade. Earlier, Teresa picked the lemons from the lemon tree beside the family's shack. Boiling the water was necessary because the well water was not potable.

Their primary income source came from the sale of burritos, which all family members, except Pepe, sold in the *barrio's* small commercial area, deemed to be neutral territory by the gangs. The burritos consisted of two corn tortillas, rice and beans, pork sausage, plantain slices, a boiled egg, and cheese. They wrapped the burritos in banana leaves and carried them on large platters, which they balanced on their heads. Susana, Teresa's mother, walked with a limp, which made her wobble from side to side when she walked. The platter balanced on her head wobbled with her, but she rarely had to grab the platter to keep it from falling.

A chorus of roosters, which sounded off throughout the *barrio*, woke the family up at four o'clock every morning and prompted them to prepare the burritos for the day's business. They made sales until about ten o'clock in the morning. Somebody had to be available to protect their home at all times, and it was Teresa's turn to watch over it today.

Pedro, Teresa's father, worked construction projects on occasions, which supplemented their income and provided money to purchase more boards to replace their shack's cardboard walls. They saved some of this money for the diabetes medicine, which Susana, Teresa's mother, had to take. Pedro was a loving husband and father. Despite the lack of formal education, Teresa looked up to him and trusted his sage advice, which he freely gave. The lack of money was a frequent issue that prompted quarrels between Pedro and Susana, but they never went to bed angry. The love they had for each other was a source of much-needed security for their children.

~.~

Susana sold most of her burritos. At 9:30, appearing out of nowhere, three boys and two girls, about 12 to 15 years of age, surrounded her. One of the boys grabbed her from behind and held a knife to her ribs. Susana screamed, and bystanders approached to help her.

The boy with the knife shouted, "Stay away, or I'll cut her!"

One of the girls reached into Susana's bosom and stole the 75 lempiras she earned from her sales. Seventy-five lempiras is about 3

U.S. dollars. The other thieves grabbed the platter with the remaining burritos, and then all of them fled. The assault occurred in a matter of seconds.

Trembling, Susana returned home and cried out to Teresa, "I was robbed. They stole my burritos, my platter, and the money I earned."

Knowing how they had to pinch every Lempira, Teresa bit her lower lip, and tears welled up in her eyes. She hugged her mother and tried to console her. Still shaking, Susana sat down, and Teresa brought her a glass of the lemonade she made earlier. Looking at her mother's face, she saw a woman who looked much older than she was. Both felt the frustration of their inadequate efforts and unattainable means to move beyond their subsistence, hand-to-mouth existence.

Such robberies were too common.

Earnings from burrito sales provided barely enough money to put food on the table. Family income was about 2,500 lempiras per month, or 100 U.S. dollars. They were poor, but not the poorest of the poor. Their typical meals consisted of one or two of the following items: beans, corn tortillas, yuca, chayotes, chilies, or avocados, along with coffee. Meat was a rare treat. On days when they didn't sell all of their burritos, they shared them among family members, which was an occasional luxury. Today there was nothing to share and, so far, no money either.

It was 10:30 now, and both Pedro and José arrived and learned about the thieves who accosted Susana. Angry, Pedro could see the hurt in Susana's eyes. Pedro and José managed to sell all of their burritos. Pepe had gone with José. They all sat at the table together for their breakfast of boiled yuca, coffee, and lemonade.

As they finished their breakfast, blaring sirens startled them and increased in intensity when police cars arrived in their *barrio*. They went outside and watched with horror and dismay while police officers stuffed the muddy, headless body of their neighbors' son into a body bag – the victim of a gang attack. His only offense was to refuse gang membership. The boy's parents shrieked with despair, and Teresa's family tried in vain to console them. Another too frequent occurrence.

Teresa turned to her brother, José, and said, "Enrique came looking for you earlier today. You need to be careful."

José's face paled, and his heart skipped a beat when he heard this, and the family also shuddered when they heard the news.

Reflecting on Enrique's insidious efforts to recruit José to join their gang, and alarmed by the day's events, Pedro, with a worried look on his face, exclaimed, "José, I'm sure you know that gang membership would be something you would regret. As a family, we must watch out for each other and be alert to the possibility of gang threats at any time. We must always be ready to defend ourselves. Whenever possible, we must be ready to help our neighbors too. And we must recognize that we live with the constant danger of gang violence. There's nothing else we can do."

With disdain in his voice, José replied, "Don't worry, Papá. I don't ever want to join any gang."

After breakfast, Susana and Teresa washed the dishes in the stream behind their shack. Not much conversation occurred. The sight of the police stuffing the neighbor's dead son in a body bag was firmly etched in their minds. The thought of Enrique's earlier visit enraged Teresa, and she loathed the idea that, due to gang threats, José might get sucked into the deceptive trap of gang membership, despite his resistance to join.

With deep melancholy, Teresa contemplated her desperate situation and that of her family. She dreamed of studying to become a teacher or a nurse, but the cost for such education was well beyond her reach. Moreover, by age eleven, she was selling burritos to help her family earn a living. So, she didn't even finish elementary school. Her dream of becoming a teacher or a nurse was as elusive as a soap bubble bouncing down the stream behind her shack.

~.~

On Fridays, at five o'clock in the afternoon, Teresa went to the San Tomás Catholic Church, where she met Raúl. Six couples, including Raúl and Teresa, practiced three Honduran folkloric dances called la mazurka, el pereke, and el jarabe yoreño.

Before departing for the church, Teresa removed her ragged dress and put on the nicest second-hand red dress she owned. Looking at her image in a mirror that hung on the outside wall at the back of the shack, she brushed her neglected hair, which looked like the hair of an abandoned Barbie doll, tangled with other toys in a forgotten cardboard box. With her slender, feminine figure, her pretty face, and her light cinnamon-colored complexion, she looked beautiful after brushing out the tangles from her long, wavy black hair.

Teresa, like most Honduran women, was a mestiza, whose recent ancestors were of Spanish and indigenous descent. Looking at her reflection in the mirror, she put her hands on her hips and smiled as she thought, *I like the looks of this pretty woman looking back at me.* Barefooted most of the time, she put on her single pair of old shoes, which she only wore when she went downtown or to church.

Before the dance practice began, all couples put on their festive, traditional garments, which church members made for them. They wore these garments when they performed their dances. The women's broad skirts included two flounces, or wide ornamental strips of material gathered and hand-sewn on the skirt, accented by braided trimming in a zigzag pattern. They also wore blouses, embellished by embroidered designs, which matched the color of their skirts.

Teresa's skirt was a vivid cobalt blue. The skirt's flounces were white, trimmed with cobalt blue braiding. The men wore white shirts and trousers adorned in colors to match the women's dresses with whom they danced. The trousers included a cloth belt of the same color. Raúl was Teresa's steady dance partner.

This evening's practice concentrated on the jarabe yoreño dance, which was Teresa's favorite. The recorded dance music featured the joyous tropical sound of marimbas with rhythmic drums. Claves, which are two pieces of hardwood struck together, made a loud rhythmic sound, heard above all the other instruments.

The jarabe yoreño is a dazzling, flirtatious dance of colonial origin. The dance begins when the women, dancing backward, reject the men's advances, each shaking their head from side to side and waving their forefinger to say no. But soon, the women take the initiative in the dance, and the men frown and act as if they've lost interest. Then the women flirt until they convince the men to dance with them. Teresa liked flirting with Raúl, and she did it well. She spread her full skirt like a peacock spreads its feathers and shook it in an energetic, sensuous way. Rocking her shoulders from side to side, she looked at Raúl out of the corner of her eye and flashed a teasing, sassy smile at him. Raúl loved the way she teased him.

After they completed their practice, the church's priest, Father Santiago, announced there would soon be a countrywide competition to select the country's best folkloric dance group. He said, "I think our dance group is so good that I suggest we should enter the competition. What do you think?"

Teresa asked, "So, you think we're good enough to compete with every dance group in the country?"

"Not only do I think you're good enough to compete, I believe you could win the competition."

Leticia Santos, Teresa's best friend, rolled her eyes. "That'll be the day."

Father Santiago replied, "You underestimate your talent. Let's give it a try."

Encouraged, everybody looked at each other with glee, and Raúl said, "I'm in. Let's go for it."

Father Santiago said, "If nobody else has anything more to say, I'll submit our application."

After the practice, Raúl treated Teresa to ice cream at a nearby cafeteria. This weekly outing was the highlight of her spartan, subsistence life.

As they ate their ice cream, Raúl, who was not so impoverished as Teresa, commented, "I'm looking forward to the upcoming church festival. It's been a while since we performed our dances. And I'm very excited about the competition Father Santiago talked about."

Teresa licked her spoon to savor one final taste of her ice cream and replied with enthusiasm, "Me too. I can hardly wait for both events."

"How's your family?"

"Struggling to get by as usual. A gang member came by looking for my brother. They're trying to get him to join their gang, and some ruffians robbed my mamá earlier in the week."

Raúl touched Teresa's hand, looked into her eyes, nodded his head, and replied, "The *Barrio* 18 gang has bothered me too. You know, your brother needs to be careful."

"We know all right. That same day, my mother was robbed, and after we finished our day's meal, we watched while the police recovered the headless body of our neighbors' son. The gangs are getting more aggressive, and things are getting worse. I'm scared."

Raúl walked Teresa almost to her home. They could only be together in neutral territory. So, Teresa could not step inside the *Barrio* 18 turf, and Raúl could not step inside the *Mara Salvatrucha* turf. Both the church and the cafeteria were in neutral territory. Raúl returned to his home, located in *Barrio* 18 turf, right before the end of twilight.

The next morning, Teresa took her turn to sell burritos. After selling the last burrito, she went to the post office and picked up a letter from Susana's older sister, Norma, who immigrated to the United States some years ago. She lived in Los Angeles with her husband, Pablo. While they were undocumented, they nevertheless managed to buy a home, and Pablo worked as a truck driver. They had two adult children. Since they were born in the United States, both of their children were U.S. citizens, and both were married and had children of their own.

After reading the letter, Susana went to a nearby store and bought a phone card to call her sister. Their opportunities to talk were infrequent, and they savored such precious moments to talk to each other.

Susana commented, "We've suffered some serious problems with gangs in the last few months. A gang member killed our neighbors' son, and they found his decapitated body a few days ago. A gang member also approached Teresa, and he wanted to talk to José. Teresa refused to cooperate with him. They're trying to recruit José to join their gang.

The gang member gave Teresa a hard time as well. As if that wasn't enough, five teens assaulted me and robbed me."

"Susana, listen to me. We see news items on TV here in Los Angeles about the gang violence that's so commonplace there. We see how bad it is right in our living room. I think we should look at bringing Teresa, José, and Pepe up here."

Susana rolled her eyes. "I have no idea how much something like that would cost, but we could never afford such a trip."

"Well, we are family. Pablo and I have talked about this, and we can help you with the money. So, I think we should act soon. Why don't you start making plans? We love you. Please be safe. Give it some thought, and let me know when you're ready."

After they hung up, Susana felt some hope that her children could escape their desperate situation, but she shuttered with the thought of seeing her children leave home with the very real possibility that she may not ever see them again.

War Tax

On the following Saturday, Teresa and her family attended an early Mass at church. It was customary for the Saturday Mass to occur at seven o'clock in the evening. But today, the Mass occurred at four o'clock in the afternoon because the church sponsored a festival, which would begin after the Mass. A heavy rain shower, very typical of this part of the rainy season, drummed on the church's tin roof, which created a reverberating roar and made it difficult to hear what was going on during the Mass. By the time the Mass ended, the rain had stopped, but conditions were now sweltering and muggy.

Some men in the church had volunteered to roast a couple of pigs, which they began before sunrise. They took turns rotating the pigs on spits over two fire pits. A tent protected them from the sun and rain during the day. Church members now gathered around the tent. The men began carving up the roasted pigs, and the savory aroma of roast pork caressed everybody's noses and made mouths water.

As they dished out servings, each person received a portion of succulent pork and crunchy chicharrones – Spanish for pork rinds. All the women in the church brought potluck dishes. Options included plantain, corn on the cob, and yuca as well as watermelon, flan, and *tres leches* (three-milk cake – a type of sponge cake soaked with milk, evaporated milk, and condensed milk and topped with cinnamon.)

José stayed home to maintain a presence at their shack. So, Susana prepared a plate to take to him. After the meal, they all sang Happy Birthday to Teresa, who celebrated her 23rd birthday. Pedro and Susana hugged their daughter. Raúl, Teresa's dance partner, hugged her too, but not as passionately as he would if Mamá and Papá were not looking.

Teresa and Raúl joined with the church's folkloric dance group to perform their dances – the highlight of the evening's events. Each of the six dance couples wore their unique traditional costumes, which featured a different color for each couple: red, blue, green, orange, purple, and yellow. Teresa's costume blossomed with a vivid cobalt blue, and Raúl's white garment complemented her flamboyant dress with cobalt blue accents. All six partners looked like the figurines on a miniature carousel music box, dancing to the rhythm of lively Honduran folkloric music. The dance group's synchronized movements created a colorful, hypnotic, kaleidoscopic effect under the bright lights illuminating the outdoor dance area.

When they finished their performance, Pedro hugged Teresa again and said, "My daughter, I think you and Raúl were the best dancers in the group. I'm very proud of you."

Never able to get enough of her father's approval, Teresa's eyes teared up, and she smiled. "Gracias, Papá."

Afterward, Raúl took Teresa by the hand, and they ran to a secluded location on the church grounds, where they sneaked a tender kiss, where Mamá and Papá couldn't see them.

The men formed two teams for a soccer match, while the women's constant chatter competed with the large speakers, which blasted loud Latin American Music.

The church was deemed to be in neutral territory between the turfs of the *Mara Salvatrucha* and *Barrio* 18 gangs. So, friends, who could only visit each other on limited occasions because they lived in different gang turfs, treasured this opportunity to enjoy each other's company. This was the case for Teresa and her friend, Leticia.

Teresa asked, "So Leticia, what's new with you?"

Leticia arched her eyebrows up, shook her head, and replied, "Last week, three young women in our *barrio*, friends of mine, disappeared. Their families filed missing person reports with the police, but they haven't found any of the women. The police think they have become victims of human trafficking. They suspect the *Barrio* 18 gang sent them to Mexico, and I'm very worried about them. The rumor is that gangs have forced the women into prostitution. I'm afraid they might come after me too."

Shuddering at the thought that she could become such a human trafficking victim, and with an anxious look on her face, Teresa replied, "Not long ago, a gang member came looking for my brother. When I told him my brother wasn't at home, he grabbed me and wanted me to go with him. Lucky for me, Manchita, a stray dog that hangs around our shack, was lying by my side, and she attacked the gang member in my defense. He cried out for help, and I got the dog to stop. The gang member took off with his arm bleeding pretty bad."

"You were lucky to have the dog with you."

Teresa also told Leticia about the ruffians who robbed her mother.

~.~

While the festival was going on, a gang member banged on the door at the family's shack. José, Teresa's brother, trembled as he opened the door and came face-to-face with another tattooed gang member, who came to extort the weekly payments that the gang demanded, known as the war tax.

"I'm here to collect 100 lempiras," he said. (About 4 U.S. dollars)

"I can only give you 65 right now; that's all I have."

He grabbed José by his shirt and pulled him close to his face. The gang member's breath smelled of stale beer. "You better not be lying to me. I'll be back the first part of the week for the rest. Remember, *plata o plomo*." (money or bullets in English)

Gang members collected the war tax throughout the *barrio*. Many complained to the police, who did nothing because they received kickbacks from the gangs.

Within the week, the gang member returned, grabbed José in the street, and demanded 135 lempiras, 35 owed from the previous week, and 100 owed for the current week.

Just two weeks later, *Mara Salvatrucha* gang members caught *Barrio* 18 gang members, who invaded their turf and tried to collect war tax from residents. Gunfire thundered and echoed throughout the *barrio* where Teresa lived, and the sounds of sirens intensified from approaching police cars. Most of the residents peeped through cracks in their doors to see what was going on, with eyes frozen with fear, unable to look away no matter how much they wished to. Five gang members died from gunshot wounds – three from the *Mara Salvatrucha* gang and two from the *Barrio* 18 gang. Police arrested several gang members, but the residents knew police corruption would ensure the gang members would soon be back on the streets.

~.~

The upcoming dance competition was now approaching. Teresa and Raúl, with other members of their folkloric dance group, worked on polishing their dance presentations in preparation for their participation in the dance competition. In addition to their routine practices on Fridays, they also began practicing on Saturday afternoons.

One day Pedro, Teresa's father, heard a hard knock at the door. When he opened the door, he had to deal with another gang member, who demanded that week's war tax.

Pedro said, "It's been a bad week. We made very little money, and I spent what I had on my wife's medicine."

The gang member warned him, "I'll be back tomorrow, and you will pay me."

Pedro held his hands out in despair, "Tomorrow is too soon. I can't have it by then."

The gang member grabbed Pedro by his shirt and scowled with clenched teeth. "I said, I'll be back tomorrow."

Returning the next day with two other gang members, they again demanded payment. Pedro was alone in the shack. Petrified, his body grew tense, and, trembling, he stuttered, "I'm sorry. I don't have any money at all right now. Please give me some more time."

Angered, they dragged him out into the street and beat him up. Two held him while the other kicked him in the groin and punched him in the face and stomach several times. The blows knocked him out, and they left him bleeding and lying in the muddy street. Neighbors called the police, but the gang members fled by the time they arrived. The neighbors helped Pedro into his shack and provided what first aid they could.

After the day's burrito sales, Teresa arrived with Susana, her mother, and they were shocked to find Pedro, holding his head in his hands, sitting on the floor in their shack. His clothes were soiled and bloody; his shirt was torn. They rushed to his side, and he lifted his head, which revealed his blood-stained, swollen face. One eye was swollen shut. He looked up at them with rage and despair.

Susana cried out, "Oh my God! What happened?"

Pedro told them the gory details. Teresa and Susana cleaned and bandaged his wounds, but it would take a few days for the swelling of his disfigured face to decrease.

As the family ate unsold burritos for a rare dinner together, they listened with despair and dismay to a news commentator on the radio who said:

> *Last night, eighteen teenagers throughout the capital were killed by gang members. Honduras owns the shameful distinction of having the highest murder rate in the world, and gang violence is the primary culprit. It is common for Hondurans to wake up and find grotesque, mutilated bodies in the streets where they live. Many Hondurans are awakened from their night's sleep because of gunfights and sirens, which are a frequent menace in their barrios. Our people live with the ever-present fear of extortion as gang members come to collect the "war tax."*

These words conjured up in the minds of the Amador family the decapitated body of their neighbor's son, the recent gunfight in their *barrio*, and the beating Pedro was now recovering from because he couldn't pay the war tax.

Susana arched her eyebrows upward and reached over to turn off the broadcast, but Pedro stopped her. Nodding with a quivering lip, he said, "I want to hear what this commentator has to say."

Gang members recruit teenage boys to join their gangs, and they kidnap young women and force them into prostitution, with the threat of death if they refuse. Nevertheless, gang membership is attractive to many because gang activities pay better than many legitimate jobs, if such jobs are even available. But gang membership is an egregious trap, and most members must pay with their lives if they try to escape.

Hearing this, tears came to Teresa's eyes as she recalled the words of Leticia, her best friend, who spoke of the women in her *barrio* who disappeared and the terrifying fear that they may be selling their bodies against their will as prostitutes. In her mind, it was clear that her family was an easy target for these ruthless gangs, and they lived with this ever-present threat.

Gang rape is common, and most rape victims do not survive. Far more women die at the hands of gangs than men. Gang members don't just kill their victims. They torture them first. Police find dead victims who have their fingernails missing, their limbs severed, their teeth broken, and parts of their bodies that have been burned.

The Amador family members shook their heads in dismay because they knew people who endured such torture.

Two of the major industries in Honduras are drug trafficking and human trafficking. And human trafficking has become more lucrative than drug trafficking. Because of corruption, it is too common for police to look the other way. And Hondurans must put up with property crime, making it more expensive to own and maintain their properties. Evil reigns.

Again, the Amador family shook their heads in desperation, knowing that corrupt police were not on the side of law-abiding people.

Almost half of our children cannot get a high school education, and when they do go to school, parents worry they may not return home. Sixty-six percent of our population lives in extreme poverty, and they are hungry. Many of our fellow citizens can only afford one meal per day. Unemployment is widespread. It is common for hundreds of people to line up to apply for a single minimum-wage job. Mister President, you have some serious work to do.

This sobering broadcast produced a somber silence among the Amador family. They understood that what this commentator said, and what just happened to Pedro, described only too well the wretched life they were living.

The very next day, the gang members returned as they had threatened. Pedro told them, "Look, I have no money at all. Please give me a break!"

Enraged, the gang members dragged him away. Three days later, neighbors found his barely recognizable, mutilated body and brought it to the Amador's shack. Teresa and her family shrieked in anguish. Their heart-wrenching cries brought more neighbors together, who tried to console them, but their efforts were futile. Having heard the blood-curdling screams of other victims who had been tortured by gangs, Amador family members gasped in horror, knowing that Pedro had endured a similar fate. The all-too-common torture that the radio commentator described just the night before was a vivid picture of the Hell Pedro endured before he finally closed his eyes in death.

Two neighbors used a blanket to cover Pedro's grotesque corpse, but now the images in their minds were even worse than reality. Emotions overwhelmed Susana, and she became so distraught that she fainted. Pepe's face became pale, and Teresa took him outside, where he vomited.

The next day, many friends and neighbors joined a procession to take Pedro to his final resting place in the cemetery, which was only two blocks from the Amador family's shack. The priest, Father Santiago, quoted the 23rd Psalm and assured attendees of the blessed hope of eternal life. A family friend sang *Ave Maria*. All Amador family members dressed in black, and Susana wore a black veil. José, Teresa, and their younger brother, Pepe, all sought their mother's touch, and she craved their touch.

The mood grew increasingly somber as memories played out in their heads like old black and white movies. Susana's memories started with the sweet love that led to their engagement to be married, their wedding, and the births of their children. For Pepe, it was the piñata that Pedro brought home for his sixth birthday, so he and his friends could beat it with sticks until it spilled candy on the floor for everybody to go after. José remembered the used bicycle that Pedro brought home for his birthday. Teresa remembered her *quinceañera* (her 15th birthday celebration), which marked her transition from a child to a woman. And then there were her father's recent loving words on her 23rd birthday and his expression of pride after her dance performance.

Mourners, with quaking shoulders and deep sobs, produced an abundance of tear-soaked tissues. Despite Father Santiago's efforts to focus on grieving and the hope of heaven, the insidious desire for revenge invaded Susana, Teresa, and José's hearts with malicious gusto. The desperation was overwhelming. Such funerals were a common occurrence.

As they departed the cemetery, Susana resolved to send her children to the United States. While they ate the day's only meal, Susana said to Teresa and José with reluctant hesitation, "The last time I talked to Norma, my sister in Los Angeles, California, she suggested you two and Pepe should immigrate to the United States. And that is what we must do."

Teresa touched her mother's hand. "Why would we do such a thing and leave you here to fend for yourself?"

"If you three go, things will be tough here. But I can't bear to think I might have to bury you as well. The fact is, it's too dangerous here."

José responded, "But, you're in danger too. I'm scared. Papá is gone, and I fear for you."

Susana replied, "As a widow and being by myself, maybe gang members will leave me alone."

Dread dominated her children's faces, and Teresa asked, "How could we even begin to afford such a trip to the United States?"

"Your Aunt Norma has offered to pay your way."

José asked, "How will you take care of yourself?"

"I'll continue to sell my burritos. When you get jobs in the United States, maybe you can send some money to me from time to time."

Teresa and José commented in unison, "Of course we'd do that, Mamá!"

A long pause haunted them, and all of them contemplated with dread and sorrow the difficult decision to break up their family.

Susana, with a depressed voice, said, "The way I see it, we have two bad options: One, you stay and endure extreme poverty, and the increasing violence, which threatens our lives; or two, you make the dangerous trip to the United States. Despite the danger, and even though the threat of deportation is real, and there is a high probability your efforts may fail, there is no doubt. The best of our two bad options is to take your chances and migrate to the United States."

While she agreed with her mother's decision, Teresa, somewhat ashamed of her selfishness, worried that she might miss out on the dance competition that she was so looking forward to. And her eyes filled with tears at the thought she would have to say goodbye to Raúl and end their relationship, knowing she would very likely not see him again. She hesitated to bring it up but commented, "Can we at least wait until after the dance competition before we do something like this?"

Understanding what a rare joy the dance competition was for her daughter and noting her reluctance to bring it up, Susana responded, "Teresa, I don't think you have to worry. That should not be a problem. I expect it will take some time for me and your Aunt Norma to work out the details for such a major undertaking."

~.~

The dance competition, organized by the *Concurso Proyección Folkloric Jade* (Jade Folkloric Projection Contest), attracted 30 folkloric dance groups from cities and towns across Honduras. Talented groups came to the National Theater Manuel Bonilla in Tegucigalpa to compete for the top prizes over three consecutive Saturdays. Most groups consisted of dancers who came from prosperous families. Despite their limited resources, the dance group from the San Tomás Catholic Church, in which Teresa and Raúl competed, was the top competitor after the second Saturday. And Teresa and Raúl were their top performers. The joy and energy with which they danced brought the audience to their feet with hearty applause and enthusiastic cheers, which reverberated throughout the theater.

On Friday, before the competition's last day on Saturday, Teresa went to the church for the normal weekly dance practice.

When Father Santiago saw her arrive, he pulled her to the side, paused as he took a deep breath, and said with a grim look on his face, "I'm afraid we have lost Raúl. *Barrio* 18 gang members tortured and killed him when he refused to join their gang."

Teresa erupted with a heart-wrenching scream, "No!" And she sobbed with bitterness and grief. "I loved him so much. Why doesn't God protect us?"

As she clung to Father Santiago, he replied, "I wish I could give you a good answer. All I can say is we must not lose faith that God will one day give us peace."

That night, Teresa cried herself to sleep. Nevertheless, on Saturday, Teresa insisted on attending the last day's events. Even if it was possible, dancing was the last thing she wanted to do, given Teresa's devastating emotional state. And there was no dance partner to take Raúl's place anyway. Because of the San Tomás Catholic Church group's top performance, large numbers of residents from Teresa's *barrio* were in attendance. Event organizers learned of Raúl's tragic gang-related death. Some complained that, since the church's dance group was now incomplete, their group should be disqualified, but the organizers refused to do so.

Two dance groups vied for first place — Teresa's group and a group from San Pedro Sula. Both groups' award-winning performances showed themselves to be head and shoulders above their competition.

The theater grew quiet as the judges deliberated. When the judges announced their decision, the members of Teresa's *barrio* erupted in cheers and applause, with tears in the eyes of many, as they celebrated their *barrio's* victorious first-place win. Raúl's mother, with tears flowing down her face, gave Teresa a photograph of her son, and a crowd from her *barrio* lifted her up and carried her to the theater's stage to join with her winning dance group.

Television crews and newspaper reporters captured the image of Teresa's tear-stained face, while she embraced Raúl's picture. Surrounded by her dance team members, it was, for Teresa, a bittersweet moment, much more bitter than sweet.

When the bus returned to San Tomás Catholic Church, Teresa walked back to her shack alone. Heartbroken, she cried all the way. A big part of her grief was over the deaths of Raúl and Pedro, her father, who missed the joy of the dance competition victory. Teresa especially regretted with deep sorrow that she would not hear her father express his approval with the words, "Well done, my daughter." In her mind, she doubted that she would ever dance again.

The Journey Begins

After selling her burritos, Susana bought a phone card and called her sister, Norma. With a tissue to dry her eyes, Susana's voice quivered when she told Norma about Pedro's tragic death. She added, "And gang members also tortured and killed Raúl, Teresa's boyfriend, when he wouldn't join their gang."

Norma replied, "I'm so sorry to hear that. Have you given more thought to sending your children to the United States?"

"Gang members are threatening José. They're trying to compel him to join their gang. And they've confronted Teresa too. I'm so afraid. If you're still willing to help us, I've decided to send them. What do we need to do?"

"I know somebody who just made this trip on the Mexican freight train, known as the beast. She traveled with her husband and son, and she tells me the cost is about 150,000 lempiras to bring them here, which is about $6,000 in American currency. The biggest cost is for the intermediaries, known as coyotes, who make it possible to travel and evade the immigration officials, who will send Teresa and her brothers back to Honduras if they're caught. This will be a financial challenge for us, and I reiterate this trip is not without its dangers. But I think it's worth it."

Susana exclaimed, "150,000 lempiras! That's a lot of money. Why can't we just put them on a plane or a bus?"

"In most cases, believe it or not, the beast is the most viable and affordable option."

"How could that possibly be?"

"Well, in the first place, a plane ride is cheaper than a bus because you can get to the United States by plane in one day. The trip on a bus takes several days. So, you have other travel expenses in addition to the cost of bus tickets, like food and lodging."

"Second, Teresa and her brothers could never get any visa to legally enter the United States. To get a visa, travelers must demonstrate they have a binding tie that compels them to return to their native countries. Such binding ties include money in the bank and property. And we both know you have neither of these. So traveling directly to the United States is not an option. Their only viable option is to reach the border between Mexico and the United States. That leads us to number three."

As I said earlier, no matter how you travel to get to the border, you'll still have to pay the coyotes to cross the border between Mexico and the United States. That one cost is the largest expense for Teresa and her brothers and will be anywhere from $4,000 to $10,000. So, as I said, travel on the beast is the most viable and affordable option, which is why so many migrants ride the beast.

Susana pondered what Norma said, and tears came to her eyes. "You understand, there's no way I can repay you."

"Don't worry about it. As I told you before, Pablo and I are aware of the escalating gang violence in Honduras, and we've been talking about this for some time. We'll provide the money."

Susana responded, "I'm afraid to send them off with so much money."

"Here's what we'll do. We'll send you $2,000 to start. When they get low on funds, Teresa will need to purchase a phone card along the way and call us so that we can wire additional funds to her."

Sobbing, Susana's voice quivered again as she replied, "Norma, I don't know how to thank you. But okay. Let's do this."

It took some time to get ready for their departure. Among other things, they obtained passports for Teresa, José, and Pepe, and they received the $2,000 from Norma.

Susana purchased two money belts, and explained to Teresa and José, "Each of you should put one half of the money in your money belts. Every day, you should take out only enough money for the day's expenses. That way, if you're robbed, the thieves will only get one day's worth of cash."

They planned to depart during the first week of December.

At church, Teresa got with her friend, Leticia, to tell her that she and her brothers planned to travel to the United States.

Leticia asked, "Are you planning to travel on the beast?"

Teresa tilted her head. "Is that the freight train that goes from southern Mexico up to the United States border?"

Leticia nodded. "Yup. Not only is it called the beast, but it's also called the train of death."

"Well, that's our plan. Why is it called the train of death?"

With raised eyebrows and a wrinkled forehead, Leticia hugged Teresa and then looked at her with hands on her shoulders. "I'll keep you in my prayers. You know there are many tragic stories about people who have tried to make this trip before. Some fall off the beast and get maimed or killed. Others become victims of gang violence. It's a dangerous way to travel."

Teresa responded with a shaky smile, "I don't think we have any other option. I understand it's the only viable option for undocumented migrants who want to cross the border into the United States."

With her mouth half-open and nodding while listening, Leticia then said, "My friend, I recommend you start taking birth control pills before you begin your trip. I've heard many stories about women who get raped during their trip."

Hearing this made Teresa's heart skip a beat, and she replied, "Now you have me even more worried."

Leticia said, "If it were me, I would still go despite the risks. There are many other dangers as well. But these days, I'd say the danger of staying here is even worse. As you know only too well, gang violence is getting worse and worse all the time."

Leticia's words made Teresa think long and hard about her decision to make this trip. With all the other necessary preparations, she never did purchase birth control pills.

~.~

December came before they knew it. On Monday, Teresa converted $500 to 3,500 Guatemalan quetzales. On Tuesday, they departed at four o'clock in the morning and made their way to the Empresa de Transportes Cristina bus station. Their bus tickets cost 375 lempiras. The bus would depart Tegucigalpa for San Pedro Sula right before sunrise. They each carried a backpack with one change of clothes, a coat, an extra pair of shoes, and minimal toiletries.

Teresa, José, and Pepe all sobbed when they said goodbye to their mother, knowing there was a high probability they might not ever see their mother again.

Susana, also with tears in her eyes, hugged her children and said, "Take care of yourselves. I'll pray for you every day. Please write to me when you can."

Teresa said, "We love you, Mamá. We'll be praying for you too. You take care of yourself also."

They got on the bus, and the bus departed. Devastating loneliness invaded Susana's heart while she watched the bus turn a corner and disappear.

The trip to San Pedro Sula took over five hours, and they arrived right before noon. San Pedro Sula, the second-largest city in Honduras after Tegucigalpa, is among the most violent cities in the world, second only to Caracas, Venezuela.

After paying 150 lempiras for some lunch at a kiosk, Teresa, José, and Pepe caught another bus for 117 lempiras, which took them to Corinto, near the Guatemalan border, a two-hour trip. There they encountered a group of about 100 Hondurans who also planned to cross the Guatemalan border. They felt some sense of security by being a part of this group. The border was a little more than a mile from Corinto.

As they began walking, the 100 people stretched out in a long caravan. The migrants separated into smaller groups. It was unclear if the 100 people would regroup later or try to make their own way with these smaller groups.

They arrived at the border at about three o'clock in the afternoon. There they encountered a sea of about a thousand migrants who waited to see a single border control agent. Nobody could cross the border into the town of El Cinchado in Guatemala until they received a visa from this border control agent. In addition to Hondurans, there were Salvadorans, Nicaraguans, and a few other nationalities as well. Everybody was tired, hungry, and not in the best mood. Afternoon temperatures were sweltering, it was very humid, and the crowd's body heat made conditions even worse. The pungent smell of body odor would now be a continuous part of their travel in this tropical heat.

Pepe went to sleep in Teresa's arms, and she and José took turns holding him. They spent the night standing in line. Stuck in this crowd of people for so many hours, they soon drank all the water in the plastic bottles they carried. José took their three bottles to a stream to get them refilled twice before they got close to the Guatemalan immigration office.

Pepe had been very patient and well-behaved until now. After being awake for a couple of hours, he started crying and reached out to Teresa, who picked him up again. He asked, "When are we going to eat? I'm hungry, and I wanna sit down."

Teresa gave him some water to drink and said, "I'm sorry, Pepe. Everybody must show their identification before they can continue into Guatemala. We're almost there, so it shouldn't take much longer."

It was almost noon when they met with the border patrol agent. They showed their passports, completed their paperwork, paid the required fee, and received their Guatemalan travel visas.

When they entered Guatemala, several flatbed trucks with guard rails waited on the outskirts of El Cinchado to provide transportation for migrants who could pay. Men, known as coyotes, worked the crowd to sell them a place on one of the trucks.

Teresa asked one of the coyotes, "How much does it cost to get a place on a truck?"

"One hundred fifty-five quetzales, per person."

After giving the coyote 465 quetzales, Teresa, José, and Pepe competed with several others who struggled to climb onto one of the trucks, where they had to stand on the truck's flatbed. Before getting on the truck, they managed to fill their water bottles with water again, but lunch in San Pedro Sula was the last time they ate.

The truck pulled away, impeded by the sea of migrants who departed the border on foot. Many families walked with their small children. While almost everybody was tired and hungry, many chanted while they walked and sang patriotic songs, including the Honduran national anthem. Many stopped and took the time to pray before continuing on. The migrants at the front of the pack carried a large banner, which depicted the Honduran flag. Those who came from El Salvador, Nicaragua, and other countries were not so enthusiastic since they had been traveling much longer. Their next stop would be Morales, Guatemala, 35 miles away. For those who walked, the trip took 14 hours. Once the trucks broke away from the migrant crowd, travel time was about 1.5 hours.

It was standing room only on the truck bed, and the dirt road was dusty and bumpy with many potholes. This trip would be like a long walk in tight shoes. It was hot. Migrants were packed together with minimal space to move around, so there was little risk of falling. Dust covered people's bodies, and their sweat soon turned the dust into a muddy paste on their skin, like peanut butter on hot toast. They also put up with the truck's choking diesel fumes, combined with everybody's nasty body odor.

Because of scorching temperatures, high humidity, lack of sleep, almost no food over the past day or longer, waiting on foot in line for long hours, and now standing on the flatbed of this truck, everybody was exhausted, in pain, and irritable. Almost no conversation occurred.

Potholes jostled everybody along the winding road and made the truck's progress slow-going. When the truck hit a large pothole, José lost his balance and lurched against another migrant.

Angry, the man shoved José against other migrants, which provoked more anger, and he said, "Don't let that happen again!"

José replied, "I'm sorry."

The migrant stared him down and cursed at him.

Victor, another migrant who was a large muscular man, said to him, "It was an accident, the man apologized, leave him alone."

Both got into an argument, and Victor grabbed the other man by the collar and said, "You either settle down now, or I'll remove you from this truck. You got that?"

There were some hard feelings, but the man did settle down.

José said to Victor, "Gracias, señor."

When they were about halfway to Morales, a swarm of wasps attacked the migrants like fighter planes in a dogfight and inflicted them with multiple stings. Trapped, with no place to flee, people screamed and tried to evade the wasps in vain. Pepe, and others, suffered a strong allergic reaction to the wasp stings, and in no time became ill.

They arrived in Morales at about 2:30 in the afternoon. After standing for over twenty-four hours, with no food, everybody rushed to get off the truck. They had the good fortune that their truck arrived ahead of the others. Teresa saw a small hotel called Pensión del Peregrino, and she said to José, "While I find a doctor for Pepe, you should see if you can get us a room at that hotel."

While all three suffered from the wasp stings, Pepe was quite sick, with flu-like symptoms. Teresa put her hand on his forehead and noted he had a fever. She saw a policeman, and, with some trepidation, she asked him, "Where can I find a doctor for my brother?"

Seeing that the boy was listless, the policeman said, "Come with me. I'll take you to see our town's doctor."

When they arrived, Teresa thanked the policeman for his help and kindness.

Meanwhile, José got them one room at the hotel for 365 quetzales. A very spartan hotel located near the bus terminal, he was fortunate to get one of the last rooms. Many had to find a place outside to spend the night.

José explained to the desk clerk that Teresa, his sister, took his brother to the doctor and said, "Please let her know what room I'm in when she returns."

The only furniture in the dark, drab room was a bed and a dresser with a cracked mirror. One stained sheet covered the bed's sagging mattress, with no pillows. The room did not have a bathroom, but it did feature a musty smell with dead flies on the window sill. Gaudy green curtains with orange flowers contributed the only color in the room. There were separate communal bathroom facilities for men and women on each of the hotel's two floors.

José took a shower and changed his clothes.

The doctor examined Pepe and removed several wasp stings. Then he explained to Teresa, "I'll give you some aspirin, which should bring his fever down, and I'll give you an antibiotic to treat the infection caused by the wasp stings. Pepe needs to drink plenty of water. He should take an aspirin every four hours and the antibiotic twice a day. He needs to take the antibiotic until it's gone. Do you have any questions for me?"

Teresa asked, "Will he be able to travel tomorrow?"

"The aspirin should bring his fever down by tomorrow morning. If you see he's not feverish, he should be able to travel, and he can also stop taking the aspirin."

As soon as Teresa and Pepe got to their room, they showered and changed their clothes. Since they had not eaten for almost two days, all three felt weakened with hunger pangs that intensified because of the aroma of cooking food that enticed them as they raced to the hotel's cafeteria.

After waiting to get a table, José said, "I never thought sitting in a chair could be such a wonderful experience."

Teresa replied, "No kidding!"

A waitress came to their table, gave them menus, and said, "The only thing we have right now is chicken and rice."

José examined the menu and replied in jest, "In that case, I think we'll choose the chicken and rice. And bring us three Coca Colas, please."

Teresa was surprised to see José still had some sense of humor.

The waitress laughed and said, "Since there's no other option, good choice."

When the waitress brought the food, Teresa asked, "What do we have to do to get a bus to El Ceibo."

The waitress explained, "I'm from El Naranjo, which is close to El Ceibo. I stay with my aunt when I come here on Mondays to work and return on Fridays. The bus you catch here goes to El Naranjo. You can reserve seats on the bus now, but it will cost you extra. When the bus approaches El Naranjo, you'll see a fork in the road, with a sign for Mexico, which points to the left. You'll want to get off the bus there instead of going on to El Naranjo, which is where the right fork takes you. After you get off the bus, you'll find frequent buses, which leave from El Naranjo and go to El Ceibo. So, you should have no trouble catching one of those buses."

"Gracias."

The waitress liked José, and, with a pleasant smile, she asked him, "Where are you from?"

José replied, "Tegucigalpa, Honduras."

"So, I suspect you're trying to get to the United States."

"That's the plan."

"How's it gone for you so far?"

"We haven't slept for almost two days. Over those two days, we ate nothing until now, and we had minimal opportunities to sit down during the last twenty-four hours. We rode standing in a truck packed with other migrants, a swarm of wasps stung us, and a layer of dust covered us, which mixed with our sweat and smeared us with mud. And this is our first meal in Guatemala. Believe me. It's good to hear your friendly voice."

The waitress smiled with a sympathetic face and said, "I hope you'll have better luck going forward. My understanding is that traveling through Mexico is dangerous."

José smiled back and said, "Gracias. Please say a prayer for us."

The waitress nodded her head. "I'll do that."

The bill came to 138 quetzales, and Teresa paid it.

They felt much better after their meal, and they went to the bus station and paid 120 quetzales to reserve seats for the bus to El Naranjo.

The lady at the ticket office explained, "I recommend you take the bus, which departs at ten o'clock in the morning. The earlier buses are so crowded that there is little probability for you to get a seat. To get a seat on the ten o'clock bus, you should get in line not later than nine o'clock, even though you have reserved your places on the bus."

Teresa asked, "So, why are we paying extra for reserved seats on the bus?"

"If you can't get on the ten o'clock bus, you'll have priority for the next bus."

Teresa replied, "Okay. Gracias."

Back in the hotel, Teresa washed their smelly, soiled clothes in the women's communal bathroom. She hung the wet clothes to dry on the room's flimsy curtain rod. Teresa and José, who never slept on a bed before, tried the bed in the hotel room but couldn't sleep until they chose to sleep on the floor with Pepe, which was more comfortable for them.

They awoke the next morning refreshed. Pepe's fever subsided.

Teresa said, "José, we should eat a good breakfast. Who knows when we'll get to eat again."

Many migrants crowded into the cafeteria. So, they had to wait for a table. The same waitress took their orders.

She greeted them, but looked at José when she said, "Buenos Días. You look like you slept well."

José smiled at her, nodded, and replied, "We did. Gracias."

When the waitress brought the food, Teresa asked José, "Please give thanks for our food."

José prayed, "Dear God, we thank you for this food, which you have blessed us with. Please protect us while we travel, and we pray that Pepe will recover from his wasp stings. Please help us to honor you in all we do, Amen."

For breakfast, they ate eggs, ham, and tortillas and enjoyed orange juice and coffee. The bill came to 66 quetzales.

Right before nine o'clock in the morning, they got in line to board the bus – a line which grew longer by the minute. By the time the bus arrived, the line extended to the point where many who hoped to catch this bus would be disappointed, even those who made reservations.

When they got on the bus, there were no seats. A man offered Teresa his seat.

Teresa smiled and said, "Gracias, señor."

She sat down, and Pepe sat on her lap.

The bus departed at ten o'clock for El Naranjo, 100 miles away, a 4-hour bus ride. The winding road was in bad shape, with many potholes and lots of traffic. The bus driver had to wait for infrequent opportunities to pass slow-moving semi-trucks on the two-lane road. When he had a chance to pass, the bus's slow acceleration made passengers pray and grab the seat in front of them as they watched oncoming vehicles racing toward the bus. The oncoming vehicles had to slow down to avoid a disaster. And passengers sighed with relief when the bus got back in its lane in time to avoid a crash. While they traveled, the bus stopped from time to time at pueblos along the way, where Guatemalans got off the bus. So, after a while, José got a seat behind Teresa and Pepe.

As they traveled, they saw many small groups of migrants making this trip on foot – a journey which would take them about two days.

José commented to Teresa, "Thank God we were able to get on this bus."

As the waitress in Morales recommended, they got off the bus when they saw the rusted sign with nearly illegible words which read, *Frontera*

Mexicana. (Mexican border) As the waitress explained, the sign displayed an arrow pointing to the left fork in the road. After dropping them off, the bus proceeded on the right fork to El Naranjo. Many others waited at this fork in the road to catch another bus to El Ceibo, a small Guatemalan pueblo on the Guatemalan/Mexican border. After the second bus approached from El Naranjo, filled with other migrants, they realized it was hopeless to expect they would be able to catch a bus, and they joined other migrants who were walking along the road, which would take them to El Ceibo, four hours away on foot.

On their way to El Ceibo, they met Rodolfo Emanuel, who was also from Honduras. He asked them, "Is this your first trip to the United States?"

Teresa answered, "Yes. How about you?"

"This is my fourth attempt."

José asked, "Have you made it to the United States?"

"I made it once. But I got caught right after crossing the border, and the immigration authorities deported me. The first two times, I ran out of money and had to return to Tegucigalpa."

"So, now you're trying again?"

Rodolfo shrugged and explained, "I had a girlfriend in Tegucigalpa, and I was about to propose marriage to her. But she cheated on me. So, yes. I'm trying again."

After El Ceibo, their next stop would be Tenosique, Mexico, and Teresa asked, "How long does it take to get to Tenosique?"

"If you have to walk, twelve hours. If you can get a ride, two hours."

"Are buses available?"

"It's possible to get a bus, but difficult. Your best bet is to find a Coyote who can get you on a truck. Otherwise, the likelihood is good that you'll have to walk."

José sighed and complained. "Another truck! What are you going to do?"

"I'll try to get a ride on a truck, but I'll be prepared to walk if I have to. By the time we get to El Ceibo, it will be about six o'clock in the evening. So, you should plan to spend the night there."

They stopped at a stream to refill their water bottles, and José asked, "Where can we get a place for the night in El Ceibo?"

"I'd say there's very little chance for that to happen. We'll have to find a place outside to sleep."

Not liking his response, Teresa tilted her head and asked, "What happens if we keep going?"

Rodolfo replied, "I don't recommend you travel at night. You'd be pretty much on your own, which would make you vulnerable to gangs. You'll be much safer if you spend the night in El Ceibo. And why would you want to walk twelve hours all night when you can ride on a truck in the morning, which may get you to Tenosique earlier than by walking? We can travel together if you like. It'll be safer that way. The further you go into Mexico, the more probable it is that you'll have to deal with gangs."

José asked, "What happens when we get to Tenosique?"

"We'll have to cross the Usumacinta River. From there, it's a short walk to the train station, where you'll meet the beast."

When they arrived at El Ceibo, the four of them went to a small restaurant to eat dinner. They all prayed together to give thanks for their food. Teresa paid 180 quetzales. Rodolfo paid for his meal.

While they ate, Teresa asked the waitress, "Where's the safest place for us to spend the night?"

Recognizing they were migrants, she replied, "There's a church nearby. A lot of migrants spend the night on the church's property."

Rodolfo remarked, "I wish I would've known this during my earlier arrivals here."

When they got to the church, there were over one hundred migrants there.

Rodolfo commented, "I expect this is the safest place we'll find."

Many migrants squeezed onto the crowded church property. The volunteers were friendly, and they fed the migrants a meager meal. They slept on the ground. In the morning, church volunteers gave the migrants sacks, which contained tacos with beans, cheese, and an orange.

A volunteer said, "Please write your names in this record book. Include the country you came from, and the name and address of a loved one who knows you're making this trip."

Teresa asked, "Why do you want this information?"

The volunteer put her hand on Teresa's shoulder and said, "You understand this trip you're making is dangerous, right? Too many people don't make it. Too many die at the hands of gangs or accidents. If something happens to you, and your loved ones try to find out what happened, they at least will be able to learn that you passed through here."

Teresa stared into the air when she heard this sobering explanation, and her hand trembled while she provided the information for herself, José, and Pepe. Then she said, "Gracias."

"You're welcome. *Buena suerte.*" (Good luck.)

Rodolfo asked, "Where can we exchange our money into Mexican pesos?"

The volunteer replied, "There's a bank down the street, which opens at nine o'clock in the morning. They can help you."

"Gracias."

The volunteer responded, "*Que vaya con Dios.*" (May you go with God.)

The next morning, after Teresa and Rodolfo returned from the bank, they all crossed the border into Mexico and waited about two hours to get through the border's immigration station.

Coyotes soon arrived and offered to get transportation for those who could pay 1,200 pesos per person. Teresa, José, Pepe, and Rodolfo found themselves on another flatbed truck. Again, standing room only.

Their truck departed at 11:30 in the morning and arrived in Tenosique at two o'clock in the afternoon. Rodolfo made some inquiries and found out the next train would not come for two days. He said, "There's a migrant refugee center here, operated by the Catholic Church, called La Casa del Migrante. If they have room, they'll provide us with food and shelter."

Teresa replied, "Great. Let's go see if they have room for us."

The crowded refugee center had minimal room for additional migrants.

Soon after their arrival, church volunteers served them beans and rice with tortillas, and they gave them orange juice to drink. While they were finishing their meal, Teresa asked, "How do we cross this river you told us about?"

Rodolfo responded, "Most people cross on rafts. It costs 600 pesos per person to get on a raft. The rafts are constructed with two large inner tubes, designed to be used in the tires of large tractors. The inner tubes are lashed together with wood, which forms the platform on which migrants ride across the river. The raft's owner propels and steers the raft with a long pole."

The church celebrated a brief Mass for the migrants, and Teresa, José, Pepe, and Rodolfo all attended, along with many other migrants. In the old picturesque church, a mariachi band played and sang some sacred songs, and the priest, a jolly, slightly obese man, prayed for those in attendance.

Teresa, José, Pepe, and Rodolfo were grateful they could stay at the refugee center, but it was crowded, hot, and noisy during the day. Meals were spartan but adequate. Volunteers handed out rugs for migrants to sleep on at night. While there, Teresa and Rodolfo went to a nearby bank to convert more money into Mexican pesos. Pepe made some friends and had a good time playing soccer with them in a field across the street from the church.

They spent two days at the refugee center. Many of the migrants were parents who traveled with their children. Almost all migrants were fleeing gang violence and poverty in their respective countries. The priest and the volunteers went out of their way to show kindness and compassion to everybody. This refugee center also asked migrants to leave their names along with family contacts in their countries of origin.

The next morning, they filled their water bottles, and everybody received a sack of food. Teresa, José, Pepe, and Rodolfo stowed the food and water in their backpacks and boarded a raft, after paying 2,400 pesos, which took them across the Usumacinta River. Other than getting their feet wet when water washed over the raft's plywood platform where they stood, the river crossing was uneventful. At nine o'clock in the morning, they then made their way to the train station. The beast had not yet arrived.

The Beast

Rodolfo explained, "We won't be able to catch the beast at this train station. The police will arrest us if we stay here. We need to walk along the tracks for about a mile. Coyotes will negotiate with the train's conductor so that they will slow the train down until we have a chance to climb aboard. So, you need to be prepared to board a moving train."

"The time will come when the train will accelerate. So, you must get on board as soon as possible. Many lose their limbs or their lives when they try to board the train when it's moving too fast. The temptation can be overwhelming when you realize you are going to miss the train, and you see you are about to be separated from your family."

With a puzzled look on her face, Teresa asked, "Why would the police arrest us? Everybody knows migrants are riding the beast."

"As you would expect, it's illegal for people to ride a freight train because it's dangerous. That's why there are passenger trains so that people can travel in comfort and safety. It's also illegal to bribe train personnel to slow the train down. So, the police patrol this passenger station for law enforcement purposes. And migrants must therefore board the train after it leaves the station, where the police look the other way."

José commented, "But it's far more dangerous to board a moving train than it is to climb on the train when it's stopped at a station."

Rodolfo shrugged his shoulders and responded, "Rather ironic, isn't it? By looking the other way, the police don't stop migrants whose goal is illegal entry into the United States. It's all a facade. The police can say they are enforcing the law by patrolling the train station. And migrants can board the train after it leaves the station, where the police won't see them. Many stations along the way don't serve passengers. The police don't patrol those stations, so it won't be necessary at those stations to board a moving train."

As they walked along the tracks, they saw many other migrants. There appeared to be several hundred of them. The train didn't show up, so they spent the night out in the open. They could see numerous flying bugs that swarmed around the lights on top of two utility poles nearby. Although the temperature was comfortable, a light rain shower occurred after midnight. With their wet clothes, everybody shivered from the cold during the early morning hours, even though the temperature was in the mid-60s.

To make matters worse, everybody suffered numerous tick bites. Rodolfo and Teresa were striving to be close to each other, and Rodolfo removed a long-sleeved shirt from his backpack and draped it over Teresa's shoulders. José could see the start of a relationship between the two of them.

At eight o'clock in the morning, coyotes approached each migrant and collected 5,000 pesos per person. After paying, Teresa guessed she and José still had a little over 26,000 pesos remaining – about $1,000 U.S. dollars.

The train of death, otherwise known as the beast, arrived at eleven o'clock in the morning. The beast roared by them, producing turbulent currents of air that buffeted them. Seeing how large the wheels were, and knowing they had to climb on board while the beast was moving, intimidated Teresa and José. And knowing this beast's reputation made Teresa and José shudder as they contemplated the dangers which lied ahead.

Pepe exclaimed, "Teresa, I'm scared!"

Teresa's voice trembled as she tried to assure him, "Don't worry. We'll be okay."

They waited about four hours for the beast to depart the station. While they waited, they met two older teenagers who were also from Honduras: Marcos and Timoteo. They were praying together.

Marcos asked, "Why don't you join us as a team?"

Rodolfo said to Teresa and José, "That's a good idea. There's safety in numbers."

They all agreed to stick together.

Rodolfo explained, "José, when you hear the train come, you need to be ready to climb on the rung of a train car's ladder. You must choose the ladder on the leading edge of the train car. Teresa, while moving along the side of the train, you must lift Pepe as soon as possible so that José can grab him. Pepe, when José grabs you, you need to hold on to him as tight as possible. Can you do that?"

Pepe nodded his head and responded, "Sí!"

Rodolfo turned to Teresa, "After you hand Pepe off to José, you must be prepared to grab onto the next available ladder, so that you all can be on the same train car together." Anticipating that they would be climbing onto a boxcar, Rodolfo continued. "José, when you climb to the top, somebody should be able to take Pepe from you so that you can get on top of the train car. Does anybody have any questions?"

Very nervous with wrinkled foreheads, Teresa, José, and Pepe shook their heads to say, "No."

When the beast left the station, Teresa, José, and Pepe could soon hear the roar of the beast's three engines and the ominous rumbling sound of the long line of train cars as the beast moved along the railroad tracks. The ground beneath their feet began to tremble. Their hearts began to race with fear. Their ride on the beast was about to begin.

When they saw the train engines come into view, the front engine's bright headlight looked like the evil eye of an iron monster, which stared them down without blinking. This intimidating sight made them feel like tiny fleas about to ride on the back of an enormous, mean dog.

The engines passed by. José grabbed onto the ladder of a gondola car, and Teresa, as instructed, moved along the side of the train and lifted Pepe so that José could grab him. More migrants followed José up the same ladder. Teresa kept moving and followed other migrants to grab onto the gondola's next ladder and climb to the top. José got to the top of his ladder and called for help. A man was quick to come to his aid and took Pepe from José's arms. Another helped José climb over the gondola's wall to get inside.

The beast began to accelerate. Teresa, who was the last to grab onto her ladder, trembled as she faced the precarious need to climb over the edge of the gondola's wall as the beast continued to pick up speed. Increasing speed also increased the side-to-side movement of the gondola. Clinging to the rusty ladder, and seeing the tracks speed by beneath her feet, made her grit her teeth, and she froze, unable to overcome her fear. Others inside the gondola grabbed her hands and helped her cross over the wall's edge and into the gondola. José made his way to the back of the gondola with Pepe to join Teresa. Both were gasping to breathe, and it took some time before their trembling subsided.

Meanwhile, Rodolfo had climbed onto the next train car – a boxcar. Instead of climbing to the top of the boxcar, he crossed over to the gondola on the coupling, which connected the two train cars – a dangerous thing to do. He went up the ladder and climbed inside the gondola, where he met up with Teresa, José, and Pepe. Rodolfo trembled also.

Most of the migrants were tall enough to see over the edge of the gondola's wall. The gondola was crowded with other migrants, and almost everybody was standing because they were curious to watch the scenery along the way. Standing was a challenge because of the constant side-to-side movement of the gondola. So, they soon welcomed the opportunity to sit down, but they soon found it uncomfortable to sit on the floor's hard and uneven steel surface. Very few people were talking. The worries on their minds did not lend themselves to idle chatter. But talking was also a challenge because of the beast's loud rumble. Most faces reflected, not only worry, but also fatigue and despair.

Rodolfo asked, "Are you okay?"

José and Teresa responded, "As good as can be expected."

In addition to this gondola car, migrants gathered on several other train cars. Many sat on top of boxcars. From inside the gondola, it was difficult to know how many migrants boarded the beast because the boxcars were much higher than the gondola.

It was now approaching noon, and the temperature was in the low 90s. The steel gondola absorbed massive amounts of heat, so the temperature inside the gondola was maybe closer to 110 degrees. With everybody crowded together, their bodies generated even more heat, and their conditions were unbearable. Everybody consumed most of their water, and it was clear they would soon have none left. Most did not touch the sacks of tacos with beans and cheese and the orange they received at the migrant refugee center. Nobody knew when they might have their next opportunity to get more food.

As the monotony of riding in the gondola set in, Teresa pondered all that had happened so far on this crazy trip. She recalled Rodolfo's comment that it was illegal for them to ride on this beast, and it bothered her that she had never done anything illegal in her life until now. She contemplated that she still had to do something else that was illegal when it came time to cross the border into the United States. Not only did she experience regret for doing something illegal, she also regretted leaving her mother behind where she, a lonely widow, was defenseless against gang violence, and she regretted that she and her brothers had to make this arduous and dangerous journey.

She recalled a time in her youth when she climbed up a tall tree, which she saw as a tempting challenge. But then, looking down and seeing how high she was, fear set in as the wind made the tree sway from side to side, and she trembled as she made the slow descent, branch by branch, to come down out of the tree. This trip was like that. It started out as a challenge, but now fear of the unknown began to afflict her. She realized that she and her brothers had reached the point of no return, and resigned herself that the only option was to keep going.

Rodolfo surprised everybody, and interrupted Teresa's thoughts, when he shouted out, "How many here are from Honduras?"

He shouted as loud as possible to be heard over the beast's rumble.

Most of the people raised their hands.

"How about Guatemala?"

Many others raised their hands.

"El Salvador?"

A significant number raised their hands.

"Nicaragua?"

Some hands.

"Costa Rica?"

Few hands.

"Panama?"

Two hands.

"Colombia?"

Three hands.

"Who hasn't raised their hand?"

Five hands went up.

"So, where are you from?"

Three replied, "Cuba!"

The last two replied, "Peru!"

Rodolfo asked, "How many of you are fleeing a home where you have lost loved ones due to gang violence?"

Almost everybody's faces reflected despair, and they fought back tears when they raised their hands.

"How many would prefer to stay in your own countries if it wasn't for the violence?"

Again, almost everybody raised their hands.

"Who would like to share a good memory from your country?"

Teresa raised her hand and, when recognized, said, "I'm from Honduras, and I loved dancing our country's folkloric dances with my boyfriend, Raúl. I must now live with the memory that gang members tortured and killed Raúl."

Another said, "I'm from El Salvador, and I'll miss being a member of our soccer team."

A woman said, "I'm from Guatemala, and nobody makes better *chicharrones* (pork rinds) than my mother."

A man stood up with tears streaming down his face and said, "I left my wife and two kids behind. I'm hoping I can get a good job and send them money from the United States. To me, watching my children grow up is the most precious thing in the world, and I'm afraid I will not get to see that."

Many others shared their bitter-sweet memories as well. All recognized many good things about their different countries, things they had in common, things they said goodbye to.

Rodolfo then said, "I presume we're all heading for the United States. While we travel together, we will face some dangerous and perilous times. Some of us will not make it. Some of us may die. I suggest we all begin to look at ourselves as the fellow countrymen we will be when we arrive in the United States. And as fellow countrymen, I hope we will all join together to support each other from this point forward. Is there somebody here who would say a prayer for us?"

Timoteo stood and said, "Let's pray. Dear God, We are strangers here, but we face a common challenge. Our resources are very inadequate. But, as much as it may be possible, please help us to support and defend each other. Most of us, dear God, have left family and friends behind – people we love, but may never see again. We pray that you would bless them and protect them from the cruelty of gang violence. We beg You to help us succeed as we seek a new and better life. May we not waver in our faith in You, and help us honor You in all we do. Amen."

Even among the most macho of men, there was not a dry eye among the migrants in the gondola. Before Timoteo's prayer and the things that Rodolfo said, everybody felt like they were on their own. But now, there was a sense of unifying camaraderie.

Teresa admired Rodolfo for showing his leadership ability, and she was glad for his friendship.

Weekend in Villahermosa

The beast arrived in Villahermosa on Friday at six o'clock in the evening and would not depart until Monday. Everybody got off the beast and made their way to a nearby stream, where they filled their water bottles. Most ate all the food they received from the refugee center, and therefore, few people had anything to eat, and almost everybody was hungry. Teresa, José, and Rodolfo decided they would try to go downtown in the morning. Many of the migrants had very little money. So, going downtown was not a luxury they could afford. Many others, however, also planned to go down town. Since they still had some food available, Marcos and Timoteo gave Teresa some money, and she promised to bring back more food for them.

Rodolfo whispered to Teresa and José, "I'll try to wake you up before dawn. If we can get a head start before all the others, we'll have an advantage when we get downtown."

Darkness set in, and people slept wherever they could find a decent place along the tracks. Pepe stayed close to Teresa. José, Rodolfo, Marcos, and Timoteo found places close by, where they could keep an eye on Teresa and Pepe. Night time temperatures decreased to the upper-50s, and Pepe and Teresa clung to each other to stay warm. José and the other companions were not so fortunate. Even though Teresa, José, and Pepe wore coats, they were cold because they were not used to the lower temperatures of Mexico's higher, northern latitude.

Rodolfo got up at about 4:30 Saturday morning and woke up Teresa, José, and Pepe. As soon as possible, they departed and headed for town, following a sign which read, *Centro*. Roosters throughout the area began to crow. After about thirty minutes, a taxi approached them, and the driver offered to take them downtown for 75 pesos. (About $3 U.S.) José sat in the front seat. Pepe sat by a window in the back seat, Teresa sat in the middle, and Rodolfo sat by the other window. Body odor revealed that all four needed a shower. While the taxi proceeded downtown, Rodolfo took Teresa's hand in his. Teresa looked at him, smiled, and moved closer to him. She rested her head on his shoulder. Their constant exposure to body odor on the beast made them oblivious to each other's stench.

José asked the taxi driver, "What's your name?"

"Benigno. Where are you from?"

"We're all from Honduras. My name's José. In the back are my little brother, Pepe, on the driver's side, Teresa, my sister, in the middle, and Rodolfo, our friend."

Rodolfo asked, "Benigno, is there someplace where we can get cleaned up?"

Benigno paused and looked at Rodolfo in the rearview mirror. "My family owns a farm nearby. If you're willing to help with some work, I'm pretty sure my dad will let you get cleaned up."

Rodolfo said to Teresa and José, "Sounds like a good offer to me. What do you think?"

Teresa responded, "Not a problem."

The trip to the farm took twenty minutes. Benigno went into the house and talked to his father. When he returned, he said, "My papá says you can spend the night here, if you don't mind sleeping in the barn. Are you hungry?"

José answered, "We've had very little to eat since early yesterday."

"Why don't you get settled in the barn, and I'll have my mamá make ya some breakfast."

Teresa, José, Rodolfo, and Pepe found places in the barn where they would sleep at night.

After about thirty minutes, Benigno returned with a tray of food. Their breakfast consisted of orange juice, eggs, *chicharrones* (pork rinds), *yuca*, tortillas, and coffee, which they devoured in no time at all.

Benigno said, "Follow me. I'll show you the work which needs to be done."

He led them to a cornfield and said, "We only want you to pick some corn."

He gave them baskets, and all four worked until noon, when Benigno came to get them.

"I'm surprised at how much corn you were able to pick. Gracias."

Rodolfo responded, "No. We thank you."

"Come with me. I'll show you where you can get cleaned up."

He took them to a small outbuilding that had a shower room. Teresa went first, and then the rest. As they finished, they gathered on the porch in front of the house.

Rodolfo commented, "I'm not used to smelling clean bodies. You all smell fresh and almost sweet." Turning to Teresa, he said, "You look beautiful."

Teresa's shyness made her blush. She covered her face with her hands and replied, "You look pretty good yourself."

Despite their hard work, they all felt refreshed.

Now that they were cleaned up, Benigno invited them into their house, and Ana, Benigno's mother, served them lunch. The house was roomy and clean. While it wasn't so impressive to Rodolfo, whose family was more prosperous, Teresa, José, and Pepe found it to be a marvelous home.

Jorge, Benigno's father, said, "Welcome to our home. I understand you have traveled here from Honduras."

José replied, "Si señor. It's been a long trip."

Teresa added, "Gracias, señor, for opening your home to us. My brothers and I have never been in such a nice home before."

Ana said, "Gracias. Tell us about your trip."

As she heard the details about their arduous journey so far, Ana asked with moist eyes, "When do you have to leave?"

Rodolfo responded, "We need to get back to the beast tomorrow, no later than six o'clock in the evening. We expect the beast to depart early Monday morning."

Jorge said, "Well, I want you to relax for the rest of the day. So, please make yourselves at home. Tomorrow, Benigno will see that you get back to the beast."

All four were overwhelmed with gratitude. Teresa said, "Gracias, señor. You have no idea how we appreciate your kindness to us."

Ana asked, "Would you want to go to church with us tomorrow morning?"

All four replied, "Sure!"

After lunch, Teresa, José, Pepe, and Rodolfo went to the barn, and everybody took a siesta.

The afternoon temperature was sweltering. After the siesta, everybody gathered on the porch in front of the house, and Ana brought ice-cold lemonade. Teresa, José, Pepe, and Rodolfo felt well-rested, and as the afternoon transitioned into early evening, a cool breeze caressed them and revived them even more.

For dinner, they ate sausage, corn on the cob, and tortillas; and they washed it down with more ice-cold lemonade. Pepe also took his last pill to finish the antibiotic which he was taking. There were no more symptoms of infection from the wasp stings he had suffered.

Teresa helped Ana with the dishes and said, "Ana, you have no idea how wonderful your generosity is for us. Back in Honduras, it was a luxury to get more than one meal per day."

Ana handed a dish to Teresa to dry and asked, "Tell me about your family."

"My mamá's name is Susana. After gang members killed my father, Pedro, my mamá decided that my brothers and I would be safer if we left. My Aunt Norma and her husband, Pablo, live in the United States, and they are providing the money to pay for our travel to the United States."

Ana hugged Teresa and asked, "So, you're all family members?"

Teresa dried the knives, forks, and spoons and placed them in their drawer. "No. José and Pepe are my brothers. We met Rodolfo during our trip. He has made this trip before, and he has been very helpful to us. He's a good man."

"It appears to me, you have feelings for Rodolfo."

"I do like him a lot, and he likes me too."

"Is there anything more to it than that?"

"I don't know. I hope so."

When they finished cleaning up the kitchen, they joined the men on the porch. The evening breeze was pleasant, and the temperature was comfortable. Jorge and Benigno played their guitars while they watched the sun go down.

The next morning, after breakfast, they went to the Santa Ana Catholic Church.

This church reminded Teresa of the last time she was in her *barrio's* church to practice with the folkloric dance group, when Father Santiago broke the news that the *Barrio* 18 gang had killed Raúl. This brought back painful memories, which raised her eyebrows and prompted her to wipe tears from her eyes with her sleeve. Despite her melancholy, she was happy to attend church with this family, which had been so good to her and her brothers.

After lunch, Teresa washed everybody's clothes. They rested up during the afternoon, knowing they would soon be back on the beast again. After dinner, Ana gave them food to take with them. There was enough for them and their two companions, Marcos and Timoteo. Teresa, José, and Rodolfo thanked Jorge and Ana again for their kindness, and Benigno took them back to the beast.

Upon arrival, they found their two companions, Marcos and Timoteo. Teresa gave them their share of the food they brought, and both were pleased to get their money back. They had very little to eat on Saturday and Sunday, and they were grateful for the food which Teresa gave them.

Rodolfo and Teresa spent the evening together. For a short while, they were clean and refreshed. They enjoyed their conversation together, and their feelings for each other deepened. Not long after sunset, Teresa joined José and Pepe. They slept along the tracks, and they woke up right before dawn. The morning temperature was in the low 60s, which was uncomfortable and chilly for them.

Tragedy Strikes

All the gondola cars had been loaded with gravel. So, all the migrants climbed ladders, which took them to the top of boxcars. Since the beast didn't stop at a passenger station, everybody was relieved to know that it was not necessary for the migrants to board the beast while it was moving. Rodolfo, Marcos, and Timoteo joined Teresa, José, and Pepe on the same boxcar.

The beast departed on Monday at eight o'clock in the morning. Since the boxcars were higher than the gondolas, it was easier for everybody to see the hundreds of migrants who traveled with them. However, the boxcar's increased height amplified its oscillation from side to side much more than a gondola as the beast moved along the tracks, which also amplified the continual annoying oscillation of everybody's bodies. Moreover, the black smoke, which poured out of the three diesel engines, was much more noxious than when the migrants occupied the gondolas, which were much lower than the boxcars. So, compared to a gondola, sitting on top of a boxcar was much more intolerable.

Very few people tried to stand or walk on a boxcar's roof because it was a dangerous thing to do, not only because of a boxcar's constant movement from side to side, but also because there was nothing available to hold on to. From time to time, the migrants dodged tree branches hanging over the tracks, which swept over them and could also be dangerous.

During the hottest part of the day, a boxcar's roof became hot to the touch. In a gondola, people could stand or sit, and they could move around. But there were very few options for shifting one's position on a boxcar. And each move required migrants to endure again the hot surface of a boxcar's roof. So, when Teresa, her brothers, and everybody else wanted to shift their position, it was necessary to choose between the pain from staying in the same position or the burn of shifting their position.

Unlike gondolas, which provided some shade from the hot sun during much of the day, a boxcar provided none. Because they rationed their water, many, including Teresa, began experiencing signs of heat exhaustion. For those who became ill because of the heat, migrants contributed a small amount of their water, which would provide a quantity of extra water to revive those who suffered from the heat. The migrants shared their water in this way with Teresa.

The beast stopped at an isolated location near Acayucan at around four o'clock in the afternoon to load and unload freight. Word spread that the beast would depart at nine o'clock in the evening and not stop until they got to Córdoba at five o'clock in the morning the next day.

Everybody got off the beast to stretch their legs and to replenish their water supplies. They also found discreet places to relieve themselves. The women took turns, forming a circle around each woman to allow her privacy while she did her business.

Teresa, José, Pepe, Rodolfo, Marcos, and Timoteo finished off the small amount of food that remained from the day's travel.

Everybody prepared to get back on the beast when gang members, who were more brutal beasts, appeared out of nowhere. All displayed tattoos which covered their arms and faces; all were armed with automatic weapons. Some gang members did not wear shirts, which revealed more tattoos – tattoos which painted on the rest of their bodies the grotesque icons of their vicious reputation.

With a sinister smile on his face, the gang leader instructed the migrants, "Remove the money you have in your pockets. We're going to take up an offering, just as if we were in church. We'll be coming by with buckets for you to contribute your offerings. Unlike church, your failure to contribute will earn you a bullet. I suggest you not try to test our resolve. It's *plata or plomo*." (Money or bullets)

Gang members then moved among the migrants, like the agile dogs that they were, to collect their offerings.

One migrant trembled as he said, "I don't have any money."

The gang member who approached him said, "Oh! You're not going to contribute an offering. That's not good." And he shoved him to the ground, aimed his weapon, and shot him in the head. The man collapsed on the ground, bleeding. His eyes were open, but they saw nothing. They only revealed the blank stare of death.

Several women shrieked with blood-curdling screams. The migrant's wife cried out in dismay and stooped to help her husband, and the gang member, with rage in his eyes, shot her in the head too. She collapsed on top of her dead husband with eyes bulging from their sockets, her face frozen with horror, grief, and anguish. In death, their contorted bodies embraced each other in a macabre final hug. All migrants stood rigid with terror, too overwhelmed to move, their faces seized with shock.

Sirens alerted the gang members that police cars were approaching, and, displaying the same malevolent agility with which they appeared, the gang members disappeared.

A couple of men gathered around the migrant couple to see if they could help them. There was nothing they could do. Both were dead. An ambulance also arrived, and migrants watched in horror while they took the dead bodies away.

The mood among the migrants was somber and tense. The gang attack shocked everybody. Since they wore money belts under their clothing, Teresa and José still had money to spend. Most migrants had not been so prudent.

At eight o'clock in the evening, everybody took their places on various boxcars. Rodolfo said, "I'm going to use the restroom one more time before we leave." And he wandered off into the jungle.

As he was returning, Rodolfo heard the train cars clash when the beast started to move. The beast was leaving before the announced nine o'clock departure time. Rodolfo came running out of the jungle, but the beast accelerated, and it was now going too fast for him to climb onto one of the train cars.

Teresa saw him come running, and when she saw he missed the beast, she covered her face with her hands and screamed, "Rodolfo!" With a mournful look on her face and a quivering lower lip, she hoped against hope that somehow he might still climb back on the beast as she lost sight of him, as he disappeared from her life. She had started to fall in love with him, and seeing him miss the beast broke her heart. She would never see him again.

It was now dark, no clouds in the sky, and there was no moon. Since there was no ambient light emanating from electric lights on the ground, the sky displayed a dazzling array of stars. The vast abundance of stars lit up the sky with a milky white hue, which fascinated the migrants with a spectacular vision to behold. Teresa, and those with her, never saw so many stars concentrated in the sky's celestial dome. Starlight illuminated their surroundings with a haunting, eerie glow. The wonder of this display of God's mighty providence blessed them with one of the few delights in their life in contrast to the unrelenting wretchedness experienced by these anguished migrant travelers.

Nobody dared go to sleep for fear they might fall from the beast. They all heard stories about migrants maimed or killed when they closed their eyes for a brief moment and fell from the beast. It was growing colder, and whereas before the boxcar's roof was hot to the touch, now the roof was quick to give up the latent heat absorbed during the day and made the cold temperatures worse for everybody. Teresa, José, and Pepe, unlike most, brought coats to wear. Nevertheless, they were still cold. Several migrants started passing bottles of mezcal around. Drinking mezcal, an alcoholic beverage made from the agave plant, was a futile way to deal with the cold temperatures.

José got up and walked toward the rear of the boxcar to get a bottle of mezcal, which one of the migrants offered to him. All of a sudden, in the darkness, the beast passed under some tree branches, which brushed over everybody on the boxcar. Teresa screamed when one of the tree branches snared José. His frantic efforts to free himself were in vain, and the branch dragged him off the end of the boxcar. José's blood-curdling scream when he fell could be heard well above the roar of the beast. Teresa watched in numbed horror as he disappeared. The shocking tragedy appeared to occur in slow motion. José's scream stopped with an ominous abruptness. The next boxcar's wheels severed his body in two, killing him in an instant.

Teresa let out a heart-wrenching shriek, and she screamed, "Nooo!" She held Pepe close to her bosom, rocking back and forth. Pepe cried with shock as well. Timoteo, Marcos, and others rallied around her, but their efforts to console her were in vain. She wept unceasing bitter tears, her eyes and face revealed her deep anguish, and she would not speak. Despite Pepe's presence, and her two remaining friends, she never felt so desperate and alone. Both Rodolfo and José were now gone from her life forever.

The beast stopped at five o'clock in the morning on the outskirts of Córdoba for a crew rest. They would only be there for about four hours. With temperatures in the mid-40s, it was cold.

Teresa noticed that Arturo, a Cuban migrant, who had spoken to her on previous occasions, gazed at her from time to time out of the corner of his eye, with an enigmatic scheming smile. Seeing that she was shivering, Arturo sat beside her, put a ragged coat over Teresa's shoulders, and showed himself friendly. A migrant woman sat down beside her on the other side of Arturo. She touched Teresa to get her attention, and Teresa leaned toward her. The woman put her hand to Teresa's ear and warned her in a whisper, "Stay away from this guy. He's no good. Other women among us have already slapped his face because of his reprehensible roving hands and his efforts to seek sexual favors."

When Arturo put his arm around her, Teresa shuddered, stood, dropped his coat on the ground without saying anything, and walked away. After this incident, Teresa sought to stay within sight of Marcos and Timoteo, confident that her Christian friends would protect her in José's absence.

Everybody replenished their water supplies and did their business. Their location, some miles from Córdoba, was isolated. Very few people had anything to eat. Not only was everybody hungry, but they were also tired, cold, and irritable because they dared not to sleep while riding the beast all night.

Still in shock after watching the beast kill her brother, Teresa said to Marcos and Timoteo, "I'm not staying on this beast. I understand our next stop is in the larger city of Apizaco, and I'm going to see if Pepe and I can travel by bus from there."

Marcos responded, "I'd say that's not a good idea. Not only will it be more expensive for you, I understand the probability is high that immigration officials will detain you. And, being by yourself, you could become the victim of human trafficking, which, in your case, means you could be forced into prostitution. And God knows what would happen to Pepe."

"That may be the case. But, after losing both José and Rodolfo because of this beast, I can't bear the thought of riding on it anymore."

At around seven o'clock, migrants were surprised to see a caravan of pushcarts approaching, loaded with food and beverages. Migrants rushed to see what they might get. Because of the gang robbery in Acayucan, most migrants had no money to purchase anything. Other migrants who, like Teresa, had money hidden, which the gang members didn't steal. They and Teresa did what they could to ensure everybody got at least something to eat.

The beast departed at nine o'clock in the morning and arrived at a train station in Apizaco at one o'clock in the afternoon. Apizaco is a larger city, and this train station also served passengers who had tickets to board passenger trains. So, to continue on the beast, Migrants had to walk some distance beyond the train station to a place where they again would have to board the beast while it moved along the tracks. And once again, they had to pay coyotes who, in turn, bribed the train conductor. As before, the train conductor would keep the beast's speed low enough, giving the migrants the dangerous opportunity to board the moving beast after it departed the train station. Coyotes demanded 7,000 pesos per person.

New Travel Plans

After saying goodbye to Marcos and Timoteo, Teresa and Pepe took a taxi into town. It was Wednesday, and they arrived in downtown Apizaco at about two o'clock in the afternoon. Apizaco, a city about 85 miles east of Mexico City, is a commercial, manufacturing, and transportation center.

When they got out of the taxi, Pepe said, "I'm hungry. When are we going to get something to eat?"

Teresa and Pepe were fatigued and dirty. Their faces were soiled with soot from the three train engines' black diesel smoke, and they reeked of body odor. Pedestrians turned their noses, stared at them as if they were from some other planet, and moved away from them as they passed by.

Seeing a taco stand, Teresa said, "Before we can sit down in a restaurant, we need to get cleaned up. Let's go over and get us a couple of tacos for now."

They spent 75 pesos ($3) for the tacos and two glasses of lemonade. Teresa and Pepe scarfed the tacos down without paying attention to how they tasted. The tacos alleviated their painful hunger pangs, and the ice-cold lemonade refreshed their parched throats.

Teresa asked the woman at the taco stand, "Where's the closest Catholic Church?"

"Go to the next block, turn left, and you'll see the steeple."

"Can you fill our water bottles, please?"

"Sure."

"Gracias."

After Teresa and Pepe finished their tacos, they headed for Saint Mary's Catholic Church. There they met Mario, who was an acolyte at the church. He wore a garment similar to that of a priest, with a long black robe, which reached to his feet, and a shorter white robe, which reached to his knees. Unlike a priest, he did not wear a clerical collar.

Teresa asked, "Can my brother and I lay down on the pews to get some sleep? We've been awake for over a day."

Their body odor caused Mario to turn his head, and he winced his nose. He replied, "No. I can't let you stay here."

Teresa begged him, "Please let us get a little sleep. We have no other place to go."

Mario responded, "Okay. But I have to close the church at five o'clock this afternoon."

Mario, who walked with a limp, went about his business. Teresa and Pepe laid down, and sweet sleep was quick to come upon them.

Mario removed his acolyte garments, which revealed the blue jeans and T-shirt, which he wore underneath. It took Mario some significant effort to wake up Teresa at five o'clock, and he said, "You're gonna have to leave now. I have to close the church."

Teresa asked, "Is there someplace where we can get cleaned up?"

Though Teresa was dirty and smelled horrible; nevertheless, Mario saw her as an attractive woman. He replied, "My aunt owns a home right outside of town. If you want, I can take you there where you can bathe."

"Gracias. That would be wonderful."

Pepe was still sound asleep, and Teresa woke him up and said, "Come on. We have to get going."

Mario led them out of town, and they turned onto a dark dirt road, lined with trees that overshadowed it – a road that screamed, beware.

With eerie uneasiness, Teresa asked, "Where is your aunt's house?"

Mario looked at her out of the corner of his eye. "It's not too far down this road."

After they moved away from the main road, Mario pushed Teresa off the dirt road into a wooded area, pulled out a knife, and said, "I want you to take your clothes off."

Fear gripped Teresa, and she pushed him away. She and Pepe ran down the road, and Mario went after them. Because of Mario's limp, Teresa and Pepe were leaving him behind. However, when they approached a stream, Teresa got stuck in some quicksand, and soon she sunk into the quicksand over her knees.

Pepe tried to help her, but Teresa yelled at him, "Stay away, or you'll get stuck in this quicksand too."

Panic took over, and Teresa struggled to free herself, but she sunk deeper into the mire. It was like trying to swim in thick, cold honey as it sucked her down some more. She removed her backpack in her efforts to escape, and it soon disappeared below the surface.

Mario caught up with them and yanked Teresa out of the quicksand. The muddy mire sucked her shoes from her feet, and smelly, filthy, cold mud clung to her clothing up to her waist.

Mario forced her to the ground, held his knife to her throat, and said with a scowl on his face and glaring eyes that reflected his lust, "Now pull your slacks down."

With eyes frozen open with terror, Teresa blurted out, "Stop! No! Don't do this!" And she struggled to free herself.

Mario, through clenched teeth, threatened her, saying with a growling voice, "Submit! Or I'll kill your brother while you watch."

Pepe started socking Mario, and he pushed Pepe away, saying, "You leave me alone, or I'll kill your sister."

Pepe was too young to know what Mario was doing, and he sobbed with fear while he watched Mario rape Teresa.

Not able to resist, Teresa closed her eyes and covered her face with her hands. Mario's heavy breathing nauseated Teresa with the foul odor from his rotten teeth, a putrid stench like a dead skunk. He grunted when he experienced his climax. After he had his way with Teresa, he abandoned them.

After he left, Teresa noted she was bleeding. Since she knew she was a virgin, she understood that bleeding was to be expected. But she feared nevertheless that Mario might have injured her. She pulled up her slacks to cover her nudity and laid still, sobbing with shame and disgust. The first thing that entered her distraught mind was her concern about what would happen to Pepe if she died. Soon feelings of humiliation, degradation, guilt, shame, and embarrassment afflicted her. She now choked and coughed as she wailed.

Along with self-blame, she contemplated how she could get revenge and make Mario pay for what he did to her. In her mind, she envisioned the fiendish pleasure of inflicting on him a violent and painful death. She became so hysterical, it never even occurred to her to worry she might become pregnant. Then, with a sense of horror and futility, she cried out in anger, "God. Why have you let all this happen to me? My father, Raúl, Rodolfo, and my brother are all gone. Pepe and I go to your church to seek help, and your acolyte now rapes me. Why should I trust you?"

Shuttering with fear, Pepe cried with eyes widened in alarm. He worried about his sister, and in his innocence he asked, "Are you gonna be all right?"

Trembling, she reached out her hand, put it on his shoulder, and took a deep breath. "Yeah. I'll be okay. Just give me a few minutes."

It was now about 6:30 in the evening, and it was getting dark. Teresa took Pepe down to the stream, where they did their best to clean themselves up in the stream's cold water. Then they went to sleep on the bank of the stream. Some hours later, the cold temperature dipped down into the lower forties and woke them up. Pepe still had his coat, but Teresa's coat was in her backpack, which she lost in the quicksand. Shivering from the cold, Teresa held Pepe close to her, and their body heat was the only source of warmth for them.

Still well before dawn, they got up and headed back downtown. Teresa hung her head like a dying flower. On the way, a large dog's threatening growl erupted into ferocious barking. Their hearts raced, and the perception of impending danger quickened their pace. The dog's chain frustrated its effort to go after them.

Since she had no shoes to wear, Teresa's feet ached and then went numb from the cold. When they arrived downtown, they found nothing was open except a hospital, and they went inside to escape the cold.

A nurse asked, "Can I help you?"

Teresa responded, "We're trying to get out of the cold. We have no other place to go. Can we please stay here for a little while?"

"I guess so." Seeing how ragged they were, the nurse asked, "Where are you from?"

"We're from Honduras. After we crossed from Guatemala into Mexico, we rode on the beast until we arrived here."

"I suppose you're trying to get to the United States."

"That's right," and she explained how her brother died when he fell from the beast. "So, I've decided we can't ride on the beast anymore."

"I'm so sorry to hear that. Would you care for some hot tea?"

"That would be wonderful. Gracias."

When the nurse brought the tea, she asked, "So, what are you going to do?"

The tea lifted their spirits. "We're going to take some time to recover. Then we plan to take a bus to Mexico City. I thank you for the tea."

"You're welcome. Give me a minute. I'll be right back."

The nurse returned with two blankets and asked, "How long have you been traveling?"

With a momentary sense of blissful security, Teresa and Pepe savored the blankets' warmth as Teresa replied. "I thank you for the blankets. We've traveled about two weeks now."

"You know, you still have a long way to go."

"Oh. We do know."

The nurse looked at her watch. "Well, I must get back to my duties now. I hope you'll have a safe trip."

"Gracias."

Teresa and Pepe stayed until the sun came up, and then they went to a nearby restaurant for breakfast. They enjoyed hot oatmeal with toast. In addition to some orange juice, Teresa drank a cup of coffee; Pepe, a cup of tea. The bill came to 170 pesos. They stayed at the restaurant until nine o'clock in the morning. The breakfast refreshed them somewhat, but they were still exhausted due to the lack of sleep.

They left the restaurant and went across the street to a small hotel and got a room for two nights at 749 pesos a night. After taking showers, they went to a store and bought new clothes and dark gray coats for both of them. Teresa also bought a new backpack to replace the one she lost. She discarded Pepe's old coat because it wasn't adequate for the colder temperatures which they were experiencing. Both got two pairs of bluejeans. Teresa purchased a white blouse and a blue blouse for herself, and she bought two cowboy-style shirts for Pepe, one red and one green. Teresa also bought a cowboy hat for Pepe and new shoes for her and Pepe. That set them back about 1,900 pesos.

After the much-needed breakfast, the showers, and some new clothes, they felt like they had re-entered civilization again. They still felt fatigued, but they now felt refreshed, and renewing energy began to emerge.

Teresa spent 125 pesos for a phone card and called her Aunt Norma. A sense of joy came over her when Norma answered, and Teresa said, "It's so good to hear your voice."

Norma asked, "How's it going?"

Teresa hesitated and began to weep while she replied, "I'm afraid I have to give you some bad news. José was killed when he fell off the beast."

"Oh, my God! How did it happen?" Norma asked with a quivering voice.

"We were riding on top of a boxcar, and José went to get some mezcal from another migrant. As he walked toward the rear of the beast, a tree branch swept over us. Because he didn't see it, the branch snared him and dragged him to the rear edge of the boxcar, and he fell to his death."

Teresa could hear her aunt weeping, and Norma responded, "How horrible. I'll send a letter to Susana right away to let her know the bad news. How are you and Pepe?"

"We could be better, but we're okay. It grieves me to tell you, José was carrying half of our money, so that money is now gone. After José's death, I must tell you. I cannot bear to ride any further on the beast. I'm hoping it will be all right with you if we take the bus for the rest of the way to get to the border."

"I guess I don't blame you. Sure. Take the bus. I expect we need to send you some more money."

"Yes, please. So far, we've spent about $1,100, and we lost $450, which José was carrying with him in his money belt. We're now in Apizaco, Mexico, and we plan to depart the day after tomorrow. So, if you can send something today, we should be able to pick it up tomorrow before we depart."

"Okay. I'll send you $1,000. Be careful and take care of yourselves."

"We will. Gracias, Aunt Norma."

They were about to hang up when Pepe asked, "Can I talk to my Aunt Norma?"

He picked up the phone, and, after greeting her, his Aunt Norma asked, "And how are you, Pepe?"

"I guess I'm doin all right. We've been traveling a long time."

"That's true. You know. You still have a long way to go."

"I know. But we'll make it."

"I'm praying that you will. You take care of yourself and your sister."

"I will. Bye-bye."

As they returned to the hotel, Teresa looked at the church they visited the day before with a cold, defiant stare. The plaguing memory of Mario's violation invaded her thoughts with repugnance and wrath.

Other than meals, they spent the rest of the day in their hotel room. Teresa and Pepe didn't even try the bed. Instead, they preferred to sleep on the floor.

That night, Teresa cried herself to sleep. In the wee hours of the morning, she cried out when a nightmare woke her up, in which she perceived Mario was raping her again. She wrestled with the sheets, and she could smell his rotten breath. The memory of the rape jumped her like muggers in the dark. Terror overpowered her, and she screamed, which woke Pepe up.

He asked, "Are you okay?"

With darting glances, Teresa looked around the room. Internal, stormy torment afflicted her. It took her a moment to realize where she was. She told Pepe, "I'll be all right. Go back to sleep now."

Teresa laid awake until dawn, tossing and turning, unable to go back to sleep. The next day, they went to pick up the money, which Norma sent them. Other than that, and the day's meals, they relaxed in their hotel room and watched television.

The Letter

Susana stopped at the post office with her friend, Luz. She rejoiced and was pleased to see that she received a letter from her sister Norma. Eager to get some news about her children, Teresa, José, and Pepe, her anxious fingers tore open the envelope. She removed the letter and began to read. She would discover that it was a fatal letter that winged its way from afar, like a bird of prey.

The letter's words brought immediate tears to her eyes, which streamed down her face, and she screamed when she read about José's death. "Oh God! No!"

Luz grabbed Susana when she started to collapse. A bystander helped Luz take Susana to a bench, and Luz sat beside her.

A small crowd gathered around Susana and Luz. While they didn't know what happened, the distress on Susana's face revealed the news to be tragic. Whatever the letter said, they guessed that it reported the death of a loved one. Susana's reaction was a too common occurrence in this Tegucigalpa *barrio*.

Luz put her arm around Susana and asked, "What is it?"

Susana leaned her head on Luz's shoulder. Through her heart-wrenching sobs, her voice quivered as she cried out, "José, my son, is dead!"

"I'm so sorry."

Many in the crowd knew Susana and laid their hands on her to express tenderness and sympathy. No words were capable of consoling her at this painful moment, so no attempt was made to say any. Words at this moment were like worthless pennies that nobody bothers to pick up after they fall to the ground.

Father Santiago came out of the post office, and, when he saw the crowd, he went over to join them.

When Susana saw Father Santiago approach, she reached out to him and cried, "José, my son, has died in Mexico."

Also, understanding that words at this time were inadequate to console Susana, the priest limited his words to say, "I'm so sorry, Susana."

He stayed among the friends who gathered to support her.

Susana started to calm down and said to Luz, "I wanna go home. Please come with me."

As she started to leave, Father Santiago said, "Come see me when you feel you're ready."

Susana looked at him with her tear-stained face, which reflected her devastation and sorrow. "Gracias, Father. I'll be by to see you soon."

The news traveled fast, as bad news does, and her neighbors brought food to her home. They took turns sitting with her to share in her grief.

A few days later, Father Santiago came to visit and said, "I'd like to have a memorial service for José. We can do it either Wednesday or Thursday evening. Which do you prefer?"

On Wednesday, many gathered at the church for the memorial service.

Among the many comforting words Father Santiago shared, he said, "José was a good man. He was a young man; he was only eighteen years old. We live in dangerous times in Honduras, with the constant threat of gang violence. And within this past year, Susana also lost her dear husband, Pedro, a victim of gang violence. After his death, Susana's options were to keep her children home and endure the real threat of more gang violence or have them risk the dangerous trip on the

Mexican freight train, known as the beast, to find a better life in the United States. Gang members were already threatening José and Teresa. So, Susana decided that the better of these two bad options was to send them to the United States."

"Susana, I see no reason to question your decision. You did the right thing, despite what happened to José. We don't know where Teresa and Pepe are in their journey, except we know they are someplace in Mexico. But I do believe they are safer there than they would be if they were here. So, Susana, I want you to know that any guilt you feel about the difficult decision you made is unjustified. And we, your friends, are gathered here to be a source of comfort and encouragement to you."

"Now, let us pray."

Everybody bowed their heads and made the sign of the cross.

Father Santiago prayed, "Dear God. We are all saddened by the loss of our dear brother, José. But we trust that You now have him with You in a better place along with his papá. I pray you would protect Teresa and Pepe while they travel. Please help them find a safe place in the United States. I pray Your presence will be a source of comfort to Susana as she grieves the loss of José. I also pray we will soon learn that Teresa and Pepe have not only arrived in the United States, but that they will also enjoy a better life there. Help us to honor You in all we do. Amen."

After this moving, bittersweet memorial service, Susana returned to her grim, humble shack, which was more like a prison than a home in which she was locked away by herself – her husband dead, her son dead, Teresa and Pepe, so far away. Forlorn, she sat at the table by herself, contemplating her seemingly meaningless life, longing for her family's tender touch. Loneliness and sorrow squeezed in on her, like a blanket tightly wrapped around her, from which, in desperation, she felt hopelessly trapped. In her self-imposed solitude, tears flowed from sunken, darkened eyes onto her hollowed cheeks, while unanswerable questions invaded her mind.

Round Trip to Mexico City

It was now Saturday, December 17th. Teresa and Pepe checked out of the hotel and ate breakfast. Teresa purchased two bus tickets for her and Pepe. She was concerned they might have problems with immigration officials, but they encountered none. They boarded the bus to Mexico City, which departed at 9:30 in the morning. Pepe sat by the window. Teresa occupied the aisle seat. They felt like they were traveling in luxury after riding on the beast. Teresa began conversing with Raquel, a young woman who sat in the aisle seat beside her. Raquel was about the same age as Teresa. They looked like they could be sisters, and they were destined to become friends.

Raquel commented, "You're not from Mexico, are you?"

"No. My brother, Pepe, and I are from Tegucigalpa, Honduras."

"So, how do you happen to be riding this bus?"

Teresa responded, "That's a long story," and she proceeded to tell Raquel about the gang violence in Tegucigalpa, the gang-related murders of her father and boyfriend, the decision to migrate to the United States, and the dangerous journey on the beast, which brought her to Apizaco, Mexico. She explained, with a tear in her eye and a quivering lip, how her brother, Jose, died when he fell from the box car they were riding on. "After that, I decided my brother, Pepe, and I couldn't continue our journey on the beast. So, that's why we're on this bus."

Raquel, a Christian, covered her face with her hands, and, with mournful raised eyebrows, she replied, "I'm so sorry. How dreadful! So, what are your plans now?"

Teresa shrugged. "Pepe and I are going to try to get to the U.S. border by bus."

After hearing what Teresa said and seeing the anguish in Teresa's eyes as she told her story, Raquel paused before she replied, "I gotta tell you, that may not be your best option. If you travel by bus, you will, almost without a doubt, have to deal with immigration officials. Your greatest risk will be when you depart from Mexico City. President Trump is pressuring the Mexican government to stop migrants who try to enter the United States in violation of the law. If they discover you're from Honduras and trying to get to the United States, they will take steps to deport you without delay."

Raquel raised and lowered her hands, with palms up, to make her point, "We see news items on television with increasing frequency about people just like you who end up back in their countries of origin. I'm going to Mexico City to meet with my brother, Don Felipe. He lives in Tijuana, just across the border from San Diego, California, and he may suggest a better option for you."

Teresa found Raquel's words disquieting, and yet, she was hopeful Raquel's brother might have a better solution for her and Pepe. She asked, "Do you live in Mexico City?"

"No. I live in Apizaco with my husband, Alejandro, and my son, Josué. My brother is in Mexico City on business. We don't see each other much. So, I'm going to visit him for the day."

Teresa tilted her head to the side. "So, what makes you think your brother might have a better option for me and my brother?"

"I don't really know for sure. But it won't hurt to ask him. As a businessman, he has some pretty good connections."

"Well, we need a better option. I hope he can help us. Tell me about your son. How old is he?"

"I'd say he's about the same age as Pepe. He's seven years old."

Pepe said, "I'm only six years old."

Raquel responded, "Well, I expect you and Josué could be good friends."

Teresa asked, "What does your husband do?"

"Alejandro is a dentist. We lived in Mexico City for a while, and he purchased a dental practice in Apizaco, so we moved there a couple of years ago. He and Josué are spending the day together while I'm away."

The bus stopped at small pueblos along the way and arrived at a bus terminal in Mexico City at 11:30. They got off the bus together, and Felipe greeted Raquel with a kiss on each cheek, "It's good to see you again, Raquel. Are these friends of yours?"

"Yes. We met on the bus. Their names are Teresa and Pepe."

Turning to Teresa and Pepe, she said, "This is my brother, Don Felipe."

Teresa extended her hand and replied, "It's a pleasure to meet you, Don Felipe."

Felipe shook hands with Teresa and replied, "It's good to meet you as well. Do you live in Apizaco?"

Teresa replied, "No, señor, we're from Tegucigalpa, Honduras."

Raquel added, "They traveled up here on the beast with the plan to arrive in the United States. It saddens me to say they lost their brother, José, who was killed when he fell from the top of the boxcar, which they were riding on. Teresa came here on the bus today because she wants to travel to the United States border by bus."

Raquel's comment about getting to the border by bus caused Felipe to pause. With raised eyebrows, he responded, "I'm so sorry to hear you're mourning the death of your brother." He paused again and then said, "It's almost noon. Would you care to join us for dinner?"

Teresa replied, "Oh yes, Don Felipe, that would be wonderful."

They got into the Mercedes-Benz, which Don Felipe rented, and, after a fifteen-minute ride, they arrived at the restaurant El Farolito. It was an unusually warm day in Mexico City, and this was the first time Teresa and Pepe ever rode in an air-conditioned car. They shivered from the air conditioning's cold air.

After being seated at a table, Felipe smiled and asked, "Have you ever eaten tacos al pastor?"

Teresa answered, "No, señor. Tell me about them."

"They're a specialty in this restaurant. You don't want to miss the opportunity to try them."

"What are they like?"

Don Felipe touched all the fingers together on his right hand, kissed them with his lips, and opened his hand to simulate an explosion of flavor. Then he said with gusto, "They're delicious. The chef slices thin strips of succulent roasted pork from a spit and places them on a corn tortilla. The tacos also include onions, coriander leaves, and pineapple. I'm sure you'll enjoy them."

In addition to the tacos al pastor, the waiter also brought elotes, which are corn on the cob, well seasoned with salt, chili powder, lime, butter, cheese, mayonnaise, and sour cream. They all drank Coca-Cola.

Before they ate, Don Felipe asked, "Shall we pray?"

Everybody bowed their heads, and Felipe prayed, "Dear God. We thank you for this food and your many blessings. I pray you would bless Teresa and Pepe's efforts to reach the United States. May they prosper there. Please comfort them and help them deal with their grief due to José's death. I pray their faith in you will be a source of hope for them for a future reunion with José in Heaven. Help us to honor You in all we do. Amen."

Teresa looked away while he prayed. Still bitter that God allowed so much tragedy in her life, Teresa was not an enthusiastic participant in the prayer.

Felipe asked Teresa, "So, why did you decide to make this dangerous trip on the beast?"

Teresa repeated what she told Raquel earlier and said, "Now that I've lost José, my brother, I don't feel I can continue traveling on the beast. So, my plan is to see if we can travel by bus."

As Raquel told Teresa earlier, Felipe responded, "I must tell you. As Honduran migrants in Mexico, traveling by bus to the U.S. border is not your best option. The probability is high that you will encounter immigration agents who will send you back to Honduras."

A single tear filled her eye and spilled onto her cheek, and Teresa replied, "Then I'm not sure what I should do."

The despair on Teresa's face touched Felipe. He paused in contemplation and watched while Raquel and Teresa continued the conversation. With the best of intentions, he touched Teresa's hand and said, "I wanna see if I can help you."

Teresa jerked her hand away. Felipe's touch awakened panic within her. Her vivid and dreadful experience with Mario, who raped her, came rushing back to her like a demon and made her wary of Felipe's offer for help. With excessive alarm, she began gasping to breathe, backed her chair away from the table, and stuttered as she said with a shaky smile, "No, Don Felipe. It wouldn't be right for me to accept your help. I need to go to the restroom. I'll be right back."

Teresa rushed off, and both Felipe and Raquel noted Teresa's strange overreaction.

Raquel said, "Let me go see what happened."

She found Teresa in the restroom, trembling and crying, and she said, "Teresa, calm down. What's wrong?"

Teresa's lower lip quivered, and she stuttered as she said, "I'm sorry. I don't know why I overreacted. I must confess to you that a man raped me in Apizaco, and Don Felipe's touch made me panic. I don't understand why I reacted that way."

Raquel put her hand on Teresa's shoulder. "I'm so sorry. I suppose I would react the same way if a man I'd just met touched me right after being raped."

"I'm so frightened, and I don't know what I'm going to do. I'd love for Don Felipe to help me, but I'm afraid to trust him."

In an attempt to put Teresa at ease, Raquel said, "I want you to know that faith in God is very important to my brother and everybody in my family, and we are very active in our church. I'm confident you can feel safe with us."

With tearful eyes, Teresa replied, "That's good to know, but I'll tell you. The man who raped me is an acolyte in the Catholic Church in Apizaco. I don't know if I could even trust a priest anymore, let alone your brother."

Raquel hugged Teresa and spoke with a gentle voice. "Well, I'll tell you what. Let's go find out what Felipe's plan is, and you can see if it's acceptable to you."

When they got back to the table, Felipe was quick to say, "Teresa, I'm sorry for the distress I caused you."

Raquel responded, "Felipe, as you know, Teresa suffered some very traumatic experiences, starting at home and during her travel. And most of those terrible experiences involved men."

Shaking like a mistreated dog, Teresa said, "Don Felipe, please forgive me. When you touched my hand, I became very frightened."

Felipe replied, "No. I ask you to forgive me. Now, let me explain the plan I propose."

She mumbled, "Please go ahead." Teresa hid her hands under the table, wrinkled her forehead, and looked at Felipe with rapidly blinking eyes, which still reflected fear, doubt, and hesitation.

Felipe took a sip of his Coke and wiped his mouth with his napkin. "I'll be taking care of some business here in Mexico City for the next two weeks. Then I fly back to Tijuana. I suggest that you and Pepe return to Apizaco with Raquel. When I finish my business, I'll come to get you, and I'll pay your airfare to Tijuana."

Pepe exclaimed, "We're gonna fly in an airplane?"

Felipe smiled and said, "Yeah. Have you ridden on a plane before?"

"Never!"

Turning to Teresa, he asked, "How do you feel about this plan?"

"Don Felipe, that's very generous of you. Forgive me for asking this, but: How can I be confident enough to trust you?"

"Well, that's a good question. I understand you're afraid. All I can say is: While you're in Apizaco, you will have the opportunity to visit Raquel's church, and she can introduce you to many people who know me well. I used to be a member there as well. I'm confident they'll be able to put your mind at ease about me."

Dreading the thought that she would have to go to the church where she met Mario, her rapist, Teresa asked, "Would that be Saint Mary's Catholic Church?"

Raquel responded, "No. We attend the *Primera Iglesia Metodista de Apizaco*." (First Methodist Church of Apizaco)

Teresa felt some relief knowing she would not have to go back to the Catholic Church, and she asked, "Will Pepe and I be able to travel with our passports?"

Felipe replied, "That's another good question. I'm afraid the use of your Honduran passports would get you in trouble with immigration agents. If we get your hair done in a similar style to the photograph in Raquel's passport, I think you can use her passport. Once we get on the plane, you won't need it anymore."

"What about my brother?"

"I'm pretty sure Josué doesn't have a passport. We'll say Pepe's your son. I think we'll be all right with that. So, how do you feel?"

Conflicted, Teresa was still torn between this free travel offer and the need to trust Felipe.

She paused and, when she didn't answer, Pepe said with an excited voice, "Come on, Teresa. I wanna fly on an airplane."

Teresa looked at Pepe, took a deep breath, looked at Felipe with a worried look on her face, and said, "Okay. Let's do it."

Raquel said to Teresa, "I'm glad my brother can help you, and I'm confident you don't have anything to worry about."

Resigned to take what Teresa deemed to be a significant risk, she sighed and said, "I thank you so much."

Felipe concluded, "Great! I'll take you back to Apizaco now. Teresa, I feel confident Raquel won't mind if you and Pepe stay with her for the next couple of weeks. Then I'll come to get you, and we'll head to the airport here in Mexico City." Felipe then turned to Raquel and confirmed, "Will that be all right with you?"

"Not a problem."

Seeing that their long, dangerous travel in Mexico would soon be over, Teresa broke down and cried. "I'm so grateful to you for your generosity."

They got back to Apizaco by 4:30. Raquel introduced Teresa and Pepe to Alejandro and Josué. After a light supper, Felipe returned to Mexico City.

Felipe made flight reservations for Teresa and Pepe for their flight to Tijuana. He also called Elvia, his wife, to tell her about Teresa and Pepe, and that they would return with him to Tijuana.

Teresa's New Beginning

That evening, Teresa and Raquel sat on a comfortable sofa. Alejandro chatted with them for a short while before going to his home office to do some work on his computer. Josué brought out some of his toys, and he and Pepe sat on the thickly carpeted floor, happy to be playing together, and they soon became friends.

Raquel and her family lived in a comfortable four-bedroom home in a neighborhood whose residents were mostly professionals – doctors and dentists, attorneys, and accountants. In addition to the living room where Raquel and Teresa sat, there was a spacious dining room and an efficient kitchen with newer, modern appliances. An unoccupied bedroom included a double bed and served as a guest room. Josue occupied one of the other bedrooms. Alejandro's office also included a twin bed.

This respite from the beast and other dangers filled Teresa with a sense of tranquility, a much-needed respite which she relished. She commented, "This is the best day I've experienced in a very long time. I'm so grateful for the kindness you and your brother have shown to me and Pepe."

Grateful for the blessing of making Teresa's burden lighter, Raquel responded, "One of the greatest joys in life is to do something for others, which they can't do for themselves. And I think you'll find Don Felipe takes great joy in serving God in this way."

Still angry that God did not protect her from the hypocritical church acolyte who raped her, Teresa replied with a tone of bitterness and disdain, "As I said, I'm grateful to you and your brother. And I see how God has blessed you. But He has not blessed me and my family at all. I see this beautiful home you live in, but my family endures extreme poverty. My mother lives in a one-room shack with a dirt floor and no electricity. You are blessed with prosperity and apparent security, and I rejoice that you have these blessings. But most of the time, my family eats one meal a day. Violence, murder, my brother's tragic death only a few days ago, and a supposed Christian who raped me are the story of my family's life. So, I ask you: Why should I trust God for anything?"

Raquel hugged Teresa. "I can't even begin to give you an answer to your very valid question. When we go to church tomorrow, I'll introduce you to our pastor. He's a great guy. His name is Frank Turner, and he's an American missionary. I think it will be worthwhile for you to meet with him. He may be able to give you some valuable advice about what to expect when you get to the United States. But what is more important, he may be able to give you some wise counsel about this question you asked me and about the despair you have lived with."

Dwelling on Raquel's words, Teresa pursed her lips. "I'm sorry. I'm not sure if I'm interested in going to your church or talking to your pastor."

"Will you pray with me about that?"

With a half-hearted smile, Teresa replied with noticeable reluctance, "I guess so."

Raquel held Teresa's hands in hers and prayed, "Dear God. I thank you for bringing Teresa and Pepe into my life. Teresa has told me about the hard times and the tragedy she and her family have endured. Hearing her story makes me grateful for the way you have blessed me and my family. While I don't know why Teresa and her family have endured such a hard life, I believe without a doubt that you love them. I pray they will come to experience your blessings in a very tangible way. Bless Teresa and Pepe while they travel to the United States. May they find a better life there. I thank You for making it possible for me and Felipe to be a source of blessing in their lives. Teresa and Pepe need to experience Your love and Your blessings in their lives, and I pray the time they spend here will be a new beginning for them. Help us to honor You in all we do. Amen."

Despite her cynicism, a sense of hope caressed her soul, and Teresa broke down, sobbed, and embraced Raquel. "I thank you so much. Nobody ever prayed for me like this."

Raquel tightened their warm embrace and said, "That gives me great joy. I encourage you to look forward to attending our church tomorrow."

There was a knock at the door, and, when Raquel opened it, there was a procession of people dressed in robes that crowded around the door, including two children who played the roles of Mary and Joseph and sang a song in which they asked, "*¿Hay posada?*" (Is there any room at the inn?) Hearing the song, Pepe and Josué came running to the door to listen.

When they finished, Raquel followed the Mexican Christmas tradition and responded, "I'm sorry. There is no room at the inn," and she closed the door.

Teresa smiled and commented, "We have *posadas* in Honduras too. But they never visited our *barrio*."

Raquel explained, "We expect to see a *posada* procession arrive at our door every evening until Christmas Eve."

After enjoying a cup of tea, they retired for the evening. Raquel showed Teresa and Pepe to separate bedrooms. Pepe would sleep on a cot in Josué's bedroom. When she saw the bed in her room, Teresa said, "What a beautiful bed. Nobody in my family ever slept on a bed in Honduras."

Raquel responded with a look of disbelief on her face. "Is that right? I pray that one day soon, you will never have to sleep anywhere else other than on a bed."

Teresa again decided to try sleeping on the bed. She failed to fight back happy tears as she pondered the joyful events of the day.

Although she found the bed to be comfortable, she could not sleep until she laid down on the floor.

Raquel heard a scream at about two o'clock in the morning, and she rushed into Teresa's bedroom. When she found her on the floor, she asked, "Did you fall out of bed?"

Teresa, bathed in a cold sweat, glanced around, not focusing on anything, and then she looked at Raquel with eyes that reflected horror and said, "No. I couldn't sleep on the bed. As I said before, I never slept on a bed during my life in Honduras. I spent the night in a couple of hotel rooms during our travels, but I couldn't sleep there either until I got off the bed and laid down on the floor. I'm sorry I woke you up. A horrible nightmare about my rape terrified me. It was as if the whole disgusting experience happened again."

"Are you going to be all right?"

"I guess so."

Raquel went back to her bedroom, and Teresa laid awake until after sunrise. She now began to worry she might be pregnant.

After breakfast, they all walked to the Primera Iglesia Metodista de Apizaco, the church where Raquel and her family worshiped.

Raquel said, "The first thing I want to do is introduce you to our pastor."

Pepe stayed with Josué and Alejandro, and Raquel and Teresa walked up to an American man, dressed in a coat and tie. A slender man, he appeared to be in his 30s. Raquel said in Spanish, "Pastor Turner, I would like you to meet Teresa. She and her brother, Pepe, are migrants from Honduras trying to get to the United States. Teresa, this is our pastor, Brother Frank Turner."

Brother Turner smiled, shook hands with Teresa, and responded in Spanish with a strong English accent, "I'm happy to meet you, Teresa. I hope you'll find this to be a good place to worship today."

Raquel then spoke in a low voice, "Pastor, I'm sure you're aware of the dangers migrants experience when they ride the beast to get to the United States, and Teresa has experienced more than her fair share of tragedy. My brother, Don Felipe, offers to help her and Pepe, her brother, get to Tijuana. But, because of some terrible things she experienced, she's afraid to let him help her. Her biggest fear is traveling with Felipe by plane to Tijuana. I've encouraged her to set up a meeting with you to discuss the dilemmas she experienced and her fears. After Teresa's very recent arrival in Apizaco, she endured an awful experience with a church acolyte, so she's also fearful about having such a meeting with you."

The pastor smiled and replied, "Teresa, I'd be happy to meet with you. Let me put your mind at ease. The door into my office has a window. So, while our volunteer secretary can't hear what you and I might talk about, she can always see us while you and I sit in my office. I hope that relieves any fear you have about meeting with me."

Teresa paused as she pondered the pastor's words, and then, nodding her head, she said, "Pastor Turner, I would very much appreciate the opportunity to meet with you. When can I come to see you?"

Pastor Turner checked the calendar on his phone. "Would ten o'clock Tuesday morning work for you?"

"Yes. I'll come to see you at ten o'clock Tuesday morning. Gracias."

It was not yet time for the church service to begin, so Raquel introduced Teresa to her close friends, Ignacio and Lupita, and other church members. The church's ambiance wasn't anything like she ever experienced in her Catholic Church, where people entered, made the sign of the cross, and sat down with little or no conversation. In this church, ongoing conversations were happy, joyous, and sounded like a flock of cackling geese.

The service started, and Teresa noted how informal everything was. She enjoyed the singing, which included hymns of praise and gospel songs of testimony. She was surprised to see how everybody clapped to the music, and she and Pepe clapped along with them.

Pastor Turner announced to the congregation that Teresa and Pepe were visiting as guests.

The pastor called on a deacon to pray. He didn't read a prayer, as Teresa expected. He prayed from his heart. In his prayer, he said, "Dear

God, our heavenly Father. We are grateful for this opportunity to come together to worship you. I pray your presence will be real for us. No doubt, there are people here today who need Your healing touch and people who are facing difficult times. I pray, dear God, that you will meet their needs. We trust You for what You will do, but we very much look forward to the time when we can thank You for what you have done. Please be with our pastor as he preaches the word of God. If there is one here today who has not come to a saving knowledge of Jesus Christ, may today be the day in which they gain assurance of eternal life. These things I ask for Jesus' sake. Amen."

Teresa's heart fluttered, and she was touched by the deacon's prayer, perceiving he directed the words of his prayer to her.

As the congregation sang another song, everybody greeted one another, and many welcomed Teresa and Pepe and thanked them for visiting the church. Teresa and Pepe were both surprised at how friendly everybody was.

A husband and wife stood, played their guitars, and sang a heartwarming song of faith.

Then Pastor Turner stood to deliver his sermon. He took his text from 1 John 5:13 and read, "These things have I written unto you who believe in the name of the Son of God, that you may know that you have eternal life."

He then explained how Jesus Christ died on the cross to be a sacrifice for the forgiveness of our sins. Furthermore, he said, "If you recognize you are a sinner and accept Jesus Christ as your Savior, God will grant you eternal life in heaven as a free gift." He quoted Romans 6:23, "For the wages of sin is death, but the gift of God is eternal life through Jesus Christ our Lord."

As he finished his sermon, Pastor Turner said, "If anyone here has not accepted Jesus Christ as his or her Lord and Savior, I invite you to come forward while we sing. And someone will take a Bible and help you understand what it means to accept Jesus Christ as your Savior."

Teresa never heard such a sermon before. After the service was over, she pondered what Pastor Turner said.

As they departed, Ignacio and Lupita, Alejandro and Raquel's friends, suggested they all meet for lunch.

Ignacio asked, "Would it be all right if we went for pizza?"

Pepe replied, "Pizza would be great!"

Ignacio responded, "Well, that settles it."

They went to a pizzeria called Sorrento's, and Ignacio ordered a large pizza with pepperoni, mushrooms, onion, and green pepper. The waitress brought Cokes for everybody. Pepe decided he didn't like mushrooms. So, he picked the mushrooms off his pizza slices and gave them to Teresa.

As they finished their lunch, Lupita said, "Teresa, your accent tells me you and Pepe are not from around here. Please tell us about yourselves."

After explaining that Pepe, her brother José, and she migrated from Honduras, she said, "We got off the beast a couple of days ago, and we are on our way to the United States."

Ignacio asked, "And José?"

With a sorrowful face, a quivering lip, and tearful eyes, Teresa answered, "Only a few days ago, a tree limb knocked him off the boxcar we were riding on and killed him."

Both Ignacio and Lupita opened their eyes wide as they looked at Teresa. Lupita put her arm around Teresa and said, "Teresa. How tragic. We've heard many stories about how dangerous the beast is. How are you doing?"

Teresa was surprised at how affectionate this stranger was to her. "We're doing the best we can."

Raquel commented, "Don Felipe offers to take Teresa and Pepe with him when he flies back to Tijuana. Because of some other traumatic experiences Teresa and Pepe have endured, Teresa is very nervous about traveling with Don Felipe, although she accepted his offer."

Ignacio wiped his mouth with his napkin and said, "Teresa, let me tell you. I don't know anybody more honorable and trustworthy than Don Felipe."

With her arm still around Teresa, Lupita added, "I myself wouldn't hesitate at all to travel with Don Felipe. I know him to be an honorable man."

Teresa took a sip of her Coke and said, "Gracias, I feel so much better about our upcoming trip now."

Ignacio looked at Pepe and Josué and said, "I hope you won't mind if I get us some ice cream."

Both Josué and Pepe brightened up and said, "Ice cream!"

Pepe turned to Teresa and asked, "Can I have some?"

Pepe's enthusiasm brought a smile to Teresa's face. "Sure. Have some ice cream."

Teresa turned to Ignacio and said, "I thank you so much for lunch. I enjoyed myself."

Pepe added with excitement in his voice, "Me too!"

Lupita responded, "You're very welcome. I hope you enjoy your visit here."

Alejandro, Raquel, Josué, Teresa, and Pepe returned home. While Pepe and Josué played, Raquel served some coffee, and Alejandro asked Teresa, "What did you think about our church service."

Teresa took a sip of her coffee and replied, "I enjoyed the service. I've never been to a church service like that." She then tilted her head. "Maybe you could explain to me a little about what the pastor said in his sermon. I must say. I've never heard anything like that before."

Alejandro felt it better for Raquel to talk one-on-one with Teresa, so he went to his home office in the spare bedroom. Raquel sat on the sofa next to Teresa and began showing her passages from her Bible. "You can see here in Paul's letter to the Romans, 'All have sinned, and come short of the glory of God.' (Romans 3:23). I'm sure you understand we all do things we're ashamed of, things which offend God. Now here, in Romans 6:23, we read, 'The wages of sin is death, but the gift of God is eternal life through Jesus Christ our Lord.' You may recall that Pastor Turner quoted this verse. Many people believe we can only get to Heaven if our good works exceed our bad works. But the Bible teaches that any sin in our lives condemns us to eternal punishment. However, Jesus died on the cross to be a willing sacrifice for our sins. All God asks is for us to recognize our sin and our hopelessness and that we must accept Jesus' sacrifice as God's gift for the forgiveness of all of our sins. That's what Paul means when he says, 'The gift of God is eternal life through Jesus Christ our Lord.' And the resurrection of Jesus from the dead confirms His victory over the grave, to give us confidence that we can trust Him for our salvation."

Teresa listened with great interest to what Raquel said and asked, "Does that mean Christians don't sin anymore?"

"No. But the Bible teaches, when you accept Jesus Christ as your Savior, God changes you. The Bible refers to this change as a new birth. So, if you are sincere when you put your faith in Jesus Christ as your Savior, you will have a compelling desire to obey God and resist the temptation to sin. That doesn't mean you won't sin from time to time. So, God tells us in 1 John 1:9, 'If we confess our sins, He is faithful and just to forgive our sins and cleanse us from all unrighteousness.' May I show you how to accept Jesus Christ as your Savior?"

There was still some strong bitterness in Teresa's heart because of the rape and other ordeals, and she replied, "I'm not sure. Let me think about that."

Raquel took Teresa's hand and said, "Teresa, I will pray that God will lead you to make this important decision. When you meet with Pastor Turner on Tuesday, I recommend you ask him about these things we talked about."

That evening, the nightly *posada* procession came knocking at the door again. After the children sang their *posada* song, Raquel let Pepe respond, and he said, "I'm sorry. There's no room at the inn," and he closed the door.

In the morning, Alejandro went to work, Josué went to school, and Raquel, Teresa, and Pepe walked to a nearby cafeteria for breakfast. The cafeteria, filled with customers, buzzed with conversations and was located downtown in a corner building at a busy intersection. Christmas lights decorated the downtown area, and there was a larger-than-life manger scene in the city's pleasant, tree-lined plaza. The plaza included benches where people sat, some chatting, some reading, some doing nothing. Mothers pushed baby carriages as they strolled; some stopped to chat among one another. Sidewalks crossed each other in the form of a large letter X and extended to the plaza's four corners.

Also located in the plaza were numerous multi-colored kiosks where vendors sold a variety of the kind of products one might find in a flea market. The pleasant aroma of taco stands attracted hungry customers. And the plaza was a place to buy lottery tickets. Customers crowded around the kiosks, with larger numbers who waited to buy lottery tickets. The cool temperature required light jackets for customers and pedestrians to be comfortable. The plaza took up an entire city block, and downtown stores, shops, and restaurants surrounded it.

Sabrina, the cafeteria's owner, came over to say hello to Raquel. They both attended the same church.

Sabrina asked, "Your friends here were in church with you yesterday, right?"

"That's correct. Sabrina, this is Teresa and her brother, Pepe."

After Teresa and Sabrina exchanged greetings, Raquel asked, "How are things going?"

As Sabrina gave them menus and tableware, she said, "Things are going all right. I'm a little short of help. My cook traveled to Puebla for a funeral, and she won't be back for a couple of weeks."

This caught Teresa's attention, and she commented, "Maybe I could help you. I used to work with my mother to sell burritos before I left Honduras."

Sabrina replied, "I'm grateful for your offer, but my cook will be back in two weeks, so this would only be a temporary job."

Teresa smiled and raised her hands as she shrugged. "Not a problem. I'm only going to be here for a couple of weeks. The only time I can't work is Tuesday morning, when I have a ten o'clock appointment with Pastor Turner."

Sabrina brightened up. "Your appointment with the pastor won't be a problem at all. I need you here at six o'clock in the morning. You got the job."

Teresa turned to Raquel. "If it's all right with you, I can start now or tomorrow morning."

Before Raquel responded, Sabrina answered, "Let's make it tomorrow morning."

Raquel said, "I'll come by to take you to your appointment with Pastor Turner on Tuesday."

"What do I do with Pepe?"

"I'll keep an eye on him, if that's all right with you."

"Gracias."

For the rest of her time in Apizaco, Teresa worked every day except Sundays, when the cafeteria was closed, and she was grateful for the money she earned.

On Tuesday, Raquel took Teresa for her appointment with Pastor Turner. When she walked into his office, Teresa noted the window on his door, which allowed the church secretary to see both the pastor and Teresa while they talked.

Pastor Turner began by saying, "Would you care for a cup of coffee?"

"I would enjoy a cup of coffee. Gracias."

The pastor called the volunteer secretary on the intercom to ask for the coffee. After she brought it in and left the pastor's office, the pastor said, "I thank you for coming to see me. I want you to understand that anything you and I talk about is between you and me. I will not discuss anything you tell me with anybody unless you want me to. How are things going for you here in Apizaco?"

Teresa stirred some sugar into her coffee. She felt she was in a safe place, and she replied, "Since I met Don Felipe and Raquel, things have been better than any time in my life. My brother, Pepe, and Josué have become friends. I understand Sabrina is a member of this church, and I'll be working in her restaurant for the next couple of weeks until I leave with Don Felipe."

"The other day, Raquel mentioned some tough times you have experienced during the year. Why don't you tell me about them?"

Teresa told Pastor Turner about the gang problems in Tegucigalpa, Honduras, that they killed her boyfriend and her father. She explained how their deaths prompted her mother to send her brothers, José and Pepe, and her to the United States, where her Aunt Norma and her Uncle Pablo live. How she met Rodolfo while they traveled, but that they were separated when Rodolfo missed the beast train. Then, with eyebrows arched upward, she broke down and said with a whimpering voice. "As the beast approached Apizaco, a low tree branch dragged my brother off the boxcar we were riding on. He fell on the tracks, and the beast cut him in half and killed him. And then ..." Teresa couldn't finish her sentence and wept with heart-wrenching sobs.

Teresa's story stunned Pastor Turner. He handed her a tissue and asked, "You were about to tell me more?"

Teresa used the tissue to dry her eyes and nodded her head as she continued her jolting cries of anguish, which made it impossible for her to speak.

Pastor Turner said with an assuring voice, "Take your time."

Teresa nodded her head again. She took another tissue out of the box on the table beside her, wiped the tears from her eyes, took a sip of coffee, and she began to compose herself.

Pastor Turner asked again, "Is there more you want to tell me?"

Teresa dried her eyes again with the tissue, and, after a pause, she answered, "Yes. When we got here, Pepe and I went to Saint Mary's Catholic Church, where we met Mario, an acolyte. Mario seemed nice at first. He let Pepe and I lay down on some church pews so that we could get some sleep. At five o'clock in the afternoon, he woke us up and said it was time to close the church. I asked him if there was someplace we could go to get cleaned up. He said he would take us to his aunt's house. We headed out of town and turned onto a dirt road."

Teresa burst into tears again while she said through her sobs, "Mario forced me off the side of the road and raped me in front of Pepe. He threatened to kill my brother and make me watch if I didn't submit. I thought God would protect me by going to the church. Why would He let a church acolyte rape me?"

Pastor Turner took a deep breath and prayed in silence, *Dear God. Please give me the wisdom to help Teresa.* Then he said, "Teresa, I wish I could give you a good answer about why God lets bad things happen to good people. The fact is: Bad things do happen to good people and bad people alike." He held up his Bible and continued, "I will tell you this, however. I believe this Bible is the Word of God. And the Bible tells us that God loves us. The Bible says, 'All things work together for good for those who love God.' (Romans 8:28) So, no matter how bad things get, good will overcome evil."

Teresa mumbled, "I wish I could believe that."

"Well, maybe a part of God's plan was to bring you into contact with Don Felipe, Raquel and her family, and this church, to restore your faith in Him. Have you ever attended a church like ours before?"

"No."

"Do you have any questions about the church?"

"I asked Raquel about your sermon on Sunday, and she explained to me about how I could know that I have eternal life."

"I suspect she asked you if you wanted to accept Jesus Christ as your Savior. Did you do that?"

Teresa shook her head. "No. I didn't."

"I'd love to help you with that if you want. Do you feel like you're ready to do that?"

Teresa paused before responding, "What do I have to do to get ready?"

"The only thing you have to do is be willing."

Teresa's memories of her Christian friends, Marcos and Timoteo, reminded her of how they tried to comfort her after José fell from the beast to his death, and how she sought their presence to protect her after Arturo, the Cuban migrant, attempted to hit on her. She shuttered to think that Arturo might have exploited her for sex, had the migrant woman not warned her about him. She remembered Marcos and Timoteo's prayers, in which they expressed their faith that God would protect and bless the migrants in their efforts to seek a better life in the United States. Teresa's experiences with Marcos and Timoteo, Raquel and Don Felipe, and now, hearing Pastor Turner's words, made her see how God was working in her life, despite the horrific tragedy she had endured. So, she replied, "Okay. Please help me."

"I'd be glad to. I will lead you in a prayer to God. All you need to do is pray the prayer with me. Can we do that?"

Teresa shrugged her shoulders and said, "Sure."

Pastor Turner and Teresa bowed their heads, and Teresa prayed the following, repeating after Pastor Turner, "Dear God. I recognize I am a sinner and that Jesus Christ died on the cross to be a sacrifice for my sins and rose again from the grave. I now put my faith and trust in Him for my salvation, and I understand I have now received the gift of eternal life. Amen."

When they finished praying, Teresa asked, "Is that all there is to it?"

Pastor Turner closed his Bible and said, "Well, the simple act of saying the words of a prayer accomplishes nothing, unless you pray the words with sincerity. Were you sincere when you said this prayer?"

Teresa wiped the tears from her eyes with her tissue and replied, "Yes. I was."

Pastor Turner then said, "Good. So, Teresa, if you were to die today, where would you go?"

"Based on what you told me, I believe I'd go to Heaven."

"That is true, and you can count on that. Now I'm going to ask you to do a very difficult thing."

Tilting her head, Teresa asked, "What's that?"

Pastor Turner nodded his head. "I'm going to ask you to forgive Mario."

Teresa scowled, looked at Pastor Turner with disdain, and asked with a defiant voice, "How could you expect me to do that?"

Pastor Turner leaned forward and nodded his head. "I'm sure you have prayed the Lord's prayer, right?"

Teresa shrugged. "Of course."

"In this prayer, Jesus taught us to ask God to forgive our trespasses as we forgive those who trespass against us. God expects us to forgive those who do wrong to us."

"What good will that do?"

"Well, Mario will never know you forgave him. But you will. And you will never have peace about the horrible thing he did to you until you forgive him."

Teresa struggled with this counsel, but then said with a determined voice, "Okay. I forgive him."

"So, there are two major things which have happened in your life today. One, God has saved you and given you a home in Heaven when you die; and two, you can now be at peace about what Mario did to you since you have now forgiven him."

Taking a deep breath, Teresa said, "Gracias, Pastor. I feel liberated, like a heavy weight has fallen from my shoulders."

"Good. Now, it's one thing to forgive Mario, but that doesn't mean you shouldn't report the rape to the police. There may be other rape victims that exist or may exist in the future. So, your willingness to file a police report may stop his criminal behavior. How do you feel about that?"

"My biggest concern is, I don't want anybody else to know that this happened to me. Also, I don't want anything to keep me from leaving with Don Felipe."

"I do understand your concerns. May I have your permission to see if you can file a police report in a way that will satisfy your concerns?"

"Sure. Go ahead."

"So, do you have any additional questions for me?"

With a worried look on her face, Teresa replied, "Yes, I do. The Catholic Church I attended in Honduras did not teach us about our salvation like you did. So, I'm concerned about my papá and my brother, who have died, and my mamá. What about their salvation?"

"The Catholic Church teaches that Jesus is our Savior, but they place more emphasis on good works, and good works are important. We feel that it is very important to understand that our salvation is a gift of

God, and that good works are the inevitable result of the new birth that we experience when we trust Jesus Christ for our salvation, as I explained to you earlier. In the Gospel of John, chapter 17, Jesus prayed for His disciples, and in verse three He prayed, 'This is eternal life, that they may know You, the only true God and Jesus Christ, Whom You have sent.' So, let me ask you. Through the Catholic Church, did your parents and brother know the only true God and Jesus Christ, Whom He sent?"

"Of course."

"Good. In John's first epistle, he wrote, 'These things have I written unto you that believe on the name of the Son of God; that ye may know that ye have eternal life.' (1 John 5:13) So, I think you can be confident that your parents and brother are saved. Does that help?"

"Yes. Thank you."

Later, Pastor Turner arranged for Teresa to file a police report documenting that Mario raped her, in a way that would protect Teresa's identity, and that would not detain her in any way. Teresa did file the police report.

Teresa and Pepe went with Raquel, Alejandro, and Josué to church each Sunday during their stay in Apizaco. On Christmas Eve, there was a special service at the church. A *posada* procession walked down the center aisle between the church pews and asked again, "*¿Hay posada?*" (Is there any room at the inn?) This time, the answer was, "No. But you can spend the night in the cave where we keep the sheep."

Church members, dressed in apostolic garb, portrayed how Mary gave birth to the baby Jesus, and they laid the baby in a manger. Afterward, a mariachi group sang Christmas songs, and a choir sang with them.

After the service, Pepe joined with Josué and other children to attack a piñata with sticks until they broke it and spilled its candy on the floor. Then, with gusto, Pepe, and the other children, grabbed all the candy they could.

As people departed for the evening, they wished everybody, "*Feliz Navidad.*" (Merry Christmas.)

As the end of the year approached, Teresa had stopped having her nightmares about the rape. During her time in Apizaco, she grew closer to Raquel, her family, and other church members. In addition to Josué, Pepe also made some other friends. They would soon leave with fond memories and would miss the church and Pastor Turner.

Arrival in Tijuana

It was now Saturday, December 31st, and Don Felipe, Raquel's brother, returned to Apizaco. Not only was it the last day of the year, but Teresa also noted that a month had passed since she and her brothers left Tegucigalpa, Honduras, but it seemed to her that it was much longer than that.

That evening, they celebrated the new year at church. Many people gave their testimonies about how God blessed them throughout the year, which was now ending. A farmer rejoiced for the abundant harvest with which God blessed him. A newlywed husband and wife praised God for the healthy birth of their first newborn child. An elderly man rejoiced that his wife's surgery was successful – a surgery that saved her life. A woman thanked God for providing her with a job after an extended period of unemployment.

Teresa listened to all of these testimonies of God's blessings while pondering in her heart the tragic year she experienced. While there was ample justification for her to be bitter and cynical, she could not dismiss how God blessed her and Pepe through the people He brought into their lives during these last few weeks of the year.

She never stood before a gathering of people to speak, and the idea of doing so terrified her. Yet something compelled her to stand. She hesitated as she looked around at all of these people who were looking at her. She was quite nervous, but Pastor Turner could see she had something on her heart, and he said, "Teresa, talk to us. We want to hear what you have to say."

Raquel gave Teresa a tissue because she could not fight back the tears, and she began, "I have listened to those of you who have told us how God blessed you, and I'm happy for you. I must tell you this past year has been a devastating time for me and my family. My brother, Pepe, who is here with me, my other brother, José, and I left our home in Honduras a month ago. If you were to see the shack where we lived, where my mother still lives, it would be clear to you how poor my family is. Until I started my travel, I had never slept on a bed. My parents slept in hammocks. My two brothers and I slept on rugs on our shack's dirt floor. I have now had the opportunity to sleep on a bed, but I'm so used to sleeping on the floor that I still can't sleep on a bed, as comfortable as it is."

"Gang violence is widespread in the *barrio* where I lived. They tortured and killed Raúl, my boyfriend, and Pedro, my father. Gang members tried to coerce my brother, José, to join their gang. He didn't want to. Refusal to join the gang often means a death sentence. Gang members also intimidated me."

Teresa paused to deal with her grief. Church members were shocked to hear the story she told.

She composed herself, dried her tears with the tissue she held in her hand, and continued. "My Aunt Norma in the United States suggested to Susana, my mother, that she should send me and my brothers to live with her and Pablo, her husband. My mamá knew the only way for us to get to the United States was to ride the beast train with the many migrants who travel up through Mexico, and she knew such a journey is dangerous. Our options were to live with the increasing threat of gang violence or choose dangerous migration on the beast."

Many in the congregation were now weeping.

Teresa continued with more tears dripping from her face. "For us, the best option between these two bad choices was migration. Our journey so far has been tragic." And she explained how her brother died when he fell from the beast. "After that, I decided my brother,

Pepe, and I could no longer continue our journey on the beast, so we changed our travel plans."

Teresa hesitated to talk about the man who raped her, but she decided to reveal this additional tragedy in her life. "Not long after that, Mario, an acolyte I met at the Catholic Church here in Apizaco, told me he would help us. But he deceived me, dragged me to the side of a dirt road, and raped me in front of Pepe, my brother."

Shocked, all the women in the congregation gasped, shook their heads, and covered their faces with their hands.

"Not long after that, I met Don Felipe and Raquel, who were strangers to me. They took me and Pepe in and showed us kindness, as we have never experienced. They also brought me to this church, and Pastor Turner told me how to be saved. And he urged me to forgive Mario, the man who raped me, which I did. And I testify to you: The events of the last few weeks of this year have been the best things which have ever happened in my life, and I will always be grateful to Don Felipe, Raquel, and this church."

There was not a dry eye in the church, and many women reached out to Teresa and hugged her.

Pastor Turner prayed, "Dear God. We thank you for bringing Teresa and Pepe into our lives. While it saddens us to hear her tell us about the terrible tragedy she and her family have endured, we rejoice that Teresa came to a saving knowledge of Jesus Christ. We thank you that we could have a small part in being a blessing to Teresa and Pepe. We pray you would bless both of them while they continue on their journey, and may they find peace and prosperity in the United States. We also pray for Susana, their mother, who is now a widow and lives alone. Bless her and keep her safe. We pray Teresa will have the means to help lift her mother out of poverty and to rescue her from the danger of gang violence. These things we ask in our Savior's name. Amen."

On Sunday morning, they attended the morning worship service. The pastor announced that Teresa and Pepe would be departing on Monday. After the service, they enjoyed a potluck dinner, and many came up to Teresa and Pepe to say goodbye – another emotional event that brought tears of joy to Teresa's eyes.

~.~

After breakfast on Monday morning, Raquel gave her passport to Teresa, and Don Felipe, Teresa, and Pepe departed for Mexico City.

While they traveled, Felipe said, "I'm glad to hear you enjoyed your time with Raquel, Alejandro, and Josué."

Teresa replied, "We enjoyed a great time. I'm so grateful to you and your family for all you have done for me and Pepe."

"Well, with some luck, we'll arrive in Tijuana today without any complications."

A tear filled Teresa's eye and spilled onto her cheek. "I find it difficult to believe Pepe and I will be so close to the end of our journey today!"

Felipe hesitated and then said, "While today will be a significant milestone for you, your next challenge will be to cross the border into the United States without getting caught."

Staring out the car's window, that comment made Teresa shudder with anxiety.

They arrived at the airport, Felipe turned in his rental car, and they went to get their boarding passes.

The woman at the ticket counter asked for identification. Felipe showed his driver's license, and Teresa showed Raquel's passport.

The woman at the ticket counter then asked, "And what about the child?"

Felipe lied, "He's traveling with his mother."

"Nevertheless, we need some form of identification."

Felipe lied again, "We're on our way to attend a funeral for Raquel's mother. It didn't occur to us that Raquel's son would need any identification. What can we do?"

The woman looked around and said, "Okay. Don't worry about it." And she gave them their boarding passes.

Felipe checked his suitcase and kept his briefcase as carry-on luggage. As Felipe suggested, Teresa and Pepe also kept their backpacks as carry-on luggage.

Their flight would depart in an hour. So, Felipe took Teresa and Pepe to a cafeteria where they enjoyed hot chocolate and churros, a sweet pastry consisting of straight, tube-shaped strips of fried dough dusted with brown sugar and cinnamon, comparable to a donut in texture and flavor.

Noting that Teresa was nervous, Felipe said, "Don't worry. Flying on an airplane is safer than riding in a car."

His words didn't help much. Teresa was still nervous about flying on an airplane. She was not, however, so worried now about traveling with Felipe.

They boarded the plane. Felipe sat in the aisle seat, Teresa sat in the middle, and they let Pepe sit by the window. Felipe helped Teresa and Pepe with their seatbelts. Pepe was excited; Teresa was even more nervous.

The airplane taxied out to the runway and waited until an air traffic controller gave them the go-ahead to take off. The plane proceeded onto the runway and began accelerating, which pushed Teresa against the back of her seat. Teresa grabbed Felipe's hand. The plane took off at eleven o'clock in the morning, began its ascent, and ran into some sudden turbulence.

Teresa screamed, tightened her grip on Felipe's hand, and asked, "Are we going to crash?"

Felipe did his best to calm her fears and said, "No. We're just experiencing some turbulence, which is normal. Everything is all right. Don't worry. We may also experience some turbulence when we arrive in Tijuana."

On the other hand, watching the airplane climb into the air fascinated Pepe.

They all began feeling pressure in their ears, making it difficult to hear. Teresa's anxiety resumed, and Felipe once again assured her there was nothing to worry about.

At flight level, a flight attendant brought them a small lunch, which consisted of a sandwich, potato chips, a brownie, and a beverage. The opportunity to enjoy this lunch put Teresa more at ease.

When they approached Tijuana, the airplane began its descent and circled the airport until an air traffic controller gave them permission to land. They experienced more turbulence, which heightened Teresa's anxiety again.

Now on the ground, the airplane braked hard, which threw Teresa forward against her seatbelt, and she grabbed Felipe's hand again. The airplane taxied up to the terminal, and passengers deplaned. It was 2:45 in the afternoon. They made their way to the baggage claim area, where Felipe waited to claim his suitcase.

Turning to Teresa, Felipe said, "Welcome to Tijuana."

Teresa asked, "What happens next?"

"As soon as I get my suitcase, we'll meet up with Elvia, my wife, and head to my home."

They departed the baggage claim area and found Elvia. Felipe said, "Elvia, this is Teresa and Pepe, who I told you about."

Elvia hugged Teresa and said, "Welcome to Tijuana." Turning to Pepe, she asked, "Did you enjoy your plane ride?"

Pepe replied, "It was great. It was really neat to see how tiny everything was on the ground."

They exited the airport and made their way to the parking garage, where Elvia parked their Mercedes-Benz. While they drove to Felipe and Elvia's home, they passed through *barrios*, which looked very much like the *barrio* where Teresa and Pepe grew up. They then entered a residential area of elegant homes with well-manicured lawns. A security fence surrounded almost every home. When they approached Felipe and Elvia's home, Felipe pressed the button on a remote control device, which caused a gate to open and allowed them to pull into their driveway. After the gate closed behind them, the garage door opened next, and Felipe parked the car in the garage. Felipe pressed another button on his remote control, and the garage door closed.

Teresa asked, "Why so much security?"

Felipe replied, "There's a lot of crime in Tijuana. Most of it is petty crime, and prosperous people are the main targets of such crime. So, these security measures are the best way to protect ourselves."

They grabbed their luggage, and Teresa and Pepe followed Felipe and Elvia into their luxurious home. Standing in the kitchen, Teresa exclaimed, "I've never been in such a beautiful home before. I'm amazed."

Elvia replied, "Gracias. I hope you and Pepe will be comfortable here." She turned to a maid and said, "Please show Teresa and Pepe to their rooms."

As they walked away, Elvia said, "We'll have dinner in about an hour, so you have some time to get rested up."

Teresa replied, "Gracias."

They walked out of the kitchen onto the marble floor in the dining room, where there was a large dining room table with fourteen chairs and an ornate chandelier, which hung over the table. In the living room, Teresa admired the hardwood floor decorated with beautiful area rugs, and there was a high, vaulted ceiling, from which another chandelier hung. A comfortable sofa faced a large fireplace, along with several over-stuffed chairs. An elegant staircase formed a semicircle from the second floor down to the living room. Beautiful works of art hung on the walls.

The maid led them upstairs to their rooms. Teresa's room was well decorated. A painting hung on the wall showing an elegant woman sitting in a garden at a table with a saucer and a dainty cup of tea. It surprised Teresa to find she had her own bathroom.

She sat on an easy chair in the bedroom. Sadness overwhelmed her as she thought about her mother, whose custom at this hour of the day was to be sitting at her wobbly table and drinking a glass of lemonade in her one-room shack, with its dirt floor, no electricity, and the single black and white water-stained photograph of her with her husband, which hung on the wall in a cheap frame. Teresa was also worried because she experienced symptoms that she might be pregnant.

Teresa dozed off in the easy chair, and the maid woke her and informed her dinner was ready. She went into the bathroom to wash her hands and was surprised to see the sink had two knobs. She looked into the shower and saw it also had two knobs. At the sink, she chose the left knob and almost scalded herself from the hot water, which came out of the spigot. She never saw a bathroom with hot and cold water before. She figured out she could adjust both knobs to get the water temperature she preferred.

As they walked downstairs, she asked Pepe, "Do you also have a bathroom in your bedroom?"

After he said yes, Teresa warned him, "The sink's knob on the left produces hot water. Be careful you don't burn yourself. You have to adjust both knobs to get the water temperature that you want."

Everybody took their seats at the dinner table, bowed their heads, and Felipe prayed, "Dear God, our heavenly Father. We thank you for this food and your many blessings. I pray Teresa and Pepe will enjoy their stay with us and that they will soon arrive at their destination in the United States without incident. Bless them as they begin their new life there. May they prosper, and help us to honor You in all we do. Amen."

The meal consisted of *carnitas*, similar to pulled pork, yellow rice with vegetables, a lettuce and tomato salad, refried beans, avocados, and tortillas. They had ice-cold orange juice to drink, squeezed from fresh oranges, and they enjoyed flan for dessert.

Teresa said, "I thank you so much for helping me and my brother. Not only have you helped us in our journey, but you've also allowed us to experience many things we've never encountered before."

Elvia took a sip of her orange juice and replied, "You're very welcome. Felipe told me about your travel from Honduras to central Mexico and about the dangers and tragedies you've experienced. So, I'm glad we could provide a safer way to get you to the border between Mexico and the United States."

"What are our options to cross the border?"

Felipe wiped his mouth with his napkin and replied, "Tomorrow, I'll check with some friends of mine to put us in touch with a coyote."

Teresa said, "When I know how much the coyote will charge, I'll need to get a phone card so that I can call my Aunt to get more money."

"Don't worry about the phone card. You can call your aunt on my cellular phone. If you want, you can call her now, right after dinner."

"That would be wonderful!"

After dinner, Felipe, Teresa, and Pepe went into the living room. After giving him the phone number, Felipe called Teresa's aunt.

Norma answered the phone, and Teresa, with tearful eyes and arched eyebrows, said, "Aunt Norma! It's so good to hear your voice."

"Where are you?"

"We're in Tijuana."

"So, you've made it to Tijuana! Your Uncle Pablo and I have been worried about you."

"Pepe and I are fine. The last time I talked to you, we were in Apizaco. As I discussed with you, Pepe and I caught a bus to Mexico City. While on the bus, I became friends with a woman about my age, named Raquel, and she introduced me to her brother, Don Felipe. He offered to take us to Tijuana on a plane, but he needed to finish some work in Mexico City first. So, he drove me, Raquel, and Pepe back to Apizaco, and I stayed with Raquel in her home for two weeks while Don Felipe finished his business in Mexico City. Yesterday Don Felipe came to pick us up, this morning we drove to the airport in Mexico City to catch our plane, and we arrived in Tijuana this afternoon."

"What happens next?"

"Don Felipe will make arrangements with a coyote tomorrow. When I know how much the coyote will charge, I'll call you back so that you can wire us the money we need."

"That'll be fine."

"If all goes well, I should be calling you soon to arrange for you and Uncle Pablo to pick us up."

"Okay. We'll be waiting for your call. Stay safe."

Afterward, they all sat in the living room and watched a movie recorded on a DVD – something else Teresa and Pepe enjoyed for the first time.

The next morning, after a breakfast of oatmeal, orange juice, and coffee, Felipe departed. When he returned in the afternoon, he explained, "A friend of mine informed me we will meet the coyote the day after tomorrow at the Restaurante Carnitas Don Ramón in the border town of Mexicali. His name is Señor Alberto. The cost for both of you to cross the border and to take you to San Diego will be 100,000 pesos."

Teresa called her aunt. "Aunt Norma, I have 37,000 pesos, and I will need 100,000 pesos for the coyote."

Norma replied, "That's about $4,000. I'll wire it to you right away."

The next day, Felipe took everybody out for lunch.

As they finished their lunch, Felipe confirmed, "Teresa, we will leave tomorrow morning for Mexicali."

On the way back to the house, Teresa picked up the cash which Norma sent to her.

Border Crossing

By ten o'clock in the morning, Felipe, Elvia, Teresa, and Pepe were on the road to Mexicali. The weather was pleasant, so they traveled with the car windows open. Pepe discovered he could stick his hand out of the window and position it in different ways so that the wind would raise and lower it aerodynamically.

Teresa grew very quiet and didn't speak a word as she pondered the events which occurred since she met Raquel. It amazed her to contemplate how kind Raquel, Felipe, and Elvia were to her and her brother. And she also contemplated the uncertainty of what was about to happen. She had no idea what lay ahead.

As his friend instructed Felipe, they went to the Restaurante Carnitas Don Ramón on the outskirts of town to meet with the coyote, Señor Alberto, at one o'clock in the afternoon. They arrived right before noon, ate lunch, and waited for him to arrive. He showed up at 1:15. Don Felipe introduced Teresa and Pepe to Señor Alberto, and they followed him in his Cadillac pickup truck down the road to a rundown warehouse.

A man and a woman were inside the warehouse, and Señor Alberto made the introductions. "Elena, Edwardo, this is Teresa and her brother, Pepe. They will cross the border with you tomorrow morning."

It stunned Teresa to hear they would be crossing the border so soon, and the anxiety that afflicted her raised the hairs on the back of her neck.

Señor Alberto occupied a small spartan office in the warehouse with two chairs, a cluttered desk, and Señor Alberto's desk chair. Teresa and Don Felipe sat in the office with Señor Alberto. Elvia and Pepe waited in the warehouse.

Señor Alberto, with an unlit cigar in his mouth, leaned back in his chair, stared at the ceiling, and asked, "Do you have the money?"

Don Felipe opened up a small leather case, removed a business card, threw it on the desk, and said, "We'll pay you $2,000 now and the rest when I get confirmation from Teresa's family that she and Pepe have arrived without incident."

Señor Alberto continued to stare at the ceiling and shook his head. "No. I don't work that way."

Don Felipe leaned forward and said with a stern voice, "Señor Alberto."

Señor Alberto looked down at him.

Don Felipe looked into Señor Alberto's eyes with intimidating intensity. "I'm a man of my word. You have my contact information on my business card. Teresa and her brother, Pepe, have endured a very tough journey so far. Others have already taken unfair advantage of them. I want to ensure the remainder of their trip goes well. So tell me. If you won't trust me, why should we trust you?"

Señor Alberto leaned forward, put the cigar in an ashtray, picked up Don Felipe's business card, and recognized the business name. Then he looked up and said, "I'll make an exception in your case."

Teresa was surprised to see how Don Felipe got his way with Señor Alberto.

Don Felipe turned to Teresa and said, "Give Señor Alberto 50,000 pesos ($2,000)."

Don Felipe then said to Señor Alberto, "I need a business card or a phone number so that I can contact you when I hear that Teresa and Pepe are safe and sound at their final destination."

Señor Alberto replied, "In this business, we don't use business cards."

As he said this, he jotted down his name and phone number on a piece of paper and gave it to Don Felipe.

Don Felipe said to Teresa, "We're going to leave now, and we'll want to say goodbye."

Hearing these words made Teresa's heart skip a beat, and she wrinkled her forehead. Sorrow also invaded her heart at the thought she might not see Elvia and Don Felipe again.

Don Felipe said to Señor Alberto, "Please give us a minute to say goodbye."

Felipe and Teresa walked out of the office. Elvia and Pepe joined them. Teresa, with tears streaming down her face, hugged Felipe and Elvia. Through her sobs, she said, "Nobody has ever shown such kindness to me in my life. How can I ever repay you?"

Felipe responded, "Don't worry about that. It's been our great joy to know you and to have a small part in helping you reach your destination. You'll always have a place in our hearts."

"I'll never forget you either."

Don Felipe shook hands with Pepe. "You take care of your sister, and do what she says. Tomorrow will be a big day for you."

Pepe replied, "I will." And he hugged Don Felipe.

Before they left, Teresa gave Felipe the remaining 50,000 pesos she owed to Señor Alberto. As she watched them drive away, Teresa never felt so alone and vulnerable in her life. Still sniffling, she returned to Señor Alberto's office with Pepe.

Noting Teresa's white blouse and Pepe's red shirt, Señor Alberto asked, "Do you have something darker to wear?"

Teresa responded, "I have a dark blue blouse, and Pepe has a dark green shirt. Will that work?"

"Yeah. We'll be doing our best to travel without being seen. So, you should change your clothes. Now I need to go over our plan for tomorrow morning."

Señor Alberto displayed a Google satellite photograph on his computer and pointed to details on the photograph as he explained to Teresa, "The walking distance to the border is about two hours. We will leave on foot at about three o'clock in the morning, and we'll arrive at the border at about five o'clock. We want to get there while it's still dark, so nobody will see us. The name of the city on the U.S. side is Calexico."

Teresa interrupted. "Why do we have to walk so far?"

"Mexican authorities watch the roads for suspicious vehicles and people who are approaching the border. The Mexican government is cooperating with the American government to catch migrants before they reach the border. So, we don't want to meet up with them. When we walk to the border, we'll avoid the main roads as much as possible."

Señor Alberto pointed at the border wall on the satellite photograph and continued, "At the border here, we have a shallow, recently dug tunnel, which goes under the wall. You can see the parking lot for the Gran Plaza Outlets shopping center on the other side of the border. The park you see to the west of the parking lot is Chapultepec Park. That's where the immigration agents, also known as ICE agents, park their truck."

He scrolled to show Teresa the U.S. Immigration and Customs Enforcement (ICE) Facility. "This facility is within walking distance of the parking lot."

Scrolling back to the parking lot, Señor Alberto said, "Through the slats in the border wall, you will be able to see this parking lot on the Calexico side. An ICE agent is always there. Always! The street you see on the other side of the parking lot is First Street. The next street up is Second Street. You will need to go to Second Street, turn right, go to Mary Avenue and turn left. Any questions so far?"

"No."

Pointing to an area on the parking lot, Señor Alberto continued, "We will have an individual here with a flashlight. He, along with others, are called polleros. As I said earlier, an ICE agent is always patrolling around this area, but he can't see everything all the time. You need to keep your eye on this pollero. The plan is for another pollero to create a diversion to attract the ICE agent's attention. When the pollero with the flashlight sees that the patrol agent has gone to investigate, he will flash his flashlight three times. That's your signal for you and Pepe to squeeze through the tunnel and crawl on the ground until you get among the cars in the parking lot."

"There won't be many cars because the only people there at that time are clerks who clean the stores and restock the shelves. Sales personnel begin to arrive at around eight o'clock in the morning, and some businesses will be opening at that time as well. At the same time they are arriving, the clerks will be departing, and some customers will be arriving. So, there will be many people coming and going. Almost everybody is Latino. So, you will blend in fine. Keep in mind, something may occur that could require us to deviate from this plan. The critical thing to remember is that your signal to move to the parking lot will come from the pollero with the flashlight."

Señor Alberto asked Teresa to repeat what he said to ensure she understood and knew what she and Pepe had to do. He then proceeded, "When you see all these people coming and going, you and Pepe need to stand and start walking as if you're a part of the crowd. Don't walk any faster or slower than the other people, try to control your nerves, and don't look around as if you're looking for somebody. Be as casual and inconspicuous as possible while you walk away. If you can do that, you won't look any different from the rest of the people in the parking lot."

Señor Alberto then took a picture of Teresa and Pepe with his phone's camera and explained, "I'm texting your photo to another pollero who will be at the corner of Second Street and Mary Avenue. When he sees you coming, he will approach you, say "*Buenos días,*' and hug you as if he were your husband. You need to make sure you play along. If your performance appears suspicious to an ICE agent, your stay in the United States will end before it begins. Do you understand?"

With a nervous look on her face, Teresa nodded and replied, "Si Señor." She then turned to Pepe and asked, "Do you think you can do all of this with me?"

With a grin on his face, he replied, "Si. It'll be like a spy movie!"

Señor Alberto laughed and said to Pepe, "That's right. Just pretend you're spies."

Looking back at Teresa, Señor Alberto continued, "After the pollero hugs you, expect him to walk with you along the street with his arm around you. You'll arrive at a house and walk in. The most scary and risky part will then be over. After you go into the house, you'll see there are other migrants inside, and the pollero will explain the travel plan to take you to San Diego."

After he finished discussing the plan to get Teresa and Pepe across the border into the United States, Señor Alberto said, "You'll have to remain in this warehouse until it's time to leave. It's not the most comfortable place, but you should try to get some sleep. There are some sandwiches and sodas in the refrigerator. I suggest you get to know Edwardo and Elena, since you will cross the border together. Do you have any other questions for me now?"

"Will Edwardo, Elena, Pepe, and I crawl together to the parking lot?"

"No. Edwardo and Elena will go first, and then you and Pepe."

They walked out of the office, Señor Alberto departed, and Teresa and Pepe joined Edwardo and Elena.

As they all sat together, they enjoyed the sandwiches and sodas, and they reviewed their plans for crossing the border. Since Edwardo and Elena were married, the only significant difference in their two plans was that the pollero who would approach Teresa would pretend to be her husband. In Edwardo and Elena's case, an older woman would approach them with a child, and the four of them would walk off together.

At 2:30 in the morning, Señor Alberto returned to the warehouse and woke everybody up. He said, "Make sure you use the restroom before we depart. It will be a long time before you have another chance to go to the restroom."

Señor Alberto warned them, "There can be no talking, and we don't want any noise to attract our attention."

They began walking at three o'clock in the morning. It was dark, cloudy, with no moon. It was also getting colder, and Teresa and Pepe were happy to have their dark gray coats, which would protect them from the cold and help keep them from being seen.

They arrived at the border wall at five o'clock in the morning, as planned. Señor Alberto reviewed again the plans, which they would have to follow. Then he said, "I need to leave you now so that I can communicate with the polleros at a location where the ICE agents won't be able to detect my presence. *Buena suerte.* (Good luck)"

Teresa, Pepe, Edwardo, and Elena would all be lying on the ground for about an hour and forty-five minutes. Teresa, Edwardo, and Elena took turns watching for the pollero's signal. Despite the coats they wore, Teresa and Pepe, as well as Edwardo and Elena, were shivering, not only because of the cold temperatures, but also because they were lying on the cold ground. Edwardo checked his cellular phone and noted the temperature was 40 degrees. It was 6:40 in the morning.

In the darkness, the light from his cellular phone startled them, and Elena whispered, "I think you need to keep your phone in your pocket."

Early twilight began, and they could now see the cars in the parking lot. But, because of the dim light, everything was in black and white. Soon they were able to discern colors as the sun rose to the point where it was below the horizon but still not visible. They became anxious, and they watched for the pollero's signal. An ICE agent startled them when he walked by on the other side of the wall where they hid.

The ICE agent continued walking and encountered another agent. Teresa, Pepe, Edwardo, and Elena could hear the two agents talking. It was not possible to know what they were saying, not only because they spoke English, but also because they were too far away. A pollero made some noise, which caught the ICE agents' attention, and they went to investigate.

Then came three blue flashes of light from the pollero's flashlight. Edwardo and Elena went first, crawling on the ground toward the parking lot. They were progressing well, but then Edwardo's cellular phone rang, which alerted the ICE agents, who came running toward them. There was no escape for them at this point. The two ICE agents grabbed them and handcuffed them. Across the street, parked along Chapultepec park, a truck's headlights came on while the ICE agents escorted them across the parking lot toward the truck. Teresa and Pepe shuddered with fear as they watched while the ICE agents made Edwardo and Elena get into the back of the truck. Teresa knew their stay in the United States would soon be over.

Suddenly, three flashes from the pollero's flashlight caught Teresa by surprise. They hesitated for a moment, trying to regain their composure. Then, after squeezing through the tunnel, they began crawling along the ground toward the parking lot. Intense fear invaded Teresa, and her heart tripped over its own rhythm, producing a stabbing pain that matched the fear she knew only too well from her encounters with gang members in Honduras.

The sun rose above the horizon. Teresa and Pepe were now hiding among the cars in the parking lot. She watched with horror and trembled as the border patrol truck took Edwardo and Elena away. Teresa guessed it was a little after seven o'clock in the morning.

Right around eight o'clock, sales personnel began arriving, and soon night clerks were leaving the stores in the shopping center. Customers arrived as well. As instructed, Teresa and Pepe stood up, mingled among the people, and walked away from the parking lot. They crossed First Street and walked to Second Street, where they turned right. When they got to Mary Avenue, another pollero walked up to Teresa, put his arm around her, and they walked up Mary Avenue together to a house which they entered. There were six other migrants inside. The pollero, who never gave his name, explained, "A car will arrive soon, which will take you to San Diego. The trip will take about two hours. Do you have somebody who will pick you up?"

Teresa replied, "Yes, my aunt and uncle. But I will need to call them. They'll be coming from Los Angeles."

"That will work out pretty well. Their travel time to San Diego will also be about two hours. When the car arrives to pick you up, you can use my cellular phone to call them."

"Gracias. Where will they find us?"

The pollero wrote on a piece of paper, *Ponce's Mexican Restaurant, 4050 Adams Ave, San Diego, CA 92116.* He handed the piece of paper to Teresa and said, "This is the restaurant where we will drop you off."

The car arrived at 8:45 in the morning, and Teresa used the pollero's phone to call her Aunt Norma.

When she answered, Teresa said, "Pepe and I are in Calexico, California. We will leave for San Diego in the next 15 to 30 minutes. The trip will take about two hours."

"Okay, Your Uncle Pablo and I will come to pick you up. Where will we find you?"

Teresa replied, "They'll drop us off at Ponce's Mexican Restaurant," and she gave Norma the address.

Norma said, "Great! I expect we'll see you at about eleven o'clock this morning."

There was no time to eat, and no food was offered to anybody. The pollero and the driver crammed two migrants in the car's trunk, five in the back seat, and one in the front seat, a total of eight migrants. To get all five people in the back seat, they put Teresa and Pepe on the floor and crammed the other three in the back seat. The stench of body odor emanated from the car's interior, which brought back vivid memories to Teresa of her travel through Guatemala and her ride on the beast. Other than the driver and the migrant in the front seat, everybody was uncomfortable with very little wiggle room. During the two-hour trip, the five migrants in the back seat found it necessary to shift their positions with some frequency to deal with the awkward, cramped, tight space.

One of the migrants complained, "I don't know which is worse: To be crammed in this back seat or stuck in the trunk."

The Ponce Mexican Restaurant was their first stop when they got to San Diego. Pablo and Norma watched from the corner of the building as the car pulled in behind the restaurant, and Teresa and Pepe got out of the car. When Teresa and Pepe came around the corner, Pablo and Norma were careful not to display excessive emotion so that they would not attract unwanted attention.

Uncle Pablo asked, "Are you hungry?"

Teresa responded, "We haven't eaten much since yesterday."

"Well, let's get something to eat," and he led them into the restaurant.

There were only a few customers in the restaurant, some brown Latin Americans, others white U.S. Citizens. Surprised by their pale skin, Pepe stared at them and asked Teresa, "Are those people sick?"

Teresa, who was not accustomed to seeing white people either, replied, "No. That's their normal color."

While they waited for their food to arrive, Teresa could no longer contain herself. She reached out, hugged her Aunt Norma, and cried out, "I'm surprised to see we made it."

Aunt Norma put her glass of water on the table, wrapped her arms around Teresa, and said, "And we're so happy to have you with us. We'll send a letter to Susana as soon as possible to let her know you arrived safe and sound and to coordinate a time when you and she can talk."

"You know, Pepe and I haven't spoken to her since we left over a month ago."

"Well, I'm sure you'll have a very happy conversation."

They arrived at Pablo and Norma's home in Los Angeles at about two o'clock in the afternoon. Pablo and Norma owned a modest but comfortable home in a community where most of the residents were of Latin American descent. After a month of perilous travel, Teresa felt for the first time that she was now safe. She felt as if a weighty burden was taken off of her shoulders. She also felt drained of energy. Aunt

Norma showed her to her room, and she laid down. She slept on the floor from the afternoon until late the next morning. When she awoke, her thoughts were, *Now what challenges await me.*

Life in the USA Begins

As they sat at breakfast, Pablo said to Teresa, "There's something I need to ensure you understand. I wish I could tell you that you can feel safe here. But you must understand, that is not the case. While there is little worry about gang violence, you must always be vigilant about the possible presence of Immigration Control and Enforcement or ICE agents. If they catch you, they will deport you back to Honduras."

With a worried look on her face, Teresa stared into the air. Her inner voice cried out with despair, *Will I ever come to the place where there is no threat hanging over me?* To Pablo's comment, she replied, "When Pepe and I arrived at the border, there were two other people with us: a married couple, Edwardo and Elena. While they were crossing the border, Edwardo's cellular phone rang. That brought the ICE agents running, and they grabbed Edwardo and Elena and took them away in a truck. So, I guess I understand this threat."

Norma poured Teresa a second cup of coffee and replied, "That is so sad. Though the circumstances may be different, that could happen to anyone of us as well, since all of us are undocumented illegal aliens."

Teresa raised her eyebrows and asked, "So, how do we protect ourselves?"

"On a day-to-day basis, you're going to be all right. About the only thing you can do is to be sensitive to what's going on around you. Continual awareness is the key. If you sense something is not quite right, you must take steps to leave the area in a way which does not call attention to yourself. That's the best you can do."

Teresa wiped her mouth with her napkin and replied, "That's kinda like what the coyote told me when I crossed the border. He said I should try to blend in with other people and not act suspicious in any way."

"Most of the time that works fine. But you never know when you might find yourself in a situation where you're trapped and can't escape. If that happens, the probability is high that you'll find yourself on a plane back to Honduras. We have to live with that. Keep in mind, however, Pablo and I have been here for twenty years now. And so have many others. So, while you need to know about such a possibility, it won't do you any good to worry about it."

Teresa responded, "That's easier said than done. Will I be able to get a job?"

Pablo took a sip of his coffee and replied, "I've got some contacts who might help us with that. Before you can get a job though, there are several things we need to do. One of the first things we must do is to get you a driver's license, a Social Security card, and a green card."

With a perplexed look on her face, Teresa asked, "Is that possible?"

"It is only possible to get fake credentials. But you must have them, so you have no choice."

Teresa looked down and shook her head. The disturbing thought that tormented her was, *Will I ever get to the place where I don't have to do something that is illegal?*

Norma said, "Another thing which is important to get a job is the ability to speak English. We're going to enroll you and Pepe in English classes, and we need to enroll Pepe in grade school."

Teresa replied, "Well, the sooner we get started on that, the better as far as I'm concerned."

Teresa then changed the subject. "There's something I need to do right away. In Tijuana, my friend, Don Felipe, put me in touch with the coyote who got me across the border. Don Felipe wouldn't let me pay the coyote his full fee until he received confirmation that I arrived here.

He has the rest of the fee. So, I need to contact Don Felipe to let him know he can pay the coyote the rest of the money I owe him."

Norma responded, "We can call Don Felipe today, and we should also be able to get a letter in the mail to your mamá today or tomorrow. Once your mamá gets our letter, I expect she'll try to call here, so that you two can talk."

The thought that she would soon hear her mother's voice made Teresa shed a tear, filled her with hopeful anticipation, and she replied, "That will be wonderful. I can't wait to hear her voice."

Pablo commented, "I'm sure she'll be pleased to hear your voice as well."

Teresa said, "I notice you have a picture of a shack on the wall in the living room. Is that by any chance the shack where you lived before you came to the United States?"

Pablo replied, "Yeah. We don't ever want to forget what our life was like before we came here. The picture is a constant reminder of how much better our life is in the United States."

Teresa said, "The shack looks very much like the shack where my mamá lives. It's amazing to compare your very comfortable home here to where you lived in Honduras."

Norma put her hand on Teresa's shoulder and responded, "I hope God will bless you one day with a comfortable home."

Teresa replied, "¡*Ojala*!" (May God be willing.)

After Pablo left for work, Norma dialed Don Felipe's phone number and gave Teresa the phone. When he answered, Teresa said, "Don Felipe. We made it."

Felipe replied, "I'm so glad to hear that. I presume I may now pay Señor Alberto the rest of the money you owe him."

With tearful eyes and a contented smile on her face, she said, "Yes. Let me say again how grateful I am for your family's kindness to me and Pepe. Please say hello to Elvia and Raquel for me."

Don Felipe's voice quivered when he replied, "I'll do that right away. You take care of yourself. I encourage you to find a good church to attend. God bless you."

They were about to hang up, when Don Felipe said, "By the way, let me bring you up to date about Mario in Apizaco. Police arrested him after another rape victim brought charges against him. Your police statement was important evidence that persuaded the jury to find Mario guilty, and he is now in prison."

The memory of her rape and this disgusting man made her raise one side of her lip as if she smelled a foul odor. She replied, "I'm sorry to hear about another victim of his crimes. Thanks for letting me know."

When they hung up, Teresa composed herself, returned Norma's phone, and said, "You have no idea how kind this family was to me and Pepe, despite the fact we were strangers to them."

After the phone call, Norma, Teresa, and Pepe walked down the street to the bus stop, which was visible from Norma's home. Many people waited for the next bus, and most of them were Latin American women. Norma introduced Teresa and Pepe to her friends.

A crowded bus picked them up and took them to MacArthur Park, a nearby commercial plaza. Aggressive street vendors sold ice cream, hot dogs, and assorted wares from carts. There was also a woman who catered to undocumented migrants who were eager to work in the United States. Always looking around to see who was within earshot, she called out with a low, discreet voice, "*Mica, mica.*" (Spanish slang for the fake identification cards, which she offered to potential clients.)

Norma approached the woman and whispered, "We need some help."

"What do you need?" asked the woman, who clutched a notebook in which she was prepared to jot down an order.

"She can get you anything fast," added a man who was with her.

"My niece, Teresa, and her brother need Social Security cards and Green cards. Teresa also needs a driver's license."

The woman looked around again to see who was within listening distance and moved closer to Norma as she whispered, "I can have them for you by the end of the week. Each card will cost $100, for a total of $500. I'll need $100 now, and you can pay the balance when you pick up the cards. I'll need to get names, addresses, and a good phone number."

Norma paid the $100, took the woman's notebook, and jotted down the information which she requested. After she handed the notebook back, she asked, "Should we look for you here on Friday?"

"No. I'll have them ready on Saturday."

"Sounds good. We'll come to see you on Saturday."

As they walked away, Teresa said, "I still have almost 38,000 pesos, which I need to return to you."

They stopped at a bank, and Norma converted the pesos to $1,530. She gave Teresa $500 back and said, "Here. You're going to need some spending money."

Norma, Teresa, and Pepe grabbed some lunch at a nearby restaurant called El Potrillo. Norma knew the waitress, and she introduced Teresa to her. "Rosita, this is my niece, Teresa, and her brother, Pepe. They arrived yesterday."

Rosita, who was about the same age as Teresa, replied, "*Mucho gusto.* (It's a pleasure) I presume you're from Honduras."

Teresa answered, "That's right. Where are you from?"

"El Salvador. Here, let me give you my phone number. Give me a call sometime."

"Gracias. I will."

Teresa noticed Rosita was pregnant, which reminded her once again there was something else she worried about, since she still experienced symptoms that she might be pregnant. Rosita and Teresa would come to be good friends.

After lunch, they stopped at a Best Buy store, where Norma purchased a cellular phone for Teresa.

Surprised, Teresa asked, "Do I need this?"

While the store clerk set up the phone, Norma replied, "Well, ya kinda do. Cellular phones dominate our lives here. For now, I'll pay the monthly bill. Once you have a job, you can start paying it. When we get home, I'll show you how to use it."

"Gracias, Aunt Norma."

As they rode back on the bus, Norma noted that Teresa appeared to be worried about something.

When they got home, Pepe sat and played in the living room. Norma and Teresa sat in the kitchen. After making some coffee, Norma asked, "It's clear something is bothering you. Is there something we need to talk about?"

Teresa pursed her lips, stared at the floor, and told Norma about the man who raped her in Apizaco. "He threatened to kill Pepe and make me watch if I didn't submit." She then became very distraught and began sobbing. It was all she could do to blurt out, "To make matters worse, I'm experiencing symptoms that lead me to think I might be pregnant."

An uncomfortable silence made Teresa's heart race while Norma gathered her thoughts. She reached out and hugged Teresa as she said, "I'm so sorry such a horrible thing happened to you."

Trembling and sobbing, Teresa asked, "What am I going to do?"

Norma took a sip of her coffee, rested her forehead on her hand, and chose her words with care when she replied, "On the one hand, a baby born in this country is a U.S. citizen. So, that could help your efforts to become a legal resident. On the other hand, dealing with a pregnancy, along with everything else which is coming your way, may very well prove to be an insurmountable challenge for you." She hesitated for a moment and then asked, "How do you feel about getting an abortion?"

Teresa backed away from Norma with a look of shock on her face. While she had no desire to have a child which was the result of rape, she never contemplated getting an abortion. Her initial reaction was, "My God! How could I kill my innocent child?"

Norma tried to express herself with confidence and concern. Hoping Teresa would understand the potential gravity of her situation, she replied, "I understand and would expect you to feel that way. I would say your decision to get an abortion would not be your sin. It would be the rapist's sin."

Teresa's eyebrows arched upward, and her eyes reflected distress. "I guess that's true."

"This rape must have occurred around mid-December. Is that right?"

"Yes."

"Well, there is still a chance you're not pregnant. The first thing we should do is to get a pregnancy test. However, if you are pregnant, the earlier you get an abortion, the better it is."

Teresa stared into the air and shook her head. "I need to think about this for a while."

Norma put her hand on Teresa's hand and said, "Please understand. I don't mean to pressure you. But we must do something before you get a job so that you have some time to recover."

Despite Norma's words, Teresa did feel more pressure to make a decision now. Her face reflected dismay, and Teresa wrung her hands as she said, "Please give me a day to think about this."

"No problem. Do you feel up to learning how to use your cellular phone? Maybe that will take your mind off of the decision you must make for the moment."

"Sure. Let's do that."

That evening, in her bedroom, Teresa called her new friend. "Rosita, this is Teresa. My Aunt Norma introduced us at the Restaurante El Potrillo today."

"Ah, yes. I thank you for calling."

After some small talk, Teresa asked, "How long have you been in the United States?"

"About three years."

Teresa said, "As you know, I only got here a couple of days ago. I rode the beast up through Mexico to get here. How about you?"

"I came on a student visa. The visa expired a year ago. So, like you, I'm undocumented."

"How long have you been pregnant?"

"About six months."

"Have you chosen a name yet?"

"My husband and I know it will be a girl, and we plan to call her Angela."

After hesitating, Teresa took a deep breath and said, "I think I'm pregnant too."

"Congratulations! So, you came here with your husband?"

After another pause, Teresa said with a quivering voice, "No. I'm not married." And she told Rosita about the rape.

"How terrible! Are you going to keep the baby?"

Rosita's question resurrected the distress which afflicted Teresa about her impending decision, and she replied with an almost inaudible voice. "I don't know. My Aunt Norma is going to help me get a pregnancy test, and then I will decide. I must tell you. This is a tough decision for me."

"Of course it is. It would be a difficult decision for anybody. But I gotta tell you. I don't know if I could have a baby, knowing that the father was some stranger who raped me."

"That is very much weighing on my mind. But the idea of killing an innocent child weighs on my mind even more."

"Well, my understanding is that even people who are strong opponents of abortion tend to make an exception when there's a rape involved."

Teresa concluded, "I suppose that's true. But I feel very troubled with this decision. I enjoyed our conversation, Rosita. I hope we can become close friends. At this point, you're the only friend I have here."

When she got off the phone, Teresa kneeled at her bed and prayed, *Dear God, I thank you that Pepe and I have arrived here and that we are as safe as we can be. I'm so grateful for all that my aunt and uncle have done for us. It grieves me that they may now have to incur additional expense if it turns out that I'm pregnant. At the same time, I feel so much shame about getting an abortion. Please, dear God, help me make the right decision. Amen.*

The next morning, Norma and Teresa went to a local drug store and purchased a pregnancy test kit. On the way home, Norma put a letter in the mail to her sister, Susana, to let her know Teresa and Pepe arrived, and they were healthy and safe.

Sure enough, Teresa was pregnant. Tears came to her eyes, spilled down her cheeks, and reached the corners of her mouth. She could taste their saltiness. Now that there was no doubt, Teresa felt horror, shock, shame, and panic. With heart-wrenching sobs, she reached out to her Aunt Norma.

Norma hugged her and did her best to console her, saying, "I think the next thing we should do is have you meet with a counselor about the question of an abortion."

After Pastor Turner counseled Teresa to forgive Mario for raping her, Teresa ceased having nightmares about her rape. But after she went to bed, a nightmare tormented her once again. In her distressing dream, she relived the brutal experience all over again, to include the foul odor from Mario's rotten teeth. Thrashing about, she screamed and woke up at three o'clock in the morning in a cold sweat, and she was tangled in her sheets.

Norma rushed into her room in a panic and found Teresa sitting up in her bed, with tears in her eyes, and hands on her cheeks. "Are you all right?"

Teresa replied, "I guess I'm okay. I had a nightmare that Mario raped me again."

After making an appointment for Monday with Mrs. Garcia, an abortion counselor, Norma got on the Planned Parenthood website and read the following about helping a woman who is struggling with the decision to have an abortion.

You are dealing with a loved one who is considering, or has decided, to end her pregnancy. Each woman approaches this experience in her own way. For some, the decision is quite straightforward; for others, this may not be the case.

Every year, thousands of women and couples face an unplanned and, in many cases, an unwanted pregnancy. Most women are helped through this experience by someone they trust.

We know that providing reassurance and support to someone you care for can be difficult, and more so, if you are both experiencing a situation, which you may find stressful.

This page aims to help you understand the consultation and treatment process and answer the most frequently asked questions and concerns which partners have.

The woman herself makes the final decision to end or continue the pregnancy. You may feel a little helpless during this process. You might feel more involved by asking your partner or loved one how she would like you to help and reassure her.

Furthermore, you should know the help you give is valuable and will, after all, be appreciated.

That afternoon, the phone rang. When Norma heard Susana's voice, she exclaimed, "Yesterday, I put a letter in the mail to you to let you know that Teresa and Pepe have arrived, and they are safe. Let me get Teresa on the phone." She covered the mouthpiece and shouted to Teresa, "Come quick. Your mother is on the phone."

Teresa came running down the stairs with a face that was full of emotion. No tears of sorrow, but abundant tears of joy, streamed down her face when she heard her mother's voice for the first time since she left Honduras.

Susana, very emotional as well, asked with a weepy voice, "How are you, my daughter?"

"I'm doing all right, Mamá." Teresa saw no good reason to say anything about the rape or her pregnancy, so she did not. She noted that Susana was weeping, and she continued, "It's so good to hear your voice, Mamá."

After chatting a while, Pepe got on the phone, also with tears streaming down his face, which he wiped with his shirt sleeve. He cried out, "Mamá. I miss you."

After their sweet conversation, it took some time for both Teresa and Pepe to overcome the melancholy they both felt, now intensified after their short conversation with their dear mother, who they loved so much.

Pablo returned home. As a truck driver, he was on the road for several days each week, and it was normal for him to return home on Fridays in the evening.

While Teresa was in her room, Norma told Pablo about the rape, that Teresa was pregnant, and that she scheduled an appointment for Monday at an abortion clinic.

Pablo pursed his lips, sighed, and commented, "I'm so sorry to hear that. How's she taking it?"

"As you might imagine, she's struggling with the thought of getting an abortion. On the other hand, she's also struggling with the thought of having a child, which is the result of rape."

Pablo hesitated and took a deep breath. "I must tell you. This effort to bring Teresa and her brothers here was far more expensive than we anticipated. Has she decided she will get the abortion?"

Norma replied, "She hasn't. I expect she intends to choose the abortion option when she meets with Missus Garcia, the abortion counselor, on Monday. I also expect Teresa will have to recover from her abortion before she can get a job."

Pablo was conflicted. On the one hand, he was sympathetic with Teresa's tragedy. On the other hand, he was concerned about the expensive responsibility he had taken on. He concluded, "Well, keep me informed."

Norma, Teresa, and Pepe returned to MacArthur Park on Saturday to meet with the woman from whom they ordered the identification cards. After paying the remaining $400 they owed, Teresa and Pepe received them.

On Monday, Teresa and Norma arrived at the abortion clinic for Teresa's appointment. The counselor, Mrs. Garcia, invited Teresa into her office. Pepe stayed with his Aunt Norma.

 Mrs. Garcia explained, "Abortion is very common, and women have abortions for many different reasons. The decision to have an abortion is a decision that you alone must make. However, we can provide you with good information and the support that will help you decide which option is best for your own health and well-being. For some people, this decision is simple. For others, it is a difficult and very stressful decision. Please tell me what prompts you to consider an abortion?"

Teresa wrinkled her forehead, and her voice quivered as she told Mrs. Garcia about the rape. She continued, saying, "My Aunt and Uncle spent a lot of money to help me and my brother escape gang violence in Honduras. I'm now living with them. Our plan was for me to get a job to help with the additional expenses resulting from our addition to their household. They have been so generous with me, and this pregnancy imposes an additional unexpected and undeserved financial burden on them. As you might expect, this grieves me. On the other hand, I feel such guilt about making a decision to abort my baby."

Mrs. Garcia responded, "You should understand your decision to have an abortion doesn't mean you don't want or love children. It doesn't mean you're a bad person. And it doesn't mean you won't have a baby later when you feel you're in a better position to be a good parent. The bottom line is, only you know what's best for you and your family."

Mrs. Garcia could see that Teresa was struggling with this decision, and she added, "Here are some additional questions to ask yourself: Am I ready to be a parent? Would I consider adoption? What would it mean for my family if I gave birth to a child now? Do I have strong personal or religious beliefs about abortion? Would having a baby change my life in a way I do or don't want?"

Teresa hesitated for some time, and Mrs. Garcia was patient with her. After pondering these questions, Teresa tightened her lips and asked, "What happens if I decide to get an abortion?"

"You have two options: You can do the abortion here at the clinic, or we can give you medication you take at home, which will induce the abortion. Both options are effective, which would not be the case for you, if you were pregnant for more than two months."

"Tell me more about using the medication."

"We make an appointment for you here at the clinic. At that appointment, we will give you the pills. They consist of two sets of pills which you take over two days. In most cases, the abortion is over within 24 hours after taking the second set of pills. Then we'll make a follow-up appointment with you to ensure the abortion was successful."

"What about recovery?"

"You will want to rest well after your abortion. In most cases, patients can go back to work the next day. However, you should avoid strenuous work or heavy exercise for a few days. I'll give you some written instructions to deal with any bleeding you might experience. Most people feel fine within a day or two, but it's common for bleeding to last several weeks after taking the abortion pills. Cramping may occur for a few days as well."

"Anything else I should be aware of?"

"It's normal to experience a variety of emotions after your abortion. Most people are relieved and don't regret their decision. Others may experience sadness, guilt, or regret after an abortion. If you're having difficulty, we are available to provide counseling."

"How much will it cost, and when can I get an appointment?"

"The cost of the abortion pill method is $300." After checking her computer, Mrs. Garcia said, "We can schedule you for next Monday. Will that work for you?"

"I believe it will. But I need to confirm this plan with my aunt."

Mrs. Garcia followed Teresa into the waiting room, Teresa confirmed the plan with her Aunt Norma, and they made the first appointment for next Monday and the follow-up appointment for the following Monday.

The entire procedure proceeded, as Mrs. Garcia explained. At the follow-up appointment, a doctor confirmed the abortion procedure was successful, and Mrs. Garcia met with Teresa. "Everything looks good. Remember, you should expect the possibility of some bleeding over the next couple of weeks. Any questions."

Experiencing feelings of guilt, Teresa responded, "Not at this time."

Mrs. Garcia followed up, "Here's a prayer which we like to give to our patients. A local pastor provided it to us, and our patients have found it helpful."

When she got home, Teresa read the prayer, which said,

Dear God, I pray for women who feel compelled to make the difficult, traumatic, agonizing decision to abort a pregnancy. If they feel alone, I pray that loved ones will rally around them, even if they oppose their decision. If guilt afflicts them, I pray that they know You are ready to grant their request for forgiveness, and may they see that their loved ones will be quick to forgive them as well. I pray that such forgiveness will help alleviate the guilt which afflicts them. I thank you that they don't have to seek out some clandestine clinic, which might cause them harm, and that there are legal clinics which optimize their safety and the prospects for their recovery — both physical and emotional. And help us to understand they are choosing an option that, in their minds, is the best among bad options. Amen.

Teresa knew only too well about making the best choice among bad options. While the prayer was a welcome source of encouragement for her, it also made her cry with a deep sense of remorse. Teresa would find herself reading this prayer many times.

Work and School

Norma and Teresa enrolled Pepe in the Grand View Boulevard Elementary School, which offered bilingual instruction to help Pepe learn English and got him started on his education, which never was an option in Honduras. The school principal showed them Pepe's classroom. She also showed Pepe where the school bus would drop him off and how to get to the classroom.

On Monday, when the school bus arrived to pick him up, Pepe said with tearful darting glances, "Teresa, I don't want to go to school. I'm scared."

"Pepe, you need to go to school. Don't worry so much. I think you'll be surprised and will learn to like school."

As Pepe got on the bus, a neighbor boy, Lucas, also got on. Lucas sat with Pepe. Both were six years old, and they became friends before the bus arrived at the school.

The teacher, Mrs. Torres, introduced Pepe to the rest of the class. She saw that Lucas already became Pepe's friend, and she asked another boy in the class, Omar, to help Pepe make more friends. Omar was popular in the class, and Mrs. Torres knew he would convince other children to welcome Pepe.

After school, Teresa asked, "So, Pepe. How was your first day of school?"

With a cheerful voice, he replied, "I think I'm gonna like it. I have two new friends, Lucas and Omar. Lucas lives very close to us. Can I go play with him?"

"Do you know where he lives?"

"Sure. I can show you."

Teresa replied, "Well, after dinner, let's go meet his family, and we'll see."

After dinner, Pepe showed Teresa where Lucas lived. It was only two doors down. They knocked on the door, and when it opened, Teresa introduced herself and said in Spanish, "Good evening. My name is Teresa Amador. It appears my brother, Pepe, and your son, Lucas, have become friends. So, I wanted to meet you."

"I'm happy to meet you. My name is Rebeca Pérez. You must be new in the neighborhood."

"Yes. My brother, Pepe, and I live with my Aunt and Uncle Gomez."

"Yeah. I know them. So, you must be from Honduras."

"Yeah. How about you?"

"I'm from Nicaragua."

"Pepe wanted to come over and play with Lucas. I hope you don't mind."

"Of course not. Why don't you come in?"

"Sure!"

While Pepe and Lucas played, Rebeca served some lemonade. Teresa and Rebeca sat at the kitchen table and began what would become another meaningful friendship.

Teresa took a sip of her lemonade and asked, "Does Lucas have other friends in the neighborhood who he plays with?"

"Sure. And I'm sure Pepe will soon get to know them too. You'll find it's a friendly neighborhood, and I'll be happy to introduce you to some of my friends."

Pepe and Lucas went outside to play. While they finished their lemonade, Teresa and Rebeca chatted and got to know each other better.

Not wanting to overstay her welcome, Teresa smiled and said, "Well, I guess we better get going. I thank you for the lemonade."

As they walked out the door, Rebeca replied, "Why don't you leave Pepe here? They're having a good time. I'll bring him back after a while."

Teresa smiled and replied, "That would be great! Gracias." Teresa then turned to Pepe and said, "Now I want you to listen to Señora Pérez, and I don't want you to go into the street. Señora Pérez will bring you home. Do you understand me?"

"No problem."

Another week went by, and Teresa felt she was making good progress in the recovery from her abortion. However, she still dealt with the emotional trauma which afflicted her, especially at night.

She began taking a course called English for Speakers of Other Languages, or ESOL. In addition to studying English, participation in the course also broadened her circle of friends, including many Latin Americans and people of other ethnic groups, such as Orientals, Africans, Muslims, and Europeans.

In a telephone conversation, Teresa's new friend, Rosita, asked, "So, what did you decide about your pregnancy?"

Still dealing with the emotions for what she had done, Teresa shuddered as she responded with a sad tone, "I did decide to go through with the abortion. My physical recovery is progressing well. I must confess that the emotional issues still torment me."

Rosita replied, "I'd be surprised if you didn't have such emotional issues. As I told you earlier, I can't imagine having a baby that is the result of a rape. I hope you will come to see that you made the right decision. And I want you to know. I believe you did."

Tears came to Teresa's eyes as she pondered Rosita's words. "Thank you, Rosita. I really needed to hear somebody say that."

Pablo told Teresa about a job opportunity with a nightclub called El Lutrón. During a job interview, the manager explained, "We cater to male customers who seek intimate encounters with our team of attractive and talented women. I think you would fit in quite well."

When she recognized the club was a clandestine brothel, Teresa stood and ended the interview, saying, "I'm not interested in sharing such talents with your customers." And she walked out.

Confident that Pablo was not aware of the club's clandestine function, Teresa replied, when asked, "I didn't have the necessary qualifications for the job."

In another of her frequent telephone conversations with Rosita, Teresa asked, "Do you know anybody who's hiring? Now that I'm feeling better, I need to find a job."

"One of the waitresses where I work quit a couple of days ago. Do you have any restaurant experience?"

Teresa replied, "I do. Do you think I could get a job interview?"

"I'm sure you could. Why don't you come to the restaurant tomorrow, and I'll introduce you to the owner?"

"I'll do that. Would right after 1:30 in the afternoon be a good time?"

"Yeah. By that time, our lunch rush is over."

The next day, Rosita introduced Teresa to the restaurant's owner, Andrés.

Andrés offered Teresa a cold Coke, and they sat at one of the dining room tables. Andrés said, "Please tell me about your experience."

"My family in Honduras operated a business where we produced and sold burritos as street vendors. My mamá now lives by herself, but she still operates the business. During my migration to the United States, I interrupted my travel through Mexico, and I worked as a waitress and a cook at a restaurant near where I stayed in Apizaco, Mexico. It was only a temporary job to fill in for an employee who traveled to attend a funeral in another city. It worked out well because the employee returned right as I was getting ready to resume my travel."

Andrés liked her pleasant disposition, and he asked, "How's your English?"

Teresa put her glass on the table and replied, "I've only been in the United States for a short while, so my English is very limited, but I'm taking classes now."

Andrés leaned forward and lowered his voice to a near-whisper. "It's pretty obvious to me that you're an undocumented alien."

With a worried look on her face, she wrinkled her forehead and replied, "That's true. Is that a problem?"

"Do you have any identification?"

Teresa leaned forward, smiled, looked to the left and then to the right, looked Andrés in the eye, and lowered her voice to a near-whisper. "I have the best identification money can buy."

Andrés chuckled. "Okay. I like your background. Can you start tomorrow?"

Teresa brightened up and said, "Yes. I only need you to tell me what time I need to get here."

"I need you here at six o'clock in the morning. Bring your money-bought identification tomorrow." He then looked around and commented in a low voice, "After I make copies of your identification cards, don't carry them with you. If the migra catches you with false identification, they will deport you with no chance of returning."

Teresa nodded her head. "I'll do that, and I'll see you at six o'clock in the morning tomorrow. I thank you for giving me an opportunity."

When she got home, she put her identification cards in her purse and told Norma, "I've got a job! I start tomorrow at six o'clock in the morning at the Restaurante El Potrillo."

"Great! I'm happy for you."

"What do you want me to do about Pepe?"

"Don't worry about Pepe. He'll be at school most of the day, and I'll take care of him. It's important for you to have a job."

Over the next several months, Teresa's English improved, customers' tips at the Restaurante El Potrillo showed their satisfaction with her performance. She was very well-liked. Pepe was also progressing well in school and with his English classes. While their vocabulary was limited, they could now carry on a basic conversation in English. However, they spoke with a very strong Spanish accent.

Teresa didn't make enough money to get a place of her own, but Norma and Pablo were content to provide her and Pepe with a place to live. Nevertheless, she did start sending money every month to her mother in Honduras. By American standards, Teresa and Pepe were quite poor. Compared to their life in Honduras, however, they lived quite well. The important thing was: They were happy.

ICE Raid

Teresa and Pepe were adapting well to their life in Los Angeles. In addition to Lucas and Omar, Pepe made more friends at school and in the neighborhood. Teresa got together with Rebeca and Rosita often, and she was also increasing her circle of friends. In addition to sending money home to her mother, Teresa bought a computer, some nice clothes, shoes, toys for Pepe, and other things which improved the quality of life for both her and Pepe – nice things which she and Pepe never dreamed of having before. Her Aunt Norma taught Teresa how to use the computer, and she used it to work on her English. Their English continued to improve, although Pepe made quicker progress than Teresa.

Teresa arranged for her mother to have a cellular phone, and they enjoyed regular and frequent conversations. Susana used the money she received from Teresa to replace all of her shack's cardboard walls with wooden boards, and she made other improvements as well. So, Teresa's presence in the United States improved her mother's quality of life as well as her own.

It was about four o'clock in the afternoon on Saturday. Pablo, Norma, and Pepe were at home. Teresa called Norma to let her know she would be late getting home.

Two Homeland Security vans pulled up in front of the Gomez home, and eight agents from Immigration Control and Enforcement

(ICE) got out of the vehicles and surrounded the house. All wore black uniforms, with white lettering on their backs, which read, *Police, ICE Agents*. Neighbors saw the vans, came out of their homes, and watched in dismay, knowing what was about to happen to Pablo and Norma. A news crew from the Spanish television station, Univision, Channel 34, arrived and started filming.

An ICE agent knocked on the door, and, when Pablo opened the door, the agent said, "We have reason to believe you are in the United States illegally."

That statement sent a shiver down Pablo's spine. Doing his best to remain as calm as possible, Pablo asked, "Do you have a warrant?"

The agent responded, "We don't need a warrant."

Nodding his head, Pablo replied, "Oh yes, you do need a warrant. I do not give you permission to enter my home." And he tried to close the door.

The agent put his foot in the door and pushed his way into the house. He said, "Show me identification which authorizes you to be in the United States."

As Pablo learned during legal seminars provided for the benefit of undocumented migrants, he replied, "I demand you leave right now. We will show you nothing unless you can show me a search warrant signed by a judge."

The agents apprehended Pablo, Norma, and Pepe.

The Univision news crew approached, started filming, and asking questions. Pablo and Norma said nothing, as they had been instructed, and the ICE agents didn't comment either. The neighbors commented to the television crew that the Gomez family were good neighbors and didn't bother anybody. When interviewed, Rebeca, Teresa's friend, said, "Pepe, the boy ICE apprehended, plays with my son Lucas, and they are good friends."

By this time, the city bus dropped Teresa off at the bus stop, which was within sight of the Gomez home. Teresa got off the bus and started walking toward the house. She had no idea why the vans were parked in front of the house until she watched in horror as she saw the

ICE agents escort Pablo and Norma to the vehicles, both in handcuffs, along with Teresa's brother, Pepe. The agents proceeded to load them into one of the vans.

Teresa stopped to ponder what she should do. Fear gripped her as she remembered how ICE agents loaded Edwardo and Elena into an ICE van in Calexico. An agent noticed when Teresa turned around and started walking away. Teresa looked over her shoulder and saw the agent walking toward her, and she ran to get away. The agent ran after her. Teresa darted between two houses near the corner of the street and hid behind some bushes. The agent followed her between the same two houses. But, when he got to the next street over and saw no trace of her, he came back and began searching for her.

As he searched, the agent started walking away from her. Hiding behind a bush, Teresa saw a car stop at the traffic light on the corner. She ran toward the car as the agent turned around, spotted her, and ran after her.

Teresa got to the car, a Jaguar, and tried to open the front door. It was locked. She pounded on the window. Surprised, the driver looked over and saw the desperate fear on her face, her wrinkled forehead, and the hunted look in her eyes. He unlocked the door, she jumped in, crouched down in the seat, and blurted out in broken English, "Please help me! Danger!"

Startled, Matthew Ward turned right and sped away just before the ICE agent reached his car. He turned left at the next intersection, and, after making additional turns, he pulled over and parked his car.

Matthew looked at Teresa and said, "Okay. Tell me what I rescued you from."

Trembling, Teresa looked up, with eyes still widened in alarm, but now with a wary look on her face. Without making eye contact, and using her cellular phone to find the English words she needed, she said with a very strong Spanish accent, "The migra arrested my aunt and uncle, and my brother, Pepe. You may have caught a glimpse of the ICE agent chasing me when I got into your car. So, I was the only one who escaped. Please help me. I don't know what to do."

Matthew didn't know any Spanish, but he understood the word, *migra*, as the word Latin American undocumented aliens used to refer to ICE agents, and he asked, "So, you're an undocumented alien?"

Her eyebrows arched upward, and her wide-open eyes reflected desperation as she answered, "Yes. But please don't turn me in. Please help me."

Matthew hesitated as he realized he committed a crime. Then he took a deep breath and asked with a rather calm voice, "Is there someplace I can take you?"

Quite distraught, Teresa shook her head in despair and said with a quivering voice, "Other than the place where I work, I don't know where I can go right now."

"Well, I don't know where I can take you either. What's your name?"

She responded, "I'm called Teresa Amador."

"My name is Matthew Ward. Have you eaten?"

"I'm not hungry at all. But I'd like to get something to drink."

"Is there a place where you like to go?"

Without a better idea in mind, she asked, "Can we go to the Restaurante El Potrillo?"

Matthew nodded, "We can, if you show me where it's at."

When they walked into the restaurant, Matthew noted that Teresa wore the same uniform as the restaurant's waitresses, and he said, "It looks like you work here as a waitress."

As they sat at a table, Teresa replied, "Si."

Andrés, the owner, spotted Teresa and noted the troubled expression on her face. He came up to the table and asked in Spanish, "Teresa, what are you doing here? Are you all right?"

After she explained in Spanish what happened to her family, Andrés responded, "¡*Dios mio*! (O my God) And who is your friend?"

Responding now in English, and still quite traumatized, she said, "This is Matthew. I jumped into his car, and he helped me escape."

Andrés, a soccer fan, did not recognize Matthew Ward, who was a well-known soccer star with the LA Galaxy soccer team. Speaking in Spanish again, Andrés asked Teresa, "So, what are you going to do?"

"I must tell you. I don't know."

After pausing for a moment, Andrés replied, "Okay, I want you to take a couple of days off. Figure out what your options are, and give me a call Monday evening."

Matthew and Teresa ordered two cups of coffee, and Matthew asked, "Are you sure you don't want to eat something?"

Teresa sipped her coffee and replied, "No, gracias. I'm too upset to eat anything right now."

"So, where are you from, and how did you happen to come to the United States?"

Teresa replied, "I'm from Honduras." And she depended heavily on her cellular phone to find the English words she needed while she told him her sad story.

Meanwhile, the ICE agents took Pablo and Norma to a detention facility. They separated Pepe from them and put him in a caged area with several other Latin American children. The news crew from Univision split up to follow Pablo and Norma, as well as Pepe.

Moved by Teresa's tale, Matthew found himself attracted to this very pretty Honduran woman.

Teresa noted Matthew's very athletic build, with his broad shoulders and his slender waist. Despite the trauma she experienced, she couldn't help noticing how handsome he was.

It was now about seven o'clock in the evening. Matthew put his coffee cup on the table and said, "We still need to decide where I'm going to take you."

Teresa pulled out her cellular phone and called Rosita. When she answered, Teresa whimpered while she explained in Spanish what happened. Then, with a quivering voice, she asked, "Can I come to stay with you for a few days?"

Rosita replied, "My husband's family is visiting us this weekend, but you're welcome to stay with me on Monday."

Teresa put her phone away and said to Matthew, "I don't have any place to go until Monday."

Matthew rubbed his chin, nodded his head in contemplation, and then said, "I know I'm very much a stranger to you, but I have a second bedroom in my apartment, and you're welcome to stay with me if that's acceptable to you."

Teresa struggled to understand what Matthew said, so Matthew relied on his phone to translate his words into Spanish.

Teresa hesitated with a worried look on her face. Memories of rape sounded a scary alarm in her head, and her fear resurged. She took a deep breath and used her telephone to translate her words to English, "Can I lock the door?"

"Sure. No problem. I promise you'll be safe with me."

Realizing she had no other option, she said, "Okay. Gracias. Do you mind if we stop someplace where I can buy a few things I'll need?"

"Not at all."

As they progressed beyond basic conversation, they found it necessary to depend, with increasing frequency, on their phones to translate between English and Spanish. After the tedious process of looking up each word, Matthew found an application they put on both of their phones, which allowed them to speak sentences in their own languages. The application would then translate the sentences between English and Spanish. The application worked well, but they still found it necessary to repeat and modify their words before the application would communicate what they wanted to say. Even then, they experienced some uncertainty that the meaning they tried to convey was also the meaning the other understood.

They drank a second cup of coffee, and Matthew said, "I go to church on Sundays. Would you want to visit my church with me tomorrow?"

For the first time, Matthew saw Teresa brighten up a bit.

Teresa smiled and said, "I'd love to go to church with you."

"Great. So, maybe we should also get you something to wear to church tomorrow instead of your restaurant uniform."

"I don't know if I could afford that right now."

"Well. Let me take care of that for you."

Matthew's thoughtfulness made her heart throb, and she felt drawn to him.

They left the restaurant and went to a department store at a shopping mall. Matthew bought Teresa an exquisite red dress, which highlighted her feminine figure and enhanced her light cinnamon-colored complexion. To Matthew, she was like a sunrise that brightened up his world.

"You look quite stunning in that dress."

Teresa covered her shy smile with her hand, looked at him out of the corner of her eye, and said, "Gracias."

Matthew liked the almost flirtatious way she looked at him.

They also stopped at a drugstore, so that Teresa could purchase some toiletry items which she needed.

They arrived at Matthew's apartment at 8:30 in the evening.

Teresa looked around at the luxurious apartment and commented, "Your apartment is very cozy. I like it."

"Thank you. Let me show you the bedroom I told you about." He also showed her that the door had a lock on it.

With a worried look on her face, Teresa asked, "Do you mind if I watch the news in Spanish at ten o'clock this evening? I want to see if they say something about my family."

"Not a problem."

Sitting in the living room, Teresa saw Matthew's extensive collection of soccer trophies and asked, "What's with all the trophies?"

"I'm a professional soccer player."

Very surprised, Teresa asked, "That would be football, right?"

"Yeah, I guess that's what you call it in Spanish."

"What team?"

"LA Galaxy. Do you like soccer?"

With a touch of melancholy, she replied, "My dad and my brother used to listen to the games on the radio. And I would pay attention whenever they scored a goal. Are you a pretty good soccer player?"

Responding with some shyness, Matthew avoided eye contact and said, "Many say I do pretty well."

At ten o'clock, Matthew found the Univision television station, and Teresa was dismayed to see the news coverage about her family. Matthew sat beside Teresa on the sofa and watched with her, although he couldn't understand a word.

The news report was as follows:

Today, Ice raided the Gomez family home and took Pablo and Norma, along with Pepe, their six-year-old nephew, into custody.

Later, after ICE locked them up in a migrant detention facility, and when our reporters asked about the raid, Pablo responded, "I did not give them permission to enter my home, but they pushed their way in anyway. I asked to see a search warrant with a judge's signature, and they refused my request."

Lorenzo Dominguez, the attorney assigned to represent them, commented, "We may have a case against ICE for forcing their way into the Gomez home against their will and arresting them without a warrant. But we have to face the very real possibility that they may be deported back to Honduras."

The Univision news anchor then cited an article from the *USA Today* newspaper, which reported.

"ICE agents can make arrests at homes, businesses and other places. Recently, reporters have found officers making arrests at courthouses and near schools. After arrest, ICE decides whether to take custody of individuals and pursue removal proceedings."

The news anchor then said, "A news crew also caught up with Pablo and Norma's nephew, Pepe, who is only six years old." The television camera showed Pepe locked in a cage, along with many other small Latin American children, many of whom were crying and screaming with desperation.

The camera then showed a close up of Pepe, who wailed with heart-wrenching cries while he called for his sister. Teresa began sobbing and became so distraught that Matthew had to grab her to keep her from falling off the sofa and onto the floor. Teresa clung to him, and he put his arms around her while she buried her head in his shoulder, trembled with anguish, and continued to wail with deep body thrashing cries of desperation.

As Teresa began to calm down, she realized Matthew had his arms around her, and she backed away and panicked as the memory of her rape afflicted her again.

Matthew interpreted her response as one of embarrassment and said, "I apologize. What happened was quite spontaneous. I hope you recognize I was only trying to console you."

Teresa didn't understand, so he made a second effort with his phone to translate his words into Spanish.

Teresa was embarrassed by this very awkward moment and said, "Please forgive me."

"There's nothing to forgive. I'm happy you had a shoulder to cry on."

"Gracias. I think I'll go to my room now."

Church and Charm

Teresa endured a very sleepless night. She tossed and turned, worried about her brother, Pepe, and her aunt and uncle. She was also afraid because she was in the home of a man she didn't know. Troubling visions of her rape invaded her mind. She finally dozed off just before dawn.

In the morning, Matthew knocked on her door and said, "I'll have some breakfast for us in about thirty minutes."

Startled, Teresa looked around until she realized where she was. She looked at the door to ensure it was still locked. It was. She replied, "Okay. Gracias."

Having not eaten since lunch the day before, Teresa realized she was quite hungry. She showered, put on her work uniform, and made her way to the kitchen.

Matthew looked up with a frying pan in his hand and said with a broad smile, "Good morning. I'm not the best cook in the world, but I think I can make some good pancakes. I hope you like pancakes."

Teresa smiled back. "I do like pancakes. Can I help you with anything?"

Matthew flipped the pancake in the frying pan. "Why don't you serve us some orange juice? The coffee is ready, I've fried some bacon, and the pancakes are almost ready."

Teresa served the orange juice, sat at the kitchen table, and watched Matthew do his thing. She was pleased and grateful to see how attentive he was.

Matthew served the pancakes and bacon, poured the coffee, and asked, "Do you mind if I say a prayer?"

Teresa took a deep breath and relaxed a little. "Please do!"

She looked at him as he bowed his head and prayed, "Dear God. We thank you for the food you have blessed us with. I pray you will help Teresa know she can trust You, and I pray she will come to know she can trust me as well. I also pray she will come to see how you will take care of her, her little brother, Pepe, and the rest of her family. Please help us to honor you in all we do. Amen."

It took a while to translate the prayer from English into Spanish, and his prayer compelled Teresa to shed a tear. She forgot all about the nightmare about her rape, and she reached out, hugged him, and said, "Gracias."

As Teresa ate her breakfast with gusto, she looked at Matthew and said, "Tell me about your family."

After more translation work, Matthew understood what she said. "Well, you might be surprised to know I'm also an immigrant. My family came here from Canada when I was a boy, and we are now U.S. citizens. We also maintain our Canadian citizenship. My parents' names are Peter and Martha, and I have a younger sister, Cynthia."

"Will we see them at church today?"

"Yes, we will. My parents don't live too far away from here. My sister is a student at the University of California at the Berkeley campus. And it so happens she's home for the weekend. I'll be happy to introduce you to them."

Teresa felt some intimidation about meeting Matthew's family.

Matthew asked, "So, do you think you'll be able to stay with your friend for a while? What's her name?"

"Her name is Rosita. She's the best friend I have right now, and I know I can stay with her for at least a short while."

"Well, let me say I hope that will work out for you. I'm happy to let you stay here, but I don't want anybody to think poorly of you if they find out you're living with me."

Teresa was pleased to hear Matthew say that, and she felt much more confident that she could trust him. She responded, "Gracias."

"So, after what happened on Saturday, how do you feel about going back to work?"

Teresa put her coffee cup on the table. "I guess it doesn't matter how I feel. I need my job."

"What else do you do?"

"I'm also taking a course called English for Speakers of Other Languages, or ESOL, so that I can improve my English. Since my mother is still in Honduras, I also functioned like a parent for Pepe, my brother. So, I feel helpless to fulfill this role, now that ICE has taken my brother into custody. Other than that, I have very little time to do anything else."

"It appears to me, you're making pretty good progress with your English."

"Gracias. I know I have a lot to learn."

They finished breakfast, and Teresa said, "Let me wash the dishes."

"Okay. You wash, and I'll dry."

As Teresa handed the soapy dishes to Matthew, their wet hands touched from time to time. They liked touching each other, and future touches were more intentional. Their eyes also met from time to time, with discreet, nearly imperceptible smiles that communicated their pleasure of being together.

They finished getting ready for church. Teresa put on her new red dress; Matthew put on a suit and tie. They departed in Matthew's Jaguar, and both were pleased to be together. Matthew found himself looking frequently over at Teresa in her red dress and said, "That is the perfect dress for you."

Teresa looked at him out of the corner of her eye and covered her shy smile with her hand. "Gracias."

When they arrived at Fellowship Community Church, Matthew showed Teresa around and introduced her to some of his friends. While he showed her around, Teresa saw a world map framed and hanging on a wall at the back of the church. On the map were small photographs of people, and she asked, "Who are these people?"

Matthew explained, "They are missionaries who receive financial support from our church."

Looking closer at the photographs in Mexico and Central America, a tear came to Teresa's eye, and her face brightened when she saw a picture of Pastor Frank Turner. She exclaimed, "I met this missionary in Apizaco, Mexico, and he showed me how to trust Jesus for eternal life!"

Pleased, and with a surprised look on his face, Matthew said, "Is that right? How amazing!"

Matthew took Teresa to meet the church's pastor, "Teresa, this is Pastor Ron Gilming."

With a touch of shyness, Teresa covered her face with her hand and said, "It's good to meet you, señor."

Pastor Gilming shook hands with Teresa and replied, "Welcome. I hope you'll find this to be a good place to worship today. Where are you from."

Teresa smiled. "I'm from Honduras."

When he heard this and her strong Spanish accent, the pastor's reaction became less than enthusiastic.

Matthew then took Teresa to meet his family and said, "Mom, Dad, Cynthia, please meet Teresa Amador. Teresa, this is my mom, Martha, my dad, Peter, and my sister, Cynthia."

After some conversation, with assistance from the translation applications on their phones, Matthew's parents welcomed Teresa. Cynthia was not so cordial, which caught Matthew's attention.

Turning to Teresa, Matthew said, "Teresa, I sing in the church choir, so I'll leave you here to sit with my parents and sister. After the choir sings, I'll come to sit with you."

Teresa replied with timidity, a shaky voice, and a shy smile, "Okay." She felt quite intimidated to be left alone with Matthew's family.

As Matthew headed for the choir, Pastor Gilming caught up with him and said, "I'd like to have a word with you after the service."

With some surprise, Matthew took his seat in the choir, and, after the choir sang, he went to sit with Teresa.

Teresa enjoyed the service, and afterward, she and Matthew went to see the pastor.

Pastor Gilming said to Teresa, "Would you excuse us for a moment?" And when they walked away, he asked Matthew, "Do you know if Teresa is a legal resident here?"

"I know she is not. Why is that important to you?"

"Well, I'm not sure if we can welcome an illegal immigrant in our church. Many members would not like it."

Offended, Matthew looked at Pastor Gilming. "You surprise me. What kind of compassion is that toward my friend, Teresa."

Pastor Gilming crossed his arms. "It's not a question of compassion; it is a question of legality."

Matthew looked over at Teresa, and his eyebrows arched downward. Then he said to Pastor Gilming, "Just a minute."

He walked over to Teresa and said, "I need to show something to the pastor, and I'll be right back."

Teresa sat on the front pew to wait for Matthew.

Matthew returned to the pastor, took him by the arm, and said, "I want to show you something. Please come with me."

They went to the world map at the back of the church sanctuary. Matthew pointed to the picture of Frank Turner and said, "Frank Turner here, a missionary which our church supports, led Teresa to a saving knowledge of Jesus Christ when she stopped in Apizaco, Mexico during her migration to the United States. So, Teresa is our sister in Christ, and I think, sir, you have an obligation to welcome her to our church."

Matthew continued with a forced smile that masked his displeasure. "She comes from a very poor family in Honduras, and she has lost family members to gang violence. After escaping gang violence in Honduras, I suspect her brief encounter with Missionary Frank Turner, on her way through Mexico, did not give her a chance to be baptized. So, Pastor Gilming, I think you should be thinking about baptizing her instead of turning your sister in Christ away. I suggest you think about that." That said, Matthew walked away.

Pastor Gilming gazed at the picture of Frank Turner and pondered what Matthew told him.

When Matthew came back, Teresa could see he was upset about something, and she asked, "Are you all right?"

Not wanting Teresa to know about the pastor's unkind words, he failed to convince her when he breathed an exasperated sigh and said with a tight-lipped smile, "I'm fine."

They caught up with Matthew's parents, and his father asked, "Do you want to join us for lunch?"

Calming down now, Matthew turned to Teresa and said, "Will you have lunch with us?"

"I'd love to."

Peter asked, "How does Chinese sound?"

When she didn't say anything, Matthew used his phone to translate and asked Teresa, "Do you like Chinese food?"

"Sure. I love it."

They all went to the Golden Dragon Restaurant.

As they waited for their food to arrive, Martha, Matthew's mother, asked, "Teresa, where are you from?"

With heavy dependence on her phone's translation application, Teresa replied, "I'm from Tegucigalpa, the capital of Honduras. Matthew tells me you are Canadian citizens."

Peter put his teacup on the table and replied, "Yeah. We moved here several years ago from Vancouver, British Columbia. We have dual citizenship in the United States and Canada."

With one eyebrow raised and eyes which reflected a peculiar spiteful gaze, Cynthia asked, "How long have you two known each other?"

Matthew narrowed his eyes, tilted his head, looked at Cynthia out of the corner of his eye, and answered, "We met yesterday."

Looking down her nose at Teresa, Cynthia asked, "How long have you been in the United States?"

Noting Cynthia's hostile attitude, Teresa avoided eye contact with her and replied, "Only a few months."

With glaring eyes, Cynthia asked with an angry tone, "Are you a legal resident here?"

Annoyed with his sister's tone, Matthew interrupted. "Why do you ask such a question?"

Cynthia crossed her arms, stuck her nose up, and looked across her shoulder. The sides of her mouth curled downward as she replied with disgust, "Because we don't need any more illegals in this country!"

Embarrassed, Teresa gazed downward, her complexion paled, and beads of sweat formed on her forehead.

Matthew touched her hand and said with a kind voice, "Teresa, you don't have to answer her question." And turning back to Cynthia, he said with a stern stare and contempt in his voice, "You leave her alone!"

Martha asked, "Cynthia, why are you so rude?"

Ignoring her mother's question, Cynthia raised the right part of her upper lip with a scowl on her face and said, "So, she is illegal here."

Also, with a scowl on his face now, Matthew pointed his finger in her face. "I told you to leave her alone." Turning to Teresa, Matthew said, "Come on, Teresa. We're getting out of here."

As they stood to leave, Matthew turned, pointed his finger in Cynthia's face again, and warned her, "If you make trouble for her, I'll never forgive you!" And they walked out.

Peter followed them outside and asked, "Matthew, why can't you stay?"

"Are you kidding me? How could we stay with Cynthia's bitchy attitude? You better have a talk with her because I will not tolerate her animosity toward Teresa."

Teresa, with tears in her eyes, cringed because she didn't understand the harsh words between Matthew and his father. There was dead silence in the car while Matthew drove back to his apartment. Teresa sat, looking out the side window with a blank stare on her face.

Back in his apartment, Matthew said, "I want you to know I've never known Cynthia to be so rude in my life. I'm so sorry."

Teresa blinked, and a tear filled her eye and flowed down onto her cheek. "And what about the argument you had with your father?"

Matthew replied, "He wanted you to stay. I told him he needed to deal with Cynthia, and I made it clear I would not tolerate Cynthia's animosity toward you."

Teresa began gasping for breath, and she arched her eyebrows upward with fear in her eyes. Her face became pale while she struggled with her phone to translate and say, "I'm afraid of what your sister might do. I feel like everything is caving in on me. I have nobody right now."

Matthew sat her down on the sofa, and he struggled with his phone to translate and say, "You'll recall I mentioned that Cynthia is a student. Maybe it will put your mind at ease to know that Cynthia will fly back to the University at Berkeley this afternoon. She has very little information about you, and she will be very busy with her studies. So, I don't think she can cause a lot of trouble for you."

Matthew continued, "I don't know what God intended when he brought you and me together yesterday, but I'm glad He did. I like you, and I like being with you. And I find it astonishing to see how we have experienced in one day the dramatic events which brought us together. You say you feel like you have nobody right now. But I'm hoping you might come to feel I am somebody in your life. I, for one, would like to see what might happen between us."

Teresa looked into Matthew's eyes and hugged him. While they held each other, she felt a welcome sense of security with him. Matthew put some music on, and they were content to enjoy the pleasure of being together.

During the afternoon, Teresa tried to call her mother to let her know about Pepe and her aunt and uncle, but there were problems with phone communications into Honduras.

It was now dinner time. Matthew said, "Since we left the restaurant without eating our lunch, you must be quite hungry now."

"When I lived with my parents in Honduras, we were lucky to have more than one meal a day."

"Well, I think we should at least have a second meal today. I was thinking about having a pizza delivered. Will that be okay with you?"

"Sure!"

As they enjoyed their pizza, they began discussing where Teresa might stay on a permanent basis, after her temporary stay with Rosita. They were unable to come up with a satisfactory option.

After Teresa went to her room, Matthew pondered the events that occurred over the weekend. The way Teresa burst into his life, her frantic supplication for his help to evade capture by ICE, her desperate vulnerability from sudden homelessness and separation from her family, and the fact that he became her savior captured his heart. He was glad that she was just a few feet away from him in her room, and that she was safe with him. And he wanted her to know she could rely on him. He prayed, *Dear God. I thank you that I was available when Teresa needed somebody to rescue her. I would like to see if there is a future for us. Please help me to keep her safe. Amen.*

That night, Teresa knelt at the bed in her room and prayed, *Dear God. I thank you for bringing Matthew into my life. He seems like such a wonderful man. I need somebody in my life, and I'd be so grateful if it could be him. Amen.*

Legal Issues

Matthew and Teresa finished breakfast and sat at the table, drinking a second cup of coffee.

With telephone in hand to translate, Matthew said, "I'm supposed to be on the soccer field for training today, but I've decided to take the day off so that I can spend it with you. I hope you'll welcome my company."

Teresa found it challenging to find the correct words to express herself in English, and she used her phone to say. "I'd love to spend the day with you. I hope you understand the risk you're taking with me. As you said last night, the events which brought us together on Saturday were quite dramatic. It should be clear to you that I live with the constant risk of deportation at any time. Are you sure you want to run such a risk with me?"

Matthew and Teresa needed their phones with some frequency to translate between English and Spanish. The applications they used on their phones helped, but sometimes they produced bizarre, unintelligible, and even humorous results. This made their conversations tedious, which might be frustrating if the conversations weren't occurring between two people who wanted to be together and enjoyed being together – conversations between two people destined to fall in love. However, such love was not something they could foresee yet, like butterflies in the dark. Every time they used their phones, they looked into each other's eyes, seeking to confirm they understood each other.

Matthew pursed his lips while he gazed at this woman who so brightened up his life in such a marvelous way. He took Teresa's hand in his while his phone translated his words, "It's way too early to know what kind of a relationship we might have. Love is an experiment. So, our decision to venture forward in pursuit of a possible relationship is a risk in and of itself. Knowing about the tragic events in your life, including what happened to you on Saturday, I want to see you stay in this country and prosper. But more than that, there's something about you that draws you to me. So, it's not enough for me to see you stay in this country. I want to see you be a part of my life. So, yes. I'm willing to run this risk with you. How do you feel?"

With a tear in her eye, Teresa replied, "You rescued me, and you have taken care of me in a devastating moment when I was in desperate need of somebody to care for me. In only two days, I have never felt such tenderness as you have shown to me. How could I not want to be with you?"

With a very happy smile on his face, Matthew brought Teresa to her feet, they embraced, and he replied, "Well then. Let this adventure continue!"

Teresa, with a smile that reached her ears, asked, "So, what do you want to do today?"

"Well. Let's start with a walk on the beach, we'll enjoy a quiet dinner someplace, and tonight, we can have a light supper here."

Teresa was shocked. The thought that she and Matthew would enjoy such a romantic interlude was not only something she had never experienced. The possibility of such a joyous interlude was something she never even contemplated. She and Raúl never had a romantic moment like this, only because it was not an option for them. Tears of joy streamed down her face. She looked at Matthew with emotions that overwhelmed her to the degree that she could not speak. She only managed to nod her head, and she reached out her arms to seek his embrace.

As they were getting ready to depart, Teresa's cellular phone rang. When she answered, a man said in Spanish, "My name is Lorenzo Dominguez. The court has appointed me to be the attorney to represent Pablo and Norma, as well as your brother, Pepe. Do you have a minute to talk?"

A shadow came over Teresa now, her euphoria abandoned her, she sat down, and replied. "Of course."

Matthew observed the anxious expression on her face as she talked.

Lorenzo said, "Before we talk about anything else, I want to put your aunt on the phone with you."

When Norma answered, Teresa burst into heart-wrenching cries and asked in Spanish, "Aunt Norma! How are you and my uncle?"

"As you might expect, we're in jail. We're as good as can be expected. The attorney tells us there is a high probability the United States will deport us, and there are some important things he will discuss with you. He will explain that we are in a situation where we will need your help. How are you?"

"You have to know I'm very worried about you two, and my brother. A man by the name of Matthew Ward let me get into his car and helped me escape capture. He's been very good to me. He even took me to his church. So, I'm all right for the moment."

"I'm glad to hear you're all right. Just be careful with this man."

"Don't worry. I will."

Their opportunity to talk was limited, and a guard came and took Norma back to her prison cell. Lorenzo got back on the phone and said, "As you heard your aunt say, there's a high probability the United States will deport them. There are some things I need to discuss with you. Is now a good time?"

Teresa looked up at Matthew with her tear-stained face and said, "I need to talk to this attorney."

Matthew replied, "Go ahead," as he left the room.

Lorenzo began. "First, I need you to identify a person you trust, who is willing to function as a power of attorney. It must be somebody who is a citizen or a legal resident. We will want to work with this person to sell your aunt and uncle's house and transfer the proceeds of the sale to them in Honduras."

"Second, you will want to find a place to stay. I don't think you can be safe from the migra if you stay in your aunt and uncle's home. I suggest you go to the house early in the morning to get your belongings."

"Third, I will soon make contact with Pepe, and I hope to arrange a telephone conversation between you and Pepe this evening. Regarding Pepe's situation, I suggest our goal should be to identify a person who would be willing to function as a foster parent. The ideal foster parent should be willing to let you and Pepe see each other. Do you know somebody who might be willing to do that?"

Hoping that Matthew might help her, Teresa answered, "I might know somebody. I'll have to see."

"Do you have any questions for me?"

"Yes. Who can function as a foster parent?"

"A foster parent must be a legal resident of the United States or a citizen, of course. The person must have adequate financial resources. He or she may be married or single. The person must also have a safe operating vehicle that is insured, and he or she must be able to take the foster child to and from appointments. The person must also have working phone service. Any other questions?"

"No. Not at this time."

"Okay. I'll try to get back with you this evening so that you can talk to Pepe."

With a downcast expression on her face and a vacant stare, Teresa replied, "Gracias."

When she ended the call, Matthew came back into the living room. Noting that she was trembling, he led her to the sofa, they sat down together, and he asked with a concerned voice, "So, what was that all about?"

"I talked to the attorney appointed to represent my brother and my aunt and uncle, and he let me talk to my Aunt Norma."

"How are they?"

"She and my uncle are in jail. I hope to have a chance to speak to my brother, Pepe, this evening. The attorney said there is a high probability the United States will deport my aunt and uncle, and he gave me some instructions I must follow. Maybe you can help me?"

Sensing Teresa needed some time to compose herself, Matthew replied, "I'll be happy to do what I can. Why don't we head for the beach? Maybe it will lift your spirits. We can talk more about this while we're there."

As they walked together hand in hand on the beach, the gentle waves covered their bare feet, and a balmy breeze caressed them while they enjoyed the warm weather. However, although she savored this pleasurable moment, Teresa was very preoccupied.

Matthew asked, "Why don't you tell me about your conversation with the attorney?"

She paused and looked up at Matthew with a somber look on her face. "As I said earlier, the attorney tells me he expects my aunt and uncle will be deported, and he suggested I stop by their house early in the morning to get my belongings."

"What time do you have to be at work?"

"Six o'clock in the morning."

"Okay. I'll drive you to the house tomorrow morning. You can get your belongings. Then I'll take you to work and head for the soccer field for my training. What else?"

"The attorney also said I should find somebody who is a citizen or legal resident here to act as power of attorney to sell my aunt and uncle's house and send the proceeds to them in Honduras."

"Well, I guess I'm eligible to do that too. Count me in."

With a sigh of relief and a tear in her eye, she reached out to Matthew for a hug and said, "Gracias."

Matthew asked, "What about Pepe?"

"That's the hard part. The attorney said I should try to find somebody who would be willing to be foster parents for Pepe."

Matthew rubbed his chin while he contemplated Teresa's words. "That is more challenging."

With a wrinkled brow, Teresa shrugged her shoulders and asked, "Do you know anybody who might be willing to help me with that?"

Matthew pressed his lips together and hummed as he pondered her question. "I don't know at this moment. How do you feel about going to church with me on a regular basis?"

"I'd love to go to church with you. The only thing which worries me is your sister."

"Cynthia is back in Berkeley. So, we won't see her for a while. Since I'm looking forward to seeing you with some frequency, I intend to have a serious conversation with her about us. As far as finding foster parents for Pepe, I'm hoping somebody in our church might be willing to help with that. By going to church with me, your presence may help persuade somebody to volunteer."

"Well, at least I can see some possible hope for my brother."

Matthew took Teresa's hands in his and said, "Let's pray about this. Dear God. It appears we have some understanding of what will happen to Teresa's aunt and uncle. If they must return to Honduras, we pray that the proceeds from the sale of their home will be adequate for them to resume an acceptable life together there. You know, dear God, how Teresa yearns to free her brother, Pepe, and to be together with him again soon. Please help us find eligible foster parents who are willing to make a home for Pepe, and I pray that such a family will make it possible for Teresa to have a close relationship with Pepe again. Please help us to honor you in all we do. Amen."

Matthew's prayer eased her feelings of desperation, awakened within her a sense of hope, and Teresa said, "I'm so thankful God brought you into my life."

Matthew kissed Teresa, embraced her, and replied, "And I thank God for bringing you into my life."

Teresa kissed him again, and they continued their walk on the beach.

On their way back to Matthew's apartment, they stopped at a locally owned restaurant. While they enjoyed a casual lunch, Matthew asked, "If I could visit you in Honduras, what would I want to experience?"

"I must tell you, if I took you to the *barrio* where I lived in Tegucigalpa, you'd be shocked. My mother, Susana, lives in a small shack. Everybody lives in desperate poverty, and you wouldn't be there long before seeing the horrendous gang violence that occurs there. As a matter of fact, you wouldn't want to stay there long because of the threat to your safety. On the other hand, I'm confident my mother, Susana, would be pleased to meet you, and I know you would like her. I'd also want to introduce you to my best friend, Leticia."

"I'd be happy to meet your mother and your friend. But I have to believe there are some nice places in Tegucigalpa."

"I think you would enjoy the Parque Naciones Unidas El Picacho in the outskirts of Tegucigalpa, located in the hills which overlook the city. The park has some pleasant walking trails, but the most impressive thing is a 20-meter-high statue of Jesus Christ. I think you would also be fascinated to see the Mayan ruins of Copán."

"Yeah. That would be very fascinating. What restaurants would we want to visit?"

Teresa had to think about that question. Going to restaurants was a rare luxury in her life in Honduras. "I would take you to the Restaurante El Patio, and you would want to try sausage and steak *pinchitos*. I've only been there once." After looking up the word *pinchitos* on her phone, she said, "The English word for *pinchitos* is shish kebab. They are skewered and grilled cubes of tender meat grilled over a wood fire and seasoned with a peppery sauce, which gives them a delightfully smoky, peppery flavor. I understand the restaurant also has great live mariachi music on Friday and Saturday nights, but I've never heard them play. So, Friday night would be the best time to go."

Matthew commented, "We'll have to find out if there's a Honduran restaurant in Los Angeles."

Back in Matthew's apartment, they watched a movie on Netflix, and they enjoyed a light supper of cold cuts and cheese.

At seven o'clock in the evening, Attorney Lorenzo Dominguez called and said, "I have Pepe here to talk to you."

He was crying when he got on the phone and asked, "Teresa. When are you coming to get me? I don't like it here."

Teresa trembled, and she wept bitter tears as she said in Spanish. "I promise I'll get you out of there as soon as possible. How are they treating you?"

"I'm in a cage with a bunch of other kids. They don't give us enough to eat, so I'm hungry. It's too hot during the day and too cold during the night. We only have blankets that look like aluminum foil. They only let us go to the bathroom three times a day, and sometimes I can't hold it. And I don't have any other clothes to wear. With so many kids here, it's very noisy. We're all crying and begging for somebody to come to take us out of here."

"Pepe, do the best you can. I love you, and I'll come to get you as soon as I can."

Lorenzo got back on the phone, and Teresa asked, "How frequently can I talk to him?"

"They're supposed to have a schedule for kids to talk to their loved ones. Tell me when's the best time to call you, and I'll give them that information."

"Evenings are best for me."

As she ended her telephone conversation with Lorenzo, Matthew could see the overwhelming grief and desperation Teresa experienced. He embraced her and said, "I'll do my best to find some good foster parents for Pepe."

Through her sobs, Teresa replied, "Gracias."

Prayers and Confessions

At five o'clock in the morning, Matthew and Teresa stopped at her aunt and uncle's home, and she went in to pick up her belongings, to include her fake identification cards. She also picked up Pepe's belongings, and she took the framed picture of Pablo and Norma's shack, which she showed to Matthew and said, "This shack is similar to the shack where my mother lives."

Matthew was shocked to think people called such places home. Before heading to the soccer field for his training, Matthew dropped Teresa off at the Restaurante El Potrillo for the start of her shift at six o'clock.

Before he departed, Teresa confirmed with Rosita the plan to stay at her apartment. Then she came out to Matthew's car, kissed him, and asked, "When will I see you again?"

Matthew said, "I'll call you tonight."

As she watched him drive away, she prayed, *Dear God. You've brought a few good things into my life, but then you took them away. I thank you for bringing Matthew into my life. Please don't take him away from me. He's been so good to me, and I need somebody like him. Please help me to honor you in all I do. Amen.*

As they started their workday, Rosita asked, "Where did you stay over the weekend?"

Teresa replied, "Matthew Ward, the man who helped me escape the migra, let me stay in the spare bedroom in his apartment."

Rosita stopped filling a salt shaker and asked, "Matthew Ward, the soccer player?"

"Yeah. That's him."

"Do you know he's one of the top players in the Major League Soccer organization?"

"Oh my goodness! He only said he was a good player."

"Well, he's being quite modest. Did he behave himself while you were in his apartment?"

"Yes. He was very good to me. And we went to his church on Sunday."

While they were talking, Andrés came up and said, "Good morning, Teresa. Are you all right?"

"I'm as good as I can be. I need to talk to you. Do you have a minute?"

"Sure. Give me a moment." He brought two cups of coffee over to a table, and he and Teresa sat down.

Teresa explained the need to find foster parents for her brother and said, "My friend, Matthew Ward..."

Andrés interrupted, "Matthew Ward, the soccer player?"

"Yeah. He just dropped me off."

"How in the world did you meet him?"

"He was the guy who helped me escape from the Migra on Saturday, and you met him when he brought me here."

Andrés slapped his forehead. "I can't believe it. Matthew Ward was in my restaurant the other night, and I didn't even recognize him. So, you were saying?"

Teresa continued, "I'm sure you're aware the government is putting migrant children in cages, and that's where they put my brother, Pepe. His attorney wants me to find somebody who would be willing to become foster parents for him. Since I know hardly any people, Matthew suggested I start going to church with him on Sundays. He thinks we might be able to find somebody there. So, I need to know if you can schedule my time off for Sundays."

Andrés put his coffee cup down and nodded with a devious smile on his face. "Yeah. I think we can work that out, but it'll cost you."

Teresa paused, raised her eyebrows, and asked, "How much?"

"You don't have to pay any money. All I want is Matthew Ward's autograph."

Teresa smiled, socked him on the shoulder, and said, "Okay. I think I can make that happen."

After work, Teresa called Susana, her mother, and explained, "I was returning home from work on Saturday, and I watched while the migra captured Norma, Pablo, and Pepe."

Susana shrieked, "¡*Dios mio*!" (Oh my God), and she asked with a quivering voice, "Where are they?"

"They put Pepe in a cage with other migrant children…"

Susana interrupted and shrieked again with more alarm, "In a cage! Is he all right?"

"He's as good as can be expected. I'm doing what I can to get Pepe back, and I'll let you know how that goes. Norma and Pablo are in prison, and I fear they will be deported back to Honduras. They may need your help if that happens."

"How can I help Norma and Pablo?"

"Well, if the United States deports them back to Honduras, I suspect they won't know where to go when they arrive. I'm sure they'll be relieved to see that you are waiting at the airport when they arrive."

"Of course I'll plan to be at the airport. Anything else?"

"At this point, I don't know."

"How are you?"

"I'm doing all right." And she explained how Matthew rescued her from the migra and that he was now her friend.

"Who is this Matthew?"

"His name is Matthew Ward. He's from Canada, but he's now a U.S. citizen. He's also a professional soccer star."

"Do you think you can trust him?"

"Well, he rescued me, bought me some clothes, took me to his church, and introduced me to his parents. So, yeah. I think I can trust him."

"He sounds like a good man. But I'd be careful if I were you."

"I don't think I have to worry about him. My bigger concern, however, is his sister, Cynthia. When I met her, it was obvious she didn't like me when she found out I'm undocumented."

"Can she make trouble for you?"

"Matthew tells me she's a student in a university located some distance from here. He's pretty confident she won't be able to make trouble for me. It looks like Matthew and I are going to be seeing each other with some frequency, and he assures me he plans to have a talk with Cynthia."

"Well, like I say, you need to be careful."

"I will, Mamá. I'll keep you posted about Aunt Norma, Uncle Pablo, and Pepe. I love you."

The next morning, Teresa sent her monthly $200 check to Susana.

Matthew and Teresa talked on the phone every night during the week and planned to see each other during the weekend. During one of their telephone conversations, Matthew brought up the subject of baptism.

Teresa said, "I'm confused. I was baptized when I was a baby. Why do I need to get baptized again now?"

Matthew replied, "Well, if you read about baptism in the Bible, you'll find that the early church baptized Christians when they accepted Jesus Christ as their Savior. So, our church believes getting baptized is a decision which new Christians make, not their parents."

Not quite convinced, Teresa asked, "And why is this so important?"

"Our church views baptism as a new believer's profession of faith in Christ for salvation and as a symbol of the new believer's entry into God's church. Our church administers baptism by immersion and sees it as a picture of the death, burial, and resurrection of Jesus from the dead. When the new believer goes under the water, it represents Jesus' death and burial, and when the believer comes out of the water, it represents Jesus' resurrection."

"People who get baptized as infants are no less Christian. But when new believers decide for themselves to be baptized, it is a very moving worship experience for them, an experience I think you would cherish. Moreover, I want you to feel you are accepted in our church. And your baptism would help compel church members to accept you because our church views baptism to be God's requirement for acceptance in the church. So, how do you feel about it now?"

"Now that I've heard what you say, I think I would like to be baptized. When can I do that?"

"I'll give Pastor Gilming a call to see if he can baptize you this Sunday."

~.~

On Wednesday, Matthew ate dinner with his parents. When he arrived, he found his mom and dad in the living room watching the news.

The news anchor said, "President Trump gave a speech on Wednesday to a gathering of officials from California who oppose the state's sanctuary law. In the speech, he called undocumented immigrants who cross the U.S. southern border drug dealers, murderers, rapists, and animals."

Matthew crossed his arms over his chest and commented with disdain, "Well, now that you met Teresa last Sunday, I hope you see how hateful it is for our president to classify all undocumented migrants as drug dealers, criminals, rapists, and animals."

Peter, Matthew's dad, blinked, looked at Matthew, and asked, "That's an interesting point. What do you know about this woman?"

Matthew told them about the impoverished conditions Teresa lived under in Honduras, the severe widespread problems with gang violence, and how gang violence directly affected her family. He explained, "For Teresa and her brothers to come here was risky and dangerous. Given the violence her family suffered from gang members, the family decided that sending Teresa and her brothers here was the best decision among their bad options."

As Matthew told Teresa's tale, Martha reached for a tissue to dry her eyes, and she asked, "How did Teresa get here?"

"You may have seen on the news how many migrants come up from Central America on a Mexican freight train called the *beast*. It's also known as the train of death. And I'm sure you've seen pictures of large numbers of migrants sitting on top of boxcars while they traveled through Mexico. Teresa and her brothers rode the beast as part of their travel to the U.S. border." And then he explained how her older brother died when he fell from the train.

After contemplating that she just met Teresa, and how Teresa witnessed the tragic death of her own brother in this horrendous way, Martha put her hands in front of her face and cried out, "Oh my God!"

Matthew continued, "Teresa tells me there are some bad people who ride the beast. But most are people like her who are escaping abject poverty and gang violence, and many of the people who travel on the beast are Christians. Teresa was an active member of the Catholic Church in Tegucigalpa, where she lived."

"After her brother was killed, she decided to leave the beast near Mexico City with her six-year-old brother, Pepe. She ran into some Christians in a town called Apizaco and stayed with them for a couple of weeks. They invited her to attend church with them, where she met Frank Turner, one of the missionaries our church supports, and he led her to a saving knowledge of Jesus Christ."

Peter, Matthew's father, commented, "That's amazing."

"When Teresa and Pepe made it to the United States, she lived with her Uncle Pablo and Aunt Norma, along with Pepe, until last week, when ICE agents arrested them. She returned from work and watched while ICE agents took them into custody. An agent chased Teresa, and she ran up to my car and pounded on the door's window. When I saw how scared she was, I let her in and helped her escape. Her aunt and uncle are now facing deportation."

Martha asked, "And Pepe?"

"They now have him locked up with other migrant children in a cage. You may have seen news items on television about many such children who our government put into cages. An attorney made it possible for Teresa to talk to Pepe on the phone for a short while. Teresa was devastated to hear how Pepe cried out for her to come and get him. She could hear the cries of numerous other children who were in the same crowded cage with Pepe. Teresa explained to me later that conditions are filthy. It's cold at night and hot during the day. Conditions are cruel and horrible."

With tears in her eyes, Martha asked, "What's going to happen to Pepe?"

"That's a good question. The attorney told Teresa that the best thing for Pepe would be to find foster parents who would accept him, and he instructed her to see if she could find somebody who might be interested."

Martha followed up, "Where's Teresa living now?"

"I let her use my spare bedroom over the weekend. Now she has a temporary place to stay with a friend of hers. So, she needs to find a permanent solution for herself."

Peter responded, "This is tragic! So, I perceive you'll be seeing Teresa again?"

"After experiencing with her the calamity which occurred this past weekend, I've come to be very fond of her, and I see the very real possibility of a relationship with her. She's a wonderful woman. She plans to start attending church with me, and I was hoping I could bring her here for dinner next Sunday."

Martha replied, "Fine. We'd love to have her."

"I'm sure both of you will become quite fond of her as well. However, I'm very concerned about Cynthia."

Peter said, "Well, she won't be home for a while. We'll have to cross that bridge when we come to it."

As they sat at the table for dinner, Peter prayed, "Dear God. We thank you for this food and your many blessings. We pray for Teresa, her brother, Pepe, and her aunt and uncle. Bless them, we pray. Deliver them from the tragedies they have experienced. And I pray You will help Teresa to avoid capture by ICE, and help her in her efforts to find foster parents for Pepe. Help us to honor You in all we do. Amen."

After dinner, Matthew called Teresa on his way home. When she answered, they talked about the day's events, and Matthew said, "I talked to my parents about having you over for dinner after church on Sunday. They're looking forward to getting to know you better."

After a significant pause, Teresa asked, "Will Cynthia be there?"

"Not at all. You'll remember I told you she returned to the university in Berkeley."

"Then, I'll look forward to Sunday dinner with your parents."

"Great! On Friday, I'll be playing in a soccer match. Do you want to come to the game?"

"That would be wonderful. That reminds me. Andrés, the restaurant owner where I work, wants your autograph. I understand you're a real star player."

With a touch of shyness, Matthew said nothing about her compliment but said, "No problem. How about if I bring a ticket for him?"

"I'm sure he'd be thrilled. Could we also get tickets for my friend, Rosita, and her husband?"

"Not a problem. When can I pick you up at work?"

"I start at six o'clock in the morning and get off at two o'clock."

"Okay. I'll pick you up at two o'clock in the afternoon."

The next morning, Teresa told Andrés that Matthew would come on Friday to pick her up, and she said. "Matthew will give you his autograph when he comes. He also plans to bring tickets for Friday night's game for you, Rosita, and her husband."

His eyes opened wide, and Andrés exclaimed, "Whoa! That's great! I'll have to get my manager to work Friday night."

Teresa explained that Matthew would take her to the stadium right after her shift. Not understanding that the game tickets specified where they would sit, she made arrangements for Andrés, Rosita, and her husband to meet up with her so that they could sit together at the game.

Matthew showed up at the Resaurante El Potrillo on Friday to pick up Teresa. Andrés purchased a brand-new soccer ball for Matthew to autograph. He had to wait his turn though because numerous customers crowded around Matthew, who also wanted autographs. Teresa was surprised to see how Matthew drew a crowd. Matthew brought four VIP tickets, one each for Teresa, Andrés, Rosita, and her husband.

It surprised Teresa to see how huge the stadium was. She never attended a professional soccer game before. Matthew and Teresa arrived well before the game started so that he could get ready for the game. As he was about to walk away, Matthew said, "By the way, I called Pastor Gilming, and he will baptize you during the upcoming Sunday worship service."

Teresa replied, "After thinking about what you said, I'm kind of excited to get baptized."

"I'm glad to hear you say that. I think it will be a memorable experience for you."

Teresa became bored until Andrés, Rosita, and her husband, Esteban, joined her. Teresa had not met Esteban before, and Rosita introduced them. While spectators spilled into the stadium, there was a dull, increasing babble of people's conversations.

Teresa looked out over the sea of people in the stadium and exclaimed, "I've never seen so many people together in one place. I'm kinda scared."

Andrés replied, "Just wait until the game gets started. You haven't seen anything yet."

Teresa spotted Matthew on the field while he and his teammates warmed up for the game. It was amazing to see his agility on the soccer field. She fought back tears as she began to wonder why somebody like Matthew would be interested in her. She had fond memories of Raúl, and always would. Now she was falling in love with Matthew, and she worried their relationship might be an illusion – a false promise of happiness. So far, in her life, all glimmers of happiness had ended in tragedy, like balmy breezes that only brought storm clouds with damaging winds. In her mind she prayed, *Dear God, may it be different this time.*

The moment came when the crowd's babble subsided, and the teams positioned themselves for the start of the game. She watched while all the players from both teams lined up, passed each other, and slapped their hands as a greeting.

The game now started. Every time a team got the ball within range for a goal, the crowds in the stadium rose to their feet, and their babble escalated into a deafening roar, which was so strong its power was almost overwhelming for Teresa.

As the game proceeded, Matthew charged down the soccer field like he was rushing into battle, and Teresa cheered when Matthew scored the first point. The crowd's uproar became even more intense – an intensity which inflicted Teresa like a contagious disease. All the LA Galaxy fans moved in unison to form a breath-taking wave that spread across the stadium. The beat of drums and the trumpet-like sounds of air horns could be heard above the crowd's uproar.

The game now neared its conclusion, and the score was 2 to 2. With only seconds remaining, one of the referees called a penalty against the opposing team, and Matthew prepared to kick what fans hoped to be the tie-breaking point. The crowd grew quiet. Matthew kicked the ball, and it shot past the goalie to score the winning point. The crowd went wild as LA Galaxy won the game. And Teresa, hoarse now, cheered right along with the other spectators.

The game ended, and the crowd began to exit the stadium. Andrés, Rosita, and Esteban departed as well. About forty-five minutes later, a very hyped up Matthew showed up. With a broad grin on his face, he opened his arms wide and said, "We won!"

Teresa jumped up and down with excitement and ran into his open arms, exclaiming, "You're amazing!"

As they drove away, Matthew said, "Why don't you spend the weekend with me?"

Teresa felt wary about Matthew's suggestion, but she smiled in a playful way and asked, "You'll let me lock the door to my room, right?"

Matthew returned the playful smile and assured her. "I wouldn't have it any other way."

They stopped by Rosita's apartment, and Teresa picked up some things she would need, to include a lovely dress to wear at church. Matthew took Teresa to a local restaurant for a quiet dinner, and they arrived at Matthew's apartment at ten o'clock in the evening. After tea and conversation, they ended their evening with an embrace and a tender kiss. Teresa locked herself in her room for the night and prayed, *Dear God. Again, I thank you for bringing Matthew into my life. I can't stop the love that is taking control of my heart, and I don't want to. Please, dear God, let him be a permanent part of my life. Amen.*

Saturday, they went to a local park for a picnic. They selected a picnic location near a babbling brook. It was secluded enough to give them some intimate privacy, but not so secluded so as to make Teresa feel uncomfortable. It was only about 10:30 now — too early for lunch. They spread a blanket out on the ground and sat together, side by side. The brook's current flowed over some nearby rocks to produce a pleasant melodic sound of rushing water, which embellished their mutual enjoyment. The canopy of trees filtered the sun in a dazzling way, which created a glimmering light show which sparkled and danced on the water. Two blue jays entertained them while they called to each other. Blue and yellow flowers decorated the varying hues of the green grassy knoll where they sat. The flowers were as soft as thoughts of budding love.

Above the rocky area, the brook's flow was like a quiet pool, and Matthew threw a flat stone that skipped several times on the water. With the use of the translator on his phone, he struggled to say, "Teresa, I understand well that you left Honduras to flee gang violence and extreme poverty. But you must have some pleasant memories of your life there."

Teresa stared into the air with a look of melancholy on her face, and she spoke her reply into her phone's translator. "The thing I miss most is the dance group organized by the church I attended. You'll recall I told you about my boyfriend, Raúl, who was killed by gang members. He was my dance partner. The dance group featured three typical Honduran dances, which we performed on special occasions. One of them is a colonial dance called the jarabe yoreño. Both the men and the women wear colorful traditional clothing provided by the church. When the dance starts, the women reject the men's advances. The men then act as if they're discouraged and have lost interest. Soon, the women begin flirting with the men and convince them to take part in the dance. It was my favorite dance."

Listening to Teresa paint the air with her words, as she spoke with eyes that reflected nostalgia, Matthew moved close to her and tenderly kissed her. Looking into each other's eyes, he asked, "Do you think I might see you do this dance someday?"

With a sad look on her face, Teresa replied, "I don't know. I'd love to teach it to you. How about you? Tell me something about your life in Canada."

With his arm around her; and Teresa, with her head on his shoulder, Matthew replied, "Where we lived in Vancouver, British Columbia, our house was located near an enormous forest. As a boy, my friends and I spent a lot of time in the forest. We used to build small huts, and we pretended to be soldiers. I dreamed of going deeper into the forest to build a log cabin with the goal of living off the land."

"It must be a beautiful place."

Looking out over the brook, Matthew replied, "Oh, it is. I'd love to take you there sometime."

Changing the subject, Teresa looked at Matthew, hesitated, and said, "I have some issues I need to discuss with you. Does it bother you that my skin color is darker than yours?"

The question caught Matthew by surprise. He looked at her, studied her face, and took her hand in his. He lifted her hand up, and both could see the contrast in their skin colors. Matthew then gazed into Teresa's eyes and said, "The fact is, I think your skin color is a major part of how beautiful I find you. So, no. The difference in our skin color doesn't bother me at all."

Teresa's eyes reflected shyness. With a tear in her eye, she glanced away, and the blush on her face erased her face's cinnamon color. Matthew's response relieved this persistent concern that afflicted her since they met. She and Matthew hugged each other.

Then Teresa hesitated again and looked into Matthew's eyes. With a troubled look on her face, she rubbed her eyebrow. "I have a more difficult issue to talk to you about, and I must deal with it now before our relationship goes any further."

Matthew tilted his head to the side and looked at her with a focused gaze.

"You know that Pastor Frank Turner helped me accept Jesus Christ as my Savior in Apizaco. But something else happened to me in Apizaco, which I think you need to know about." A tear filled her eye and spilled onto Teresa's cheek, and she looked down with shame while she told Matthew how Mario raped her.

Matthew's face became pale as he listened to her words, and, with dismay, he started to speak.

Teresa stopped him, looked up at him with eyebrows that arched upward and with a face now bathed with tears, and she said, "There's more."

With an expectation of impending doom, she hesitated and then blurted out, "As a result of the rape, I became pregnant. And soon after I arrived in Los Angeles, I agreed to an abortion, which was the most difficult decision I ever made. So, can you forgive me? And, are you sure you want to continue our relationship now that you know about this?"

In his inner being, Matthew reeled from this devastating revelation. His hesitation produced deep despair for Teresa. But then he took Teresa in his arms and said, "Let me put your mind at ease. I see this as another tragic event that has afflicted you. While it grieves me to hear about the rape and your decision to get an abortion, there's so much more about you, which compels me to want you in my life. So, believe me when I say, I see nothing to forgive."

It was time for lunch now, and Matthew prayed, "Dear God. Thank you for this wonderful day and the meal we're about to enjoy. Please give Teresa peace about these issues, which have caused her grief and have weighed so heavily on her heart. I suspect Teresa would agree with me when I ask You to bless this relationship of ours, which is in its infancy. Amen."

Matthew and Teresa hugged each other with a tight embrace. Teresa's deep cries produced a catharsis for her, and her tears soaked Matthew's shoulder. They did not break their embrace until her sobs subsided. They would never talk about this again.

For lunch, they ate sandwiches, potato salad, and watermelon. While they brought out the food, their hands touched from time to time – a touch which both savored. Afterward, they embraced each other again, which was for Teresa like the warmth of the blanket she received from the nurse in Apizaco, which she wrapped around her to produce serene tranquility. They chatted away well into the afternoon hours. On the way back to Matthew's apartment, they stopped at a local restaurant for fish and chips.

Back in Matthew's apartment, they watched a movie, and then, each went to their separate bedrooms, ready to hug a pillow, but wanting to hug each other.

Teresa Visits Matthew's Parents

On their way to church, Peter commented to Martha, "I was thinking about our prayer the other day when Matthew ate dinner with us. I can't escape the thought that maybe we are the answer to the part of our prayer where we asked God to help Teresa find foster parents for her brother, Pepe. How do you feel?"

Martha stroked her chin and looked at Peter. "Are you suggesting we should take on the responsibility to be foster parents for Pepe?"

Peter shrugged. "That's exactly what I'm suggesting."

Martha looked out the car window, pressed her lips together, and hummed in contemplation. Then she looked back at Peter and asked, "Do we want to take on such a large burden?"

"I'm not so sure whether we would be taking on such a large burden. With our five bedrooms, we have plenty of room in the house. You'll recall Matthew told us Teresa needs a permanent place to live. In addition to our bedroom and the bedroom I use for an office, we have three available bedrooms: One, where Teresa could stay, one for Pepe, and one for Cynthia when she visits."

Martha played with her hair and hummed again. "So, now you're suggesting we should also give Teresa a place to live?"

Peter shrugged his shoulders. "Well, it only makes sense. If Pepe comes to stay with us, then he and Teresa could be together. I think that would be wonderful for them. And I'm certain Teresa's presence would alleviate much of any burden we would have if we agree to become Pepe's foster parents."

"But we don't know anything about Teresa."

"We know she accepted Jesus Christ as her Savior at a church in Mexico, pastored by a missionary who receives financial support from our church. We know Matthew is fond of her, and it appears they have feelings for each other. Like I said, it keeps occurring to me that we may be the answer to the prayer, which we said for Teresa and Pepe."

Martha pursed her lips, took a deep breath, and said, "I guess I'm not opposed to the idea. She and Matthew will be coming over for lunch today. Let's see how that goes."

When they arrived at church, Peter said, "Let's pray about this matter before we go into the church."

Martha put her hand in Peter's, and they bowed their heads. Peter prayed, "Dear God. Please give us wisdom about this matter. If it's your will for us to become foster parents for Pepe, we pray that You would give us peace and confidence on how to proceed. Please help us to honor you in all we do. Amen."

They waited in the vestibule for Matthew and Teresa and watched while they arrived. Teresa wore a stylish white dress. Matthew wore dark blue trousers and a white shirt with gray pinstripes.

Martha commented, "They look good as a couple."

Peter responded, "I agree."

Matthew and Teresa paused at the door. Teresa appeared to be nervous. Matthew took her by both hands, and she looked at him with adoring eyes. Peter and Martha could see that Matthew said something to her, which put her at ease. Teresa smiled, and her face brightened.

When they stepped inside, Matthew said hello to his parents, but Teresa reached out, embraced both of them, and said with her very strong Spanish accent, "I'm so happy to see you. I look forward to coming to your home for lunch after church."

Both Peter and Martha were surprised by her heartwarming display of affection. They went into the sanctuary together. Matthew explained,

"Teresa, as we did last week, please sit here with my parents, and I'll come to sit with you after I sing in the choir."

Teresa sat down, and Martha touched her hand and asked, "How was your week?"

Although she was a little shy, she depended on her phone to translate and responded, "I understand Matthew told you about what happened with my brother and my aunt and uncle. I worked all week, which was good because the work took my mind off of their dilemma." Then she brightened up in a delightful, almost childlike manner, and she said, "Matthew took me to the stadium to watch him play soccer. I've never experienced anything like that! It was spectacular."

As the service began, Peter commented, "I'm glad you had a good time at the soccer match."

The music director announced the page number for the first congregational song, and Martha opened a hymn book to the correct page and handed it to Teresa.

Teresa smiled ear-to-ear and replied, "Gracias."

As the congregation sang, it was apparent that Teresa's limited English would not permit her to sing. She looked over at Martha, shrugged her shoulders, smiled, and put the hymn book back in the pew's rack in front of her. Then she clapped to the rhythm of the music with enthusiasm. Both Peter and Martha looked at each other and smiled. Even though clapping to the music was not customary in their church, they found her joyful participation to be amusing and delightful.

The song leader gave the page number for another hymn, and the pastor instructed the congregation to greet people. Peter and Martha introduced Teresa to the people around them and observed how Teresa greeted everybody with cordial exuberance and a smile.

After the choir sang, Matthew sat with Teresa. They held hands during the rest of the service, and Martha noted they could not resist the urge to gaze at one another with some frequency.

Peter and Martha were surprised when Pastor Gilming announced after his sermon that he would baptize Teresa.

A deacon stood with angry eyes, a scornful look on his reddened face, and said, "Pastor Gilming, before you baptize this woman, I want to know if she's legal here."

Pastor Gilming pressed his lips together, took a deep breath, and asked, "And what does this have to do with a person who has accepted Jesus Christ as her Savior and now wants to obey Him by being baptized?"

The deacon replied with an angry tone and a curled lip, "I suspect she's a Central American immigrant who is here illegally, and our president tells us that such illegal immigrants are drug dealers, murderers, rapists, and animals."

When she heard this, Teresa buried her head in Matthew's shoulder, and, through her sobs, she said, "Please take me away from here."

Matthew, with his arm around her, whispered, "I don't blame you for wanting to leave. But let's not be too hasty. Let's see how Pastor Gilming handles this matter."

Pastor Gilming replied, "It is true that some migrants coming to the United States from Central America may be drug dealers, murderers, and rapists. But most of them are, in fact, decent and honorable people who are escaping extreme poverty and gang violence. And..."

Pointing his finger at Pastor Gilming, the deacon interrupted and said, "That may be true, but they're all here illegally, which makes all of them criminals."

Pastor Gilming pursed his lips as he struggled to control his anger and replied, "Well, in the first place, Saul, in the book of acts, persecuted Christians, and he was complicit in the murder of at least one Christian, who happened to be a deacon, whose name was Stephen. Today, we would deem Saul to be a criminal. If you were alive in apostolic times, would you have opposed Saul's baptism, who became the Apostle Paul? I don't think so."

At this point, the deacon stomped out of the church and slammed the door behind him.

Pastor Gilming turned toward Teresa and, when he called her name, she looked up at him with her tear-stained face. "Teresa, my sister in

Christ, it grieves me to hear this deacon make such hateful comments about you. He has called migrants coming from Central and South America drug dealers, murderers, and rapists. Am I correct in my understanding that you are none of these?"

Filled with shame and sobbing, she was too embarrassed to say anything, and, to confirm that he was correct, she nodded her head to say, "Yes."

Pastor Gilming told the story of how gang members in Honduras killed her father and her boyfriend, how they threatened her and her brother José, and how José fell to his death from the Mexican freight train known as the beast. He then said to the congregation, "If you had to choose between the constant danger of gang violence or the danger of fleeing as an undocumented alien to come to the United States, I have to believe you would decide that the best of your bad options would be to come to the United States. Yes. Entering the United States as an undocumented migrant is illegal. But stealing bread is also illegal. And I ask you. How many of you would punish a man who steals bread because he has no money to feed his hungry family? I think we would forgive such a man and try to help him improve his desperate lot in life."

Many in the congregation now had tears in their eyes.

Pastor Gilming continued, "Why, then, would we not forgive Teresa here, who also faced desperation – and danger as well? I spoke to Frank Turner, the missionary in Mexico who led Teresa to a saving knowledge of Jesus Christ – a missionary who receives financial support from this church. He testified that Teresa and her brother Pepe are good people. And it was our missionary who told me the story of their desperate plight. And even now, Pepe, Teresa's innocent six-year-old brother, is imprisoned in a cage with other migrant children."

With tears in Pastor Gilming's eyes now, he concluded, "If the church was willing to baptize the apostle Paul, despite his hateful crimes against Christians, then I feel compelled to baptize Teresa, my sister, today. And my conviction is such that, if we, as a church, are unwilling to stretch out our arms to embrace, welcome, and protect my sister, Teresa, then I'm afraid I will have to resign as your pastor."

Another deacon stood and said, "Pastor, we're with you. Please baptize Teresa now."

When she saw how everybody in the church stood and applauded, Teresa's tears of shame became tears of joy.

A woman accompanied Teresa to a dressing room where she changed into a baptismal garment, and Pastor Gilming invited her to descend into the baptistery.

Matthew moved closer to take photographs, and Pastor Gilming repeated to the congregation much of what Matthew explained to Teresa about baptism. Then he asked her, "Teresa, have you accepted Jesus Christ as your Lord and Savior?"

Still with a tear-stained face, Teresa replied with a bright smile, "Si señor."

He then instructed Teresa to cover her nose and mouth. He raised his right hand over his head and said, "I now baptize you, my sister, in the name of the Father, Son, and Holy Spirit." When he lowered her into the water, he said, "Buried in the likeness of Jesus' death." And when he brought her back out of the water, he said. "Raised in the likeness of His resurrection to walk in newness of life."

The baptismal water washed away the tears from her tear-stained face, the church rejoiced with wholehearted applause, and Teresa was moved to tears of joy. Martha and Peter also had tears in their eyes, as did Matthew and almost everybody else in the Church.

Right after the service ended, and while Teresa got dressed, Pastor Gilming came up to Matthew and said, "Do you have a minute? I want to talk to you."

"Sure."

They stepped to the side, and Pastor Gilming spoke in a low voice in an effort to be discreet. "First, please forgive me for my earlier comments about Teresa."

Matthew replied, "No problem. Thank you for baptizing her. I hope you'll come to see what a wonderful woman she is."

"You can count on that. As you heard me say, I called Frank Turner, the missionary in Apizaco, Mexico. He only had good things to say about Teresa. He explained how she came to trust Christ as her Savior, and he also concurred with the conviction that I should baptize her."

"I'm so happy to hear that. I expect Teresa will continue to come to church with me. Do you think that is possible without jeopardizing her safety?"

"Well, I can't guarantee anything, but I'll have a good talk with today's angry deacon. After today's events, I don't think anybody else in this church would dare to betray her."

~.~

Matthew and Teresa arrived at Peter and Martha's home, and Teresa exclaimed, "Wow! What a beautiful home you have!"

After thanking Teresa for her compliment, Martha embraced Teresa and said, "I would not have blamed you for walking out of our church today, and I'm so glad you stayed. I hope it's clear to you that the church as a whole welcomes you to be a part of our congregation."

Teresa replied, "Not only was I tempted to leave because of the shame I experienced, but also for fear that somebody would report me to ICE. I'm still worried about the man who walked out of the church."

Matthew replied, "Pastor Gilming assured me he would talk to the deacon, and he's confident he can convince the deacon to welcome you as a member of our church."

"I hope the pastor will be successful."

In the living room, Teresa saw Matthew's pictures hanging on the walls and sitting on tables. Her smile reached her eyes, and she said to Martha, "Please tell me about these pictures of Matthew!"

Filled with pride, Martha told how Matthew played in the forest when they lived in Canada, about his Boy Scout activities, fishing trips, and of course, his star performance with his school soccer teams from grade school through college.

Matthew's shyness prompted him to look away while his mom told Teresa about his life history. But Teresa couldn't hear enough about

Matthew. Then Martha said, "Well, if we're going to have dinner, I better get in the kitchen."

In response, Teresa said, "Oh! Let me help!"

"No. You don't have to do that. Why don't you sit here in the living room with Matthew?"

But Teresa insisted, "No. I wanna help."

"Okay. Come on."

When they went into the kitchen, Teresa exclaimed, "Oh my! I've never seen such a beautiful kitchen. It's so big! I think your kitchen is bigger than my mamá's whole house."

Martha tried to imagine how a whole house could be smaller than her kitchen and replied. "Thank you. Would you wanna mash the potatoes?"

"Sure."

After she finished with the potatoes, Teresa went over to stir the green beans on the stove. It impressed Martha to see how efficient Teresa was in the kitchen.

As Martha stirred some flour into the gravy she was making, she asked, "So, how do you feel about my son?"

Teresa sat at the kitchen table and stirred sugar into the iced tea. She spoke her response in Spanish into her phone. Then, after looking around to see if anybody else was listening, she played back the English version. "I'm not ready for Matthew to know this yet, but I'm starting to fall in love with him. Your son is such a wonderful man, and I can see you're very proud of him. And I'm so proud to be with him. Not only did he rescue me, but he makes me feel so special. How could I not fall in love with such a man? Please don't tell him I told you these things. Maybe you could pray that God would show us what He wants for us."

A tear came to Martha's eye, and she walked over to Teresa and drew her close. Teresa put her arms around Martha's waist. Martha prayed, "Dear God. I thank you for bringing Teresa into Matthew's life. I know she has faced many challenges in her life, and I pray Matthew will be good for her. I'm also happy to see how Matthew brightens up when Teresa is with him. And I pray You will show us what their future will be together. Amen."

Teresa looked up at Martha, and both women now had tears in their eyes. This was their bonding moment.

Martha dried her eyes and said, "Well, I guess we better get this dinner served. I'm sure Peter and Matthew must be getting hungry by now."

They sat down to dinner, and Peter said, "Matthew, why don't you say the prayer?"

They all bowed their heads, and Matthew prayed, "Dear God. Thank you for this food and your many blessings. I'm grateful to see Teresa join us, and I pray she will always feel welcome here. Amen."

Peter stood, everybody passed their plates to him, and he served them a portion of roast beef. Teresa poured iced tea into everybody's glasses.

As they passed the green beans, mashed potatoes, and gravy around, Peter asked, "Teresa, what did you think of our church service today?"

"Other than the argument that occurred before Pastor Gilming baptized me, I enjoyed the service. I only wish I could sing along with everybody else."

Martha buttered her bread and asked, "Did you understand anything the preacher said in his sermon?"

"Very little. But I did understand a few things."

Matthew put some gravy on his potatoes and asked, "How different is our service compared to the church you attended in Apizaco?"

"The services were much the same, but they didn't have a choir in Apizaco, except at Christmas. In Apizaco, everybody clapped with the music, they used tambourines, and the songs were more like Mexican ballads."

After dinner, Teresa helped Martha clear the table and watched while Martha put the dishes in the dishwasher. Surprised, she said, "I can't believe you have a dishwasher. I've never seen a dishwasher in a house before."

Martha, with a surprised look on her face, said, "I can't imagine my life without a dishwasher. I hate washing dishes. I can't remember the last time I washed and dried dishes."

"How wonderful! One day, I hope I will have a dishwasher."

After cleaning up the kitchen, Teresa joined Matthew in the living room to watch a movie, and Peter and Martha said they were going to take a nap.

Upstairs in their bedroom, Peter asked, "So, now that we've gotten to know Teresa a little better, what is your impression?"

Martha brightened up with a dimpled smile and exclaimed, "I love her; I think she's wonderful. And I know what you're going to ask, and my answer is yes. I'm all for the idea. After our nap, let's let them know Pepe can have a home with us."

An hour later, Peter and Martha came downstairs and watched the last part of the movie.

Peter then said, "I want to suggest an idea to you two. Martha and I have talked it over, and we've decided we are willing to be foster parents for Pepe."

With a very perplexed look on her face, Teresa wrinkled her brow and asked, "Matthew, what did they say?"

Matthew took her by the hands and said, "My mom and dad want Pepe to come and live here. Is that okay with you?"

Teresa screamed and started sobbing, which startled everybody. She ran to Martha, embraced her, and said, "Oh! I thank you. Gracias. God bless you. This is so wonderful. I don't know what to say!"

Peter said, "We haven't told you the rest of it yet. Teresa, we want you to live here too."

Teresa screamed again with even more emotion, turned to Matthew, hugged him, buried her face in his shoulder, and continued sobbing. Everybody sobbed with her now, and they all rejoiced.

Matthew said, "Well, it's only 3:30. How about if Teresa and I go to get her things so that she can spend her first night here?"

Peter replied, "Might as well."

By seven o'clock in the evening, Teresa had moved into her room.

Matthew and Teresa sat at a laptop computer and figured out which buses Teresa now had to take to get to her job. She was glad to see it was only necessary to transfer once to a different bus.

It was time for Matthew to return to his apartment. Teresa went with him to his car, and, before he got in, he kissed and embraced Teresa and said, "With all this great news, I hope I can say something else which we can celebrate."

Teresa looked at him with red eyes and her tear-stained face. "I don't know if I can handle anymore. This is just too good to be true."

"Well, I suppose I could tell you later that I've fallen in love with you."

Teresa started crying again with joy, wrapped her arms around Matthew, kissed him, and said, "Oh, I love you too. This is the best day of my whole life!"

Day in Court

Anxious to start the process to get Pepe out of his cage, Teresa felt like her work shift took forever. When she got back to her new home, Martha asked her, "How do we find out what we must do to become foster parents?"

Happy that Martha took the initiative, Teresa responded, "I couldn't wait to get home to give the attorney a call. I'll call him right away."

"No problem, I'll be in the kitchen when he needs to talk to me."

A secretary put Teresa through to Lorenzo Dominguez, and he asked, "Teresa, how are you?"

"I'm fine. I found a husband and wife who are interested in being foster parents for Pepe. Can we talk about that?"

"Of course. Tell me about the people who are interested."

"I'm dating Matthew Ward, the soccer player, and it's his parents who are willing to be foster parents."

"You're dating Matthew Ward! Well, you know you're gonna have to get me some soccer tickets."

"I'm sure that won't be a problem."

"Is one of his parents available to talk?"

"Yes. That would be Matthew's mother, Martha. Let me get her."

When Martha picked up the phone, Lorenzo introduced himself and said, "Teresa tells me you and your husband have offered to be foster parents for her brother, Pepe."

"That's correct."

"I'm sure Teresa is deeply grateful that you're willing to do this. Let me explain the process. You must obtain a license to operate a foster home. I'll schedule a social worker to visit your home to meet with you and your husband. What is his name?"

"Peter."

"Let me explain the qualifications to be foster parents. You must be citizens or legal residents of the United States. You must also demonstrate you have adequate financial resources. In addition, you must have a safe operating vehicle that is insured so that you can take the foster child to and from appointments. Oh. And you must have a working phone service. Do you have any questions?"

"I think we meet all of those qualifications. What will the license cost?"

"Nothing. I forgot to explain. As foster parents, you'll receive a monthly payment to feed Pepe, clothe him, and meet his material needs."

"Is that right? I didn't expect that."

There was a pause on the phone, and Lorenzo asked, "By the way, do you speak Spanish?"

"No. We don't. But Teresa tells me Pepe is speaking English pretty well. And Teresa is now living here with us, and she will be here when she's not working. Do you expect any complications?"

"I don't anticipate any. I'm sure you won't have any problems."

"How long does the licensing process take?"

"The normal licensing process takes between two and four months. Given Pepe's unfortunate situation, I think I can get it down to a couple of weeks."

"For a child stuck in a cage, that's still a long time."

"I do agree. I'll do whatever I can to speed up the process. Do you have any other questions?"

"Not at this time."

"You can get my phone number from Teresa. Please feel free to call me if you have any additional questions. I'll get back with you as soon as possible to set up the licensing appointment. By the way, you'll want to ensure Peter is also available for the licensing appointment. Let me talk to Teresa again."

When Teresa got back on the phone, Lorenzo said, "I think Pablo and Norma's trial is coming up soon. Have you identified somebody to be their power of attorney?"

"Yes. That will be Matthew Ward."

"Okay. I'm beginning to think there's something special going on between you and Matthew."

Teresa brightened up and replied, "Yes. We are in a promising relationship."

"I'm glad to hear that. Regarding the power of attorney, I'll need some information, and then I'll start the paperwork for the power of attorney right away."

"Let me go get Martha again." Teresa went into the kitchen, handed her phone to Martha, and Martha gave Lorenzo the information he needed for Matthew.

By the end of the week, Lorenzo set up the licensing appointment. He also called Matthew to explain how he would use the power of attorney.

Matthew asked, "When will we want to put the house on the market?"

"We won't want to do that until we get the court's decision regarding Pablo and Norma, Teresa's aunt and uncle. If, for some reason, the court should agree to let them stay in the United States, the need to sell their home will no longer be necessary."

~.~

Pablo and Norma appeared in court during the following week on Wednesday. The case was the Department of Homeland Security Versus Pablo and Norma Gomez. This first hearing, called the master calendar hearing, was called to order.

The immigration judge began recording the hearing and said, "We are here for a master calendar hearing for Mister Pablo Gomez and Missus Norma Gomez, today, Wednesday, March 8th, 2017, at the Los

Angeles Courthouse. My name is Judge Clyde Blankenship. Attorney Lorenzo Dominguez represents Mister and Missus Pablo Gomez. Attorney William Peterson represents the United States Government. Miss Maritza Lopez has been sworn in, and she will be the court clerk and interpreter."

Turning to Mr. and Mrs. Gomez, the judge asked them, "Which language do you speak best?"

Although they spoke English well, Pablo and Norma responded, "Spanish, your honor."

"What language did you first speak, growing up as a child?"

"Spanish."

The court clerk said in Spanish, "Please raise your right hands. Do you swear the testimony you are about to give is the truth, the whole truth, and nothing but the truth?"

With hands raised, both Pablo and Norma replied, "I do."

The judge asked, "What are your true names?"

"Pablo Gomez."

"Norma Sánchez de Gomez."

After verifying the reference number assigned to the written Notice to Appear, the judge asked, "Did you receive a copy of this notice?"

Both Pablo and Norma replied, "Yes, your honor."

The judge marked the Notice to Appear as exhibit 1 and explained, "You are appearing here today because you are accused of residing in the United States illegally. Do you understand?"

Both Pablo and Norma replied, "Yes, your honor."

The judge said, "I hereby inform you that all forms of relief available to you will be lost for a period of 10 years if either of you lies or fails to appear for any upcoming hearings, including adjustments of status, changes of status, cancellations of removal, voluntary departures, and registry."

Turning to the court clerk, the judge said, "Please ensure the written record shows that attorney Lorenzo Dominguez represents Mister and Missus Pablo Gomez."

The judge looked at Mr. and Mrs. Gomez and asked, "Do you understand the charges against you?"

Both replied, "I do, your honor."

"Do you admit or deny the charges?"

Attorney Dominguez said, "My clients do not deny the charges."

The judge asked, "Do your clients have anything to say or present in their defense?"

Attorney Dominguez said, "They do."

"Please proceed."

Attorney Dominguez stood and began, "Your honor, Mister and Missus Pablo Gomez have lived in Los Angeles for twenty years. They own the home they live in, and they have ten years remaining on their mortgage. I have submitted a document from the mortgage company, which shows they have never missed a payment. There are no records to show they have ever received any public assistance from any governmental entity. Mister Gomez has worked as a truck driver for many years. I have submitted statements from their neighbors, who testify that they hold the Gomez family in high esteem. Neither has any record of problems with the police, neither civil nor criminal. Other than the fact that they are undocumented immigrants, they are otherwise honest, hardworking, and honorable people. Your honor, with all due respect, my clients request you grant them relief from removal."

As Attorney Dominguez made his case in favor of Mr. and Mrs. Gomez, the judge propped his head on his hand, yawned, and looked at his watch frequently. It seemed the judge already decided the case and was not paying attention to what Attorney Dominguez said. It was as if Attorney Dominguez was arguing with a statue. When Attorney Dominguez finished making the case for relief from removal, Judge Clyde Blankenship cleared his throat, looked down at his desk, and declared without making eye contact, "Your request for relief from removal is denied, the charge against you is sustained, you will be deported."

Both Norma and Pablo jumped when the judge slammed his gavel on his desk. Norma burst into tears, and Pablo grabbed her to keep her from falling to the floor. Pablo's chin quivered, and tears were in his eyes as well.

After they walked away from the judge, Lorenzo said, "I'm so sorry. I must tell you, if it weren't for President Trump's crackdown on undocumented immigrants, the judge would probably have granted you relief. I think it was obvious to you, the judge made up his mind before the hearing began. I hope you understand I did my best for you."

An ICE agent took them back to their prison cells. Within the next two weeks, Pablo and Norma would be put on a plane and sent back to Honduras. They would not have a chance to see Teresa before their departure.

After Lorenzo gave Teresa this sad news, she hung up and called Matthew right away. Her nearly inaudible voice reflected resignation. Through her sobs, she said, "The judge decided against my aunt and uncle. The United States will soon deport them back to Honduras."

Matthew said, "I'm so sorry to hear that. Where will they go when they arrive in Honduras?"

"I'm not sure. I talked to my mamá earlier to let her know the probability was high that my aunt and uncle would be deported and may need my mamá's help. As soon as we hang up, I'm going to call her again."

In her phone conversation with her mother, Teresa explained that Norma and Pablo would be arriving soon in Honduras. She also said, "My boyfriend's parents have agreed to become foster parents for Pepe, and they've invited me to live with them as well. So, Pepe and I will be back together soon, and we'll be safe."

Susana, Teresa's mother, replied with a quivering voice, "I'm so glad to hear about you and Pepe. I've been so worried about you two. How are Norma and Pablo dealing with the judge's decision?"

"I must believe they are devastated. I'm not able to see them, and I don't think I'll be able to see them at all, not even at the airport when they leave the country."

"How cruel! Please keep me posted about Norma and Pablo."

In the meantime, Peter and Martha completed their licensing to be foster parents, and Attorney Lorenzo Dominguez accelerated the release of Pepe into their custody. Lorenzo took Peter and Martha to pick up Pepe. When they arrived and saw the many children crowded into the cage with Pepe, Martha covered her face with her hands and cried out, "Oh my God. I can't believe this is happening in the United States."

Lorenzo went in to get Pepe released. When he returned with Pepe, Peter and Martha got a better look at him. He was a dirty, unwashed child. Pepe looked at them with darting eyes, and his muscles stiffened, as if ready to flee. His only change of clothes was tattered. He smelled of urine. His gaunt and sickly appearance revealed that the food offered to him was inadequate.

Lorenzo stooped to Pepe's level and said, "This is Mister and Missus Peter Ward. They will take you now to see Teresa, your sister. You will be staying with Mister and Missus Ward, and Teresa will be there with you."

Even after he explained these things to him, Pepe clung to Lorenzo, and his heart-wrenching cries broke Peter and Martha's hearts.

Lorenzo said to him, "Don't worry. You are safe now, and you'll be seeing Teresa very soon."

When they got close to home, Martha called Teresa to let her know they would soon arrive. Teresa was standing at the door when they pulled up to the house.

Filled with excitement, Pepe jumped out of the car and ran into Teresa's arms. They sobbed together for some time.

There was a room with a bed for Pepe, but he didn't use his bed that night. Instead, he slept with Teresa, and, after the insecurity he endured during his captivity, his restorative sleep was both sound and sweet. While his caged confinement left him traumatized, he regained his former playfulness within days, and his frequent boyish grin stole the hearts of Peter and Martha.

Pablo and Norma Back in Honduras

Immigration Control and Enforcement (ICE) agents shackled Pablo and Norma's hands and feet, put them on a bus, and took them, with other migrants, to the Los Angeles International Airport. At the airport, ICE agents escorted them to a plane, which would take them to the Toncontín International Airport in Tegucigalpa, Honduras. All migrants remained shackled, and they occupied every seat on the plane.

As the plane took off, Pablo and Norma experienced troubling and conflicting emotions. Norma leaned her head on Pablo's shoulder, and, with eyebrows arched upward and eyes that stared into the air, her voice quivered as she asked, "What will become of us?"

On the one hand, their red, tear-filled eyes and the downcast expressions on their faces reflected their desperation and their grief because they were leaving behind their home of twenty years and their many friends. They also worried about whether they might lose the investment in their home. And they were anxious, and uncertainty gripped them, not knowing what awaited them when they arrived in Honduras. Then there was the question of where they would live and how they would make a living. The threat of widespread gang violence, which was not so prevalent when they left Honduras, frightened them. They had no ability to contact family members in Honduras. The insecurity they felt was overwhelming.

On the other hand, there was also some curious anticipation about being in their native country again after their long absence. They had family and friends they had not seen in twenty years, and they experienced some nostalgic recollection of the life they left behind when they immigrated to the United States. Though they lived a life of poverty in Honduras, they always cherished some fond memories and missed their homeland during the time they lived in the United States – twenty years in which going home to Honduras was impossible without sacrificing the prosperity they achieved in the United States.

The plane touched down in Tegucigalpa. A charitable organization's volunteers escorted Pablo, Norma, and other returning undocumented immigrants to a processing area in the airport, where they completed some necessary paperwork.

Teresa called Susana the day before her aunt and uncle's departure. So, Susana took a taxi to the airport, and she was waiting for them now. Susana saw Pablo and Norma emerge from the processing area, and she shouted, "Norma!"

Surprised to hear her name called, Norma looked around until she spotted Susana, and she ran to embrace her. After not seeing each other for twenty years, the two sisters buried their heads in each other's shoulders as they wept. Pablo also brushed tears from his eyes as he rejoiced to see their happy reunion. Susana's presence alleviated their uncertainty, knowing now they were not abandoned to fend for themselves. The happy reunion between Norma and Susana was joyous and emotional.

With her arm around Norma, Susana said, "My tiny shack isn't much, but you're welcome to stay with me until you're ready to get your own place."

"Gracias, Susana. You have no idea how relieved we are to see you here."

They took a taxi to Susana's shack. Both Pablo and Norma were shocked to see the poor conditions in which Susana lived, bringing back their recollection of the poor conditions in which they once lived. But they were grateful to have a place to stay. After settling in, they helped Susana with the burritos which she made and sold in town. After their long absence, they once again had to get used to one meal a day, which was all they could afford.

Meanwhile, Matthew and Teresa worked on Pablo and Norma's home in Los Angeles to put it on the market. Within two weeks, they received an offer of $480,000 for the home.

When Pablo and Norma purchased the home twenty years ago, they paid $90,000 for a house that required a significant amount of work. They did most of the work themselves and turned it into a comfortable home.

After Matthew closed on the house, Teresa called Susana and asked to talk to Pablo. When he answered, Teresa said, "Uncle Pablo, I'm glad to tell you the house sold for $480,000. After paying off the $48,600 mortgage, the realtor's fee of $28,800, and other closing costs, your profit from the sale is a little over $400,000."

Norma and Susana watched as tears came to Pablo's eyes. With her eyebrows arched upward, Norma put her hands on her cheeks and asked, "Is it bad news?"

Teresa heard Pablo's quivering voice as he replied, "No! We'll receive $400,000 from the sale of the house."

Norma exclaimed, "¡*Gracias a Dios!*" (Thank God)

After coordinating with Pablo, Matthew wired the proceeds from the home's sale to him.

Pablo and Norma purchased a comfortable home in one of the better neighborhoods of Tegucigalpa. Pablo also invested in a truck, which set him up in business to haul freight.

During a telephone conversation with Teresa, Susana told her about Pablo and Norma's new home and said, "The home has maid's quarters, and they have invited me to come live with them. The maid's quarters are larger than my shack, and I even have a bed to sleep on instead of a hammock. The street is paved. There's no garbage in the streets. The neighborhood is quiet. And there is not much gang activity here. The only bad thing is that I still have trouble sleeping on a bed."

With tears of joy, Teresa replied, "I'm so happy for you, Mamá."

Pablo's business soon became successful, and Susana and Norma continued making and selling burritos.

Disneyland

Soon after Pepe settled in with Matthew's parents, Matthew showed up one day with a soccer ball and said, "Pepe, why don't you and I kick this ball around for a while."

That started a close relationship, which would grow stronger with time. Pepe was showing some talent for soccer. Watching them play was a source of contentment and joy for Teresa. Matthew and Pepe were bonding, and both enjoyed the time they spent together.

Matthew ensured Teresa and Pepe had seats at the soccer stadium for all home games. They also traveled with Matthew to some of the away games when the games didn't interfere with work or school.

Teresa and Pepe's English skills showed marked improvement. Matthew was also learning some Spanish. Their need for the translation application on their phones decreased and only required occasional use.

Matthew and Teresa took Pepe to church every Sunday, and Pepe was making some good friends there. One day, Matthew sat down with Pepe and asked, "Do you know what it means to accept Jesus Christ as your Savior?"

"In Sunday school, the teacher told us how Jesus died on the cross to save us from our sins. Is that what you're talking about?"

"It is. Did your Sunday school teacher also explain what sin is?"

"She said the reason why we sometimes do bad things is that we are sinners. And sinners can't go to Heaven if they don't get saved."

"That's true. Would you like to get saved?"

With a concerned look on his face, Pepe replied, "Yes. What do I have to do?"

"All you have to do is say a prayer in which you ask God to save you. I can help you say this prayer. Shall we do that now?"

Pepe looked up at Matthew and nodded his head.

Matthew put his arm around Pepe, instructed him to repeat his words, and they prayed together, "Dear God, my Sunday school teacher taught me that I am a sinner and that sinners can't go to Heaven if they don't get saved. I want to go to Heaven when I die, so I accept Jesus Christ as my Lord and Savior, and I promise to live a life that pleases You. Amen."

Matthew asked, "Did you mean what you said in this prayer?"

Pepe replied, "Yes."

"Good. That means you are now saved. You know, your sister got saved when you two were in Mexico. And not long ago, Teresa got baptized. So, that's the next thing you must do."

"My sister got baptized? When did that happen?"

"Pastor Gilming baptized her while you were still locked in the cage. How do you feel about getting baptized?"

Pepe nodded his head and replied with raised eyebrows, "I'm a little scared."

"Well, I'll tell you. I was a little scared when I got baptized, and so was your sister. But sometimes we must do some things which scare us."

"I remember I was scared when Teresa made me go to school. But that's when I met my friend, Lucas."

"So, you found out you didn't need to be so scared, right?"

"Yeah!"

"If I go with you. Would that make it easier for you?"

"Sure."

"Good. I'll call Pastor Gilming and ask him to baptize you this Sunday. Okay?"

Still a little uneasy about the idea, Pepe replied with a shaky voice, "Okay."

On Sunday, Matthew went with Pepe to get him ready for his baptism. Teresa, Peter, and Martha watched with joy while Pastor Gilming confirmed that Pepe had professed his faith in Jesus Christ as his Savior and baptized him. Matthew took pictures of the baptism, which Teresa sent to Susana and her aunt and uncle. And she called her mother, eager to give her all the details about the baptism.

Whenever Matthew came over to see Teresa, Pepe ran to him and hugged him. And Matthew would pick him up and ask, "How are you doing, guy? How's school?"

Pepe was always eager to show him what he was up to, and Matthew was interested in listening to him.

Teresa and Martha's relationship grew closer with time, and one day, while preparing a salad for lunch, Martha commented, "Teresa, You, Pepe, and my son are starting to look like a family."

Teresa's cheerful smile reflected joyous contentment as she responded, "I'm so happy to see Matthew and Pepe play soccer and to see them spend so much time together. I've never seen Pepe so happy in my life."

Martha and Teresa sat down at the kitchen table for their lunch. "So, how're things going with you and Matthew?"

"I've never been so happy in my life as well."

~.~

The soccer season came to a close in May. Matthew, Teresa, and Pepe went out for pizza after the season's last game. Matthew took a sip of his Coke and asked, "Pepe, how do ya feel about going to Disneyland one of these days soon?"

Teresa brightened up and looked over at Pepe to hear what he would say. He asked, "What's Disneyland?"

Astonished, Matthew asked, "You don't know what Disneyland is?"

Pepe shrugged his shoulders, "No. What is it?"

"Well, it's a fun place. I guess there's no better way to know what Disneyland is than to go see it for yourself."

Teresa commented, "Pepe's seventh birthday is coming up soon. Why don't we go to Disneyland for his birthday."

"Sounds good to me."

Pepe's birthday was on June 15th. Martha, Matthew's mother, baked him a birthday cake, and they invited some of Pepe's friends over. Matthew, Martha, and Peter sang *Happy Birthday* in English, and Teresa sang *Las Mañanitas* in Spanish. They ate cake and ice cream and watched with gusto while Pepe tore the gift wrap paper off of the many gifts he received. Afterward, they gathered by the swimming pool and watched while Pepe and his friends attacked a piñata with sticks until it spilled its candy. Teresa, Matthew, and his parents laughed with joy while the children struggled to get as much candy as possible.

On Saturday, Matthew, Teresa, and Pepe went to Disneyland. When they walked into the park, the first thing they saw was Mickey Mouse and Minnie Mouse standing in front of a castle.

Pepe wrapped his arms around Matthew's waist and cried out, "I'm scared!"

Matthew replied, "There's nothing to be scared of. Let's watch and see what happens."

Pepe watched while other children rallied around Mickey Mouse and Minnie Mouse, and he saw how they all enjoyed a good time.

Still a little timid, Pepe asked Teresa, "Will you go with me?"

"Of course," and she took Pepe by the hand and went with him to meet Mickey Mouse and Minnie Mouse.

As they approached, Minnie Mouse kneeled to Pepe's level and said, "Hello. I'm Minnie Mouse. What's your name?"

"Pepe."

"I like that name. How old are you?"

"I'm seven. My birthday was on Thursday."

"Thursday! Well, happy birthday, Pepe," and she gave him a bag of candy.

They spent the day going on the rides, listening to music, watching parades of robots, and other fantasy things. They enjoyed Adventure Land, Fantasy Land, Main Street USA, Mickey's Toontown, among other amusements. Teresa took an abundance of pictures with her phone.

As they watched while Pepe rode on a flying elephant, Teresa saw how he was having such a good time, and she said to Matthew, "I thank you so much for bringing Pepe here today and for the time you spend with him. I see how he brightens up when he's with you. I'm so happy you are a part of his life."

Matthew put his arm around Teresa and replied, "Well, the fact is, I get a kick out of playing with Pepe. I like knowing that he likes being around me. I think he shows promise to be a good soccer player someday."

After piloting the flying elephant, and while Pepe rode a horse on the King Arthur Carousel, Matthew took Teresa to the side and said, "I have something I want to give you."

Not sure what to expect, she smiled and asked, "What might that be?"

Matthew got down on one knee in front of a small crowd of people and took a small box out of his pocket. Teresa and the small crowd now knew what was about to happen. The crowd got quiet and moved in closer. Teresa put her hands over her face as tears came to her eyes.

Matthew removed an engagement ring from the box and said, "Teresa, I'd be the happiest man in the world if you'd agree to be my wife."

Jumping with child-like joy now, she extended her left hand and exclaimed, "Oh, Si!"

While the crowd burst into applause, Matthew placed the ring on Teresa's very willing finger, stood, and gave her a passionate kiss. The enthusiasm of the crowd's applause increased in intensity, and people congratulated the newly engaged couple. Using Teresa's phone, a bystander took several photos that captured their embrace and showed off the ring on her finger. Matthew kneeled again to get a picture that showed him proposing to Teresa.

Pepe finished his ride, and, while they walked to Big Thunder Ranch, their last stop for the day, Teresa appeared to float on air with jubilation.

They enjoyed barbecued chicken for dinner and got home at around six o'clock in the evening. When they walked in the door, Martha said, "So, Pepe, tell me all about Disneyland."

"I love Disneyland. When we got there, Mickey Mouse and Minnie Mouse said hello to me, and Minnie Mouse gave me this bag of candy for my birthday. We went to Adventure Land, and we rode on a boat that took us to a house in a tree. There were some birds at the treehouse which sang songs. Then we went to Fantasy Land, and I rode on the back of a flying elephant, and we saw Pinocchio."

"So, what did you like the best?"

"I liked Pinocchio. He was funny."

"And then what?"

"We watched a parade, and I got to sit in a fire truck. We took a ride on a spaceship. And there was a boy who played the guitar and sang songs in Spanish. His name was Pepe, just like me!"

"Was there anything you didn't like?"

"Yeah. We left too soon. I wanted to stay longer."

"So, I guess you'd like to go back again someday."

Pepe nodded his head up and down with a wide grin on his face.

Pepe went off to play, and Matthew said, "Mom, there's something I need to tell you and Dad."

They went into the living room where Peter was reading. When he looked up from his book, Matthew extended Teresa's left hand and said, "Mom, Dad, I'm happy to announce that Teresa has agreed to become my wife."

Peter stood to shake hands with Matthew as he put his arm around Martha and said, "Congratulations."

Martha went over to Teresa, hugged her, and said, "Well, I must tell you. This is no surprise to us. We expected you two would soon be announcing your engagement. We're thrilled and so happy to see this day come."

Peter said, "Let me get a closer look at that ring."

Teresa's grin could not have been brighter as she showed off her ring.

Before the evening was over, Teresa called her mamá.

"Teresa! How are you, my daughter? And how is Pepe?"

"Pepe is fine. We took him to Disneyland to celebrate his birthday, and he enjoyed a marvelous time."

"How wonderful. Can I talk to him? I want to wish him a happy birthday."

"Sure, Mamá. But I have some exciting news to tell you. Matthew has proposed marriage to me."

"Oh, my daughter, I'm so happy for you. Congratulations. Have you set a date?"

"Not yet. We only got engaged a few hours ago, and we haven't made any plans yet. But I'll let you know as soon as possible."

Teresa could hear while Susana, with a happy voice, said to Pablo and Norma, "Teresa has gotten engaged!"

Teresa also heard as Pablo and Norma shouted, "Congratulations, Teresa!"

Teresa called Pepe to the phone to talk to his mother, and he told her all about his Disneyland adventure.

Susana longed to see her son. She wept as she listened to his words, and she said, "Happy birthday, my son. I love you."

"I love you too, Mamá."

After talking for a brief while, Susana said, "Well, I want you to be a good boy. Listen to your sister."

Pepe's eyes opened wide, and he started to cry. His lower lip protruded as he replied, "I will, Mamá."

"You're not in school right now, are you?"

"No. It's summer vacation."

"When school starts, I want to know you're studying hard. Do you hear me?"

"Yes, Mamá. I promise."

After Teresa's additional short conversation with Susana, she promised to send the pictures they took. Their conversation made Susana realize how much she missed her children, and she broke down and cried for some time.

The next morning at church, Peter spoke to Pastor Gilming to inform him that Matthew and Teresa were now engaged.

During the announcements, Pastor Gilming said, "It gives me great pleasure to announce that Matthew Ward has proposed to Teresa Amador, and she has agreed to become his wife."

The congregation applauded. And when it came time to greet one another, many crowded around Matthew and Teresa to congratulate them, and they insisted that Teresa show them the ring.

Teresa couldn't wait to get to work on Monday, and she showed off her ring to Andrés, Rosita, and everybody else to celebrate with her that she was now engaged. Everybody shared her excitement and congratulated her. Rosita hugged her as she said, "I'm so happy for you."

Cynthia Comes Home; Teresa Goes Home

It was Friday, and the semester at the University of California at Berkeley ended. After a one hour and fifteen-minute flight, Cynthia's plane landed at the Los Angeles International Airport. Martha, Cynthia's mother, arrived at the airport with Pepe to pick her up.

After retrieving her luggage, Cynthia walked out of the baggage claim area, and Martha approached her, hugged her, and said, "Hello. It's good to have you home."

Cynthia looked down, saw Pepe, and asked, "Who's he?"

Pepe, with a big grin on his face, said, "I'm Pepe!"

Without acknowledging his presence, Cynthia asked Martha, "What's he doing here?"

Watching to see how Cynthia responded, Martha replied, "He lives with us. We are his foster parents."

Pepe asked with boyish curiosity, "Did you like flying on the airplane?"

Cynthia looked down her nose at him but otherwise ignored him again and asked, "Why would you do such a thing?"

Embarrassed by Cynthia's coldness toward Pepe, Martha explained, "You'll recall when you were here before that Matthew introduced Teresa to us. Pepe is Teresa's brother. We rescued him from the cage the government sent him to when they arrested Teresa's aunt and uncle. Her aunt and uncle have now been deported back to Honduras. Teresa also lives with us, so that she and Pepe can be together. And Matthew and Teresa have now become engaged."

With a look of shock on her face, Cynthia asked, "Are you kidding me? So, you're letting a criminal live in our home?"

Pepe's lower lip stuck out, and he fought back tears as he said, "Teresa is my sister. She's not a criminal!"

Cynthia ignored him again.

Martha became angry and said, "I've had enough of your hateful attitude. You need to get over it now!"

As Martha drove them home, the silence in the car was hostile and severe. They arrived home at ten o'clock in the morning.

Cynthia grabbed her suitcase and, with a snooty attitude, went straight to her room.

With a frown on his face, Pepe asked, "Cynthia doesn't like me. Does she?"

Martha kneeled to his level and hugged him, "Don't worry. She'll get over it."

At noon, Martha called for Cynthia and Pepe to come downstairs for lunch. The cold silence continued with hostile tension. Pepe finished his lunch and went outside to play.

Martha commented, "I don't know what your problem is. Pepe is a great little kid, and we like having him here. You don't even know Teresa, and you have no idea about the hardship she has endured. Your dad and I are happy to have her here as well, and we're pleased she and Matthew have become engaged."

With disdain and a twisted scowl on her face, Cynthia replied, "Engaged. How is it possible that he would want to marry a Latin American woman? I gotta believe there are any number of white women who would love to be in a relationship with a soccer star."

"So, you're prejudiced against Latin American people. Are you also prejudiced against blacks?"

Cynthia cleaned her mouth and threw her napkin on the table. "The fact is, I'm just indifferent. Let them live in their world, and let me live in mine. I'm going back up to my room." And she stomped off.

While she was in her room, Cynthia called several of her friends and invited them over for a pool party. At the same time, Martha called Matthew and said, "I picked up Cynthia from the airport earlier this morning, and she was very rude to Pepe. I expect we will have to deal with a rather volatile situation now that Cynthia knows that Teresa and Pepe live with us. You may want to come to visit us this evening."

Martha's words caused Matthew some significant distress. He took a deep breath and paused before answering. "Thanks for letting me know. I'll come over after I finish my training day."

At 3:30 in the afternoon, Teresa returned from work and walked in the door. Martha was waiting for her. "You and I need to talk."

Cynthia heard when Teresa came through the front door, and it was evident to her that Teresa returned from work on the bus.

Teresa went with Martha into the kitchen, and Martha asked, "Can I make some tea for us?"

Teresa looked at Martha with a wary stare. "Yeah. I'd enjoy a cup of tea."

With a worried look on her face, Martha said, "Teresa, you know Cynthia is now home, and I'm afraid she is infuriated to find you and Pepe living here."

Though she knew Cynthia had arrived home, Teresa's eyebrows arched upward, and she felt vulnerable due to this sudden revelation about Cynthia's hostile attitude. Fear gripped her, and she shrugged her shoulders as she asked, "So, what's going to happen?"

"Matthew is coming over, and, when Peter gets home, I expect we're going to have some kind of a showdown."

Looking down at the floor, Teresa's eyes teared up, and she asked, "Are Pepe and I gonna have to leave?"

Martha put her teacup on the table. "I don't see that happening. Peter and I have a responsibility as foster parents for Pepe, which we must live up to, and I will not allow you and Pepe to be separated. I'm very disappointed in my daughter. For all I know, she may decide she doesn't want to stay here."

Even greater insecurity invaded Teresa's heart, and she said, "Oh my God! I don't want to see your family divided over me and Pepe!"

Teresa's comment touched Martha's heart, and she hugged Teresa. "Knowing you, I would expect you to worry about something like that. But let's not be too hasty now."

As they were talking, Cynthia came downstairs, and, when Teresa saw her, she said with the friendliest tone possible, "Welcome home, Cynthia."

Cynthia stuck her nose in the air, turned around, and went back upstairs.

Matthew and Peter now arrived, and dinner was almost ready. Teresa and Martha were finishing up in the kitchen, when Peter and Matthew walked in. Matthew kissed Teresa; Peter kissed Martha and asked, "Where's Cynthia?"

Martha replied, "She's been in her room, pretty much since she got here. I'm afraid we're going to have some trouble with her. She's been downright snooty about Teresa and Pepe living with us."

Peter pursed his lips as he contemplated Martha's words. "I recall she was very rude when she met Teresa at church before she went back to college. Do you have any idea what her problem is?"

"I think she's prejudiced against people of color."

Matthew was upset and worried. "I hope she doesn't do something stupid, which could put Teresa in jeopardy."

Peter said, "Well, let's see if we can have a quiet dinner, and we'll talk about this matter afterward."

Peter went upstairs and knocked on Cynthia's door. When she opened the door, Peter hugged her and said, "Welcome home. Come join us. Dinner is ready."

Cynthia raised one side of her upper lip and asked with a defiant tone in her voice, "Are those two people there?"

Peter struggled to subdue his anger and replied, "Of course. They're a part of our family. Now, are you coming or not?"

"I'll eat my dinner up here."

Peter's icy stare signaled erupting wrath. He nodded, his face now reflected both anger and dismay, and He responded with clenched teeth, "Fine. But you're gonna have to go get your food." And he turned around and went downstairs.

As Peter finished praying to give thanks for their food, Cynthia walked through the dining room with her attitude, went into the kitchen, got her food, went back upstairs, and slammed her door. The electrifying tenseness in the dining room robbed everybody at the table of an enjoyable meal of delicious food.

After dinner, Peter told Cynthia to come downstairs.

Cynthia scowled and said, "Hell no!"

Peter demanded, "You will come, or there will be consequences. Do you hear me?"

Cynthia pushed past Peter and stomped downstairs. Peter struggled to control his temper and made a deliberate effort to slow his pace while he walked downstairs into the living room. The fiery tenseness in the room made everybody shudder. Teresa fought back tears. Matthew's facial muscles tightened. Martha stared into the air. Peter clenched his jaw. Cynthia sat with her nose in the air. Pepe went to Teresa's side, and his face grew pale. This was not a happy family.

Peter spoke with a soft but stern voice, "Cynthia, your mother and I, as foster parents, have brought Pepe here to live with us. We saw it as our Christian duty to bring Teresa here also so that she and her brother could be together. What was, at first, a duty, is now a joy for us. Both Pepe and Teresa have won our hearts, we love them, and they are welcome here. I think you know, Matthew and Teresa have fallen in love, and they are now engaged to be married. Your mother and I rejoice to see them together because we see how happy they are. I want you to understand what I'm about to say. We love you. But Teresa and Pepe are welcome members of this family, and they aren't going anywhere. You have two options. One, embrace and love them as members of our family. Or two, you may leave. Because I repeat. They're not going anywhere."

This ultimatum brought tears to Cynthia's eyes, and, with disdain in her voice, she screamed, "So, they're more important to you than I am!"

"Not at all!" Peter pointed his finger at Cynthia and declared, "As members of our family, they are as important to us as you are. And you have the option to accept that or go elsewhere."

Abundant tears now flowed down Cynthia's face, and rage seized her as she ran upstairs and slammed her bedroom door.

After this confrontation, Teresa was distraught. Matthew walked her out to the pool, embraced her, and said, "I don't know what's going to happen now. I love you. And you heard my dad affirm that my parents love you too, and they see you and Pepe as members of our family. I'm determined we must not let Cynthia tear us apart as a family."

Teresa looked up at Matthew with adoring eyes and said, "I love you so much, Matthew."

Matthew returned to his apartment. Teresa endured a sleepless night. Despite Matthew's effort to assure her that she was a part of the family, she felt alone, and she felt like she was an intruder.

On Saturday, Teresa sat in the living room with Pepe. Pepe was watching Saturday morning cartoons. There was a knock at the door, and Cynthia walked by them as if they weren't there. She opened the door, and three of her lily-white friends came in and followed Cynthia to the pool.

As they lounged around the pool, one of the three women, Priscilla, asked, "The woman in the living room, is she a maid?"

Cynthia replied, "I wish! Her name is Teresa. The boy who is with her is her brother, and both are illegal aliens in our country. My parents care for the boy as a foster child, and they invited Teresa to live here, so that she and her brother could be together. The worst part is my brother, Matthew, has asked Teresa to marry him, and my parents are treating me like a second-class citizen!"

Cynthia's friend, Linda, rolled her eyes, tilted her head to the side, and commented with a tone of arrogance, "How horrible!"

Cynthia teared up and said, "I don't know what to do. I don't even feel welcome in my own home."

Deborah said, "Well. I know what I would do. I'd turn them in to ICE."

Cynthia responded as if a light came on in a dark room, "Yeah! Why didn't I think of that?"

All four women huddled together to discuss how to turn Teresa over to ICE.

Cynthia said, "I understand Teresa comes home from work on the bus. I could tell ICE to grab her when she gets off the bus. Then, problem solved!"

The next day, everybody went to church, except Cynthia. She searched the internet and found information about how to turn an undocumented alien in to ICE. She found it was very straightforward. All she had to do was contact the Department of Homeland Security at 1 866-DHS-2ICE.

On Monday, Cynthia watched while Teresa left for work. She went into the kitchen and made herself a cup of coffee. When her mom walked in, Cynthia asked, "Where did Teresa go this morning?"

Martha replied, "She goes to work as a waitress at the Restaurante El Potrillo."

"What time does she get home?"

"Between 3 and 3:30 in the afternoon."

"Is she always off on Sundays?"

"Yeah. They give her Sundays off so that she can go to church with us."

"Is that the only day off she has?"

Martha wondered why Teresa's schedule was so important to Cynthia and asked, "Why so many questions?"

With her back to Martha, Cynthia looked over her shoulder with a devious smile, feigned an air of curiosity, and replied, "Just asking."

While Martha was downstairs, Cynthia went to her room with a face contorted with rage and called the ICE number. When she got an answer, she told a ruthless lie. "We have a part-time maid who works for us. She comes on the bus and arrives here at about 3:30 in the afternoon. We suspect she is stealing from us, and I'm pretty sure she's an illegal alien. Can you check that out for me?"

The agent replied, "Sure." And he proceeded to get the additional information he needed.

On Wednesday, Teresa didn't show up after work. An hour passed, and Martha began to worry. She dialed Teresa's cellular phone. No answer. She called the restaurant and asked Andrés, "Did Teresa leave work on time?"

"Yeah. She should be home by now."

"But she isn't."

Andrés asked, "Did she say she had something to do before she came home?"

"No."

"Hmm. That doesn't sound good."

Martha hung up, texted Matthew, and asked him to call her.

When she received his call, Martha said, "I'm worried. Teresa has not come back from work yet. I called Andrés, and he confirmed she left work on time."

Matthew trembled when he heard this and said, "Let me make a phone call."

When Attorney Lorenzo Dominguez answered the phone, Matthew said with a quivering voice, "Something has happened to Teresa. Can you find out if ICE has her?"

"I'll look into it. I'm afraid it might take a couple of days. Let me know if she turns up."

Matthew called Martha back, and, when she answered, he asked, "Any signs of her?"

"No. Nothing."

"I called Attorney Lorenzo Dominguez. He tells me it will take a couple of days to find out if ICE has grabbed her. I'm leaving now, and I'll come to see you."

As he drove to his parent's home, he prayed, *Dear God. I pray that Teresa is all right. Please let her turn up soon. I love her so much. Don't let me lose her. Amen.*

Despite his faith in God, he couldn't help but fear the worst.

At dinner that evening, like a satisfied cat that just swallowed a mouse, Cynthia, with shifting eyes, asked, "So, where's Teresa? She should have been here a while ago."

It was so surprising for Cynthia to show any interest in Teresa that Matthew became suspicious. Staring at her, he responded, "I don't know, and I'm very worried about her."

Late Friday afternoon, Lorenzo called Matthew and said, "I've confirmed ICE does have Teresa. It does not look good for her. I expect she will be deported."

Dread gripped his heart, and Matthew's voice again quivered as he asked, "Do you have any other details?"

"Well, ICE is not supposed to disclose this, but it appears somebody tipped them off."

Matthew called his mom. "ICE has Teresa in custody. I'm afraid she'll be deported."

Martha cried out, "Oh God! No!"

"The attorney tells me somebody tipped ICE off."

Martha sat down. "Who would do such a thing?"

"Well, I hate to say this, but there's only one person I can think of."

Without his saying so, Martha knew right away that Matthew was referring to Cynthia.

Matthew asked, "Do you mind if I come over for dinner? I don't want to be alone right now."

"Please do come."

Martha saw that Cynthia was asleep on a chaise lounge near the pool. Her phone was on a table beside her, and Martha tiptoed over and picked up the phone. Looking through the list of recently dialed numbers, she saw a toll-free 866 number and re-dialed it. When an ICE agent answered, she hung up, having confirmed her daughter's betrayal.

She yelled with a stern voice, "Cynthia."

Cynthia stirred, stretched, and woke up.

Martha confronted her. "Matthew confirmed that ICE grabbed Teresa. And I re-dialed ICE's phone number on your phone. So, I know you betrayed her, and you betrayed your family. Do you have any idea what you've done?"

Cynthia stood and waved her hand in defiance with an angry glare. "Yeah! I got rid of a woman who committed the crime of entering our country as an illegal immigrant – a woman who was taking advantage of my brother and my parents so that she could evade capture."

Martha shuddered with anguish and anger and pointed her finger in Cynthia's face. "No! What you have done is to separate a Christian woman from her only remaining brother. Why would you do such a cruel thing? You have no idea the horror Teresa has experienced. Not only did Teresa flee extreme poverty in Honduras, but she also fled the atrocities of vicious gangs. These gangs killed her father and her boyfriend, and they threatened her and her brother, José. Her mother, a widow, made the agonizing decision to put her children, Teresa, José, and Pepe, on the infamous Mexican freight train, which travels up through Mexico. This train, known as the beast, helped them get to the United States."

Cynthia, shaken from this confrontation, replied, "I had no idea."

"Oh, but that's not all. When José fell off of that beast, which is a common occurrence, it cut him in two and killed him. Teresa and Pepe made it to the United States, where their aunt and uncle provided them refuge. ICE deported her aunt and uncle and put Pepe in a cage with other migrant kids. And to know Pepe is to recognize that ICE inflicted cruel and unusual punishment on a dear, innocent child. Matthew rescued Teresa from being captured, and he is, without doubt, the most wonderful person that Teresa has had in her tortured life. And, Teresa is the most wonderful person that Matthew has had in his life. And all that wasn't enough! Your shameful betrayal is yet another dagger in Teresa's back."

Martha threw the phone at Cynthia and walked away. Cynthia's heart raced with such a painful force that it scared her and filled her with nausea, not knowing what consequences she might face for her betrayal.

Martha got with Pepe and sat him down. "Pepe, I'm afraid the same people who took your aunt and uncle away now have your sister as well. I'm sorry to say you will not see her for a while."

Pepe began to cry, and Martha held him close to her.

Pepe asked through his sobs, "What's going to happen to me?"

"We'll do everything we can to keep you here with us, and I'm sure you'll be an important part of Matthew's life as well."

With wide-open eyes, and a tear-stained face, the corners of Pepe's mouth drooped to a deep frown. "But I want my sister back."

"I know you do, Pepe. I want her back too."

When Matthew arrived, Pepe came running to him. Matthew kneeled and hugged him, and Pepe cried out, "When will I see my sister again?"

Weeping as well with low wails, like a violin playing a sad song, Matthew looked at Pepe's frightened face and his sorrowful frown, which reflected deep despair, while tears dripped from his chin. Matthew hugged him again and said, "I'm sorry this happened, and I miss her as much as you do. I don't want you to worry. One way or another, I will bring Teresa back again. Okay?"

Matthew looked at him again. Pepe nodded his tear-stained face, with only the slightest ray of hope.

Matthew stayed the night, and he let Pepe sleep with him. Pepe clung to him all night long.

ICE would not let Matthew or anybody else see Teresa, and they sent her back to Honduras two weeks later.

Wedding in Honduras

Although Susana, Teresa's mamá, was sad to see her daughter deported from the United States, she and Teresa's Aunt Norma and her Uncle Pablo were overjoyed to see her again. Tears flowed without ceasing when Susana and Teresa embraced each other.

Having not seen her mamá for many months, Teresa noticed how much her mamá had aged over the short time since she and her brothers said goodbye, when they departed Honduras for the United States. Her mamá's wrinkled forehead and the lines around her eyes and mouth had deepened; her hair was much whiter than before. Tragedy and loneliness had not been kind to her mamá.

While Teresa was in the United States, she worried that she would never see her mother again. So, Teresa was happy to be with her again, but she was also devastated and filled with despair. Sitting alone in the veranda of her aunt and uncle's home, the questions in her mind, which tormented her, were, *Will I ever see Mathew again? What will happen to Pepe? And: Why, Oh God, must I face this new tragedy in my life? Why!?* Memories flooded her mind of the sweet love that she and Matthew shared. She shuddered to think his love was yet another loss she would have to endure. It seemed to her that, every time happiness appeared on the horizon, some demonic force always came a long to tear it away from her.

When the international press learned Teresa Amador was Matthew's fiancé, the headline was, *Professional soccer star, Matthew Ward, separated from his fiancé – an undocumented Honduran migrant, deported by ICE.* The news story appeared on all the U.S. networks, and Teresa sobbed when she saw the news story in Honduras.

~.~

Cynthia stood before her family as they expressed how ashamed they were that she would betray them. Peter, her father, asked her, "So, why should any of us forgive your betrayal of our family?"

Matthew scowled, "What kind of a sister are you? Are you such a hateful person? Is this who you are?"

With deep remorse, Cynthia broke down and recognized what a dastardly thing she did and responded, "You're right. I don't deserve your forgiveness. Matthew, I know my actions have devastated you and Pepe more than anybody. If I could undo what I did, believe me, I would. I'm so sorry."

Peter continued, "It is only because we understand that God teaches us to forgive you that we do find it in our hearts to grant forgiveness to you. I suggest you need to do your best to make necessary restitution."

From that point on, Cynthia treated Pepe as if he were her brother and came to love him. Strange enough, after the hateful prejudice she displayed, she became a peculiar replacement for Pepe's sister. However, she was an inadequate and unsatisfactory substitute, which was a relentless source of guilt for her.

Matthew spent much time with Pepe. And Pepe came to rely on Matthew as a crucial source of much-needed security. He took Pepe with him to the soccer field where he trained, and his teammates made Pepe an honorary member of the team. Matthew bought him a team uniform, which Pepe wore with pride.

They also went to Disneyland again. While they enjoyed a great time, Teresa's absence robbed them of the best of Disneyland's charm. They both yearned to have Teresa back in their lives again.

Matthew arranged for Teresa to get a cellular phone in Honduras, and they talked almost every day. After every conversation, Matthew found himself reliving many precious moments with Teresa, which were now only bittersweet memories. Devastated, he missed her uninhibited, child-like exuberance, and he longed to hold her in his arms again. With undeterred determination, he planned to travel to Honduras as soon as possible.

Anticipating that the United States might not permit Teresa's legal re-entry into the country, Matthew called his dad's brother in Vancouver, Canada – Matthew's Uncle Wilbur Ward.

When Wilbur answered, Matthew said, "You may have heard on the news that my fiancé, Teresa Amador, has been deported to Honduras. I'm determined to marry her and bring her back to the United States. Due to the fact she lived here as an undocumented migrant, her direct re-entry into the United States may not be possible."

"I did hear the news report. What do you propose to do?"

"That's why I'm calling. I'm hoping you can help me. Since I'm a Canadian citizen, it might be easier for me to bring Teresa to Canada. If that's an option, may I bring her to stay with you for a short period of time while I arrange for her to immigrate into the United States from Canada?"

Wilbur responded, "Sure. I don't see why not. If you can get her here, bring her. So yes, she can stay with us."

A couple of weeks later, after evaluating his options with greater care, Matthew called Teresa and told her with a voice that reflected unyielding determination, "I'm coming to get you. I want to marry you there with your family present, and one way or another, you will leave with me."

With tears of joy, Teresa responded, "I love you, Matthew. A wedding here with my family present would be a dream come true for me. But what about your family?"

"I regret that my family will not be present, but the bigger regret for me would be to lose you. And I'm not going to let that happen. And, I will be overjoyed to see your dream come true. I figure we can have a wedding reception for my family and friends here after you return with me to the United States."

Matthew booked a reservation on Copa Airlines. He checked his baggage at the Los Angeles International Airport, and he carried both his Canadian and U.S. passports.

When airline personnel recognized who Matthew was, they alerted Copa airline personnel in Tegucigalpa that Matthew Ward, the soccer star, would be arriving at their location. One of the agents in Tegucigalpa leaked the news to the news media in Tegucigalpa, who made plans to be present when Matthew's flight arrived. Before his flight departed, Matthew called Teresa. "My flight arrives in Tegucigalpa today at three o'clock."

"We'll be at the airport when you arrive. May God give you a safe flight."

~.~

The flight crew informed the passengers that the tower at Toncontín International Airport cleared them for landing, and Matthew tightened his seatbelt. Surrounded by mountainous terrain, the Toncontín International Airport has the reputation of being one of the most dangerous airports in the world. The plane experienced some significant turbulence during its descent.

Because of the treacherous terrain around the airport, the pilot made the necessary sharp turn as the plane came in for a landing. This maneuver was flawed, and the pilot took evasive action to accelerate the plane and climbed to avoid a crash.

Matthew saw with horror how close the wing on his side of the plane came to striking the ground, which startled Matthew and caused panic among all the passengers. The plane circled the airport and made another attempt to land, which was successful this time.

The Toncontín International Airport only has four gates, and only two of the gates have boarding bridges, which were both occupied when Matthew's flight landed. So, airport personnel moved a stairway up to the airplane and required passengers to exit the airplane onto the tarmac and walk to the terminal. Matthew arrived in the hottest month of the year, and, not having ever been in Central America, he was not accustomed to the stifling temperatures and the near-100 percent humidity. When he stepped out of the plane, the high humidity made him cough, and sweat was quick to drench his clothing.

After processing through customs and retrieving his baggage, he emerged to find a crowd of people, including news reporters, who surrounded him, taking pictures and asking questions. Frenzied fans rushed him to get autographs. When he spotted Teresa, he finished an autograph, returned the pen and paper to the fan, and pushed his way through the crowd. The crowd opened up a path, and Teresa ran into his arms. Abundant tears of joy poured from Teresa's eyes, and during their passionate kiss, the crowd burst into applause, and the photographers fought each other to capture the kiss on film.

Teresa and Matthew were together again.

As they exited the airport, Matthew met for the first time Teresa's mother, Susana, her Aunt Norma, and her Uncle Pablo. Susana hugged Matthew and kissed him on both cheeks. Teresa's aunt and uncle said, "Welcome to Honduras."

A taxi took them to the Gomez home, and Pablo showed Matthew to his room. Since he was occupying Teresa's room, Susana shared her maid's quarters with Teresa.

Pablo was quick to thank Matthew for arranging the sale of their home in Los Angeles, and he said, "The money from the sale allowed us to buy this home, my truck, and made it possible for me to go into business. For the first time in our lives, we are debt-free."

Matthew replied, "I'm so happy to see you have been able to prosper here."

Teresa, Norma, and Susana began preparing dinner. The home had no air conditioning. Drenched in sweat, Matthew asked, "May I take a shower before we eat?"

Pablo replied, "Sure," and gave him a towel.

In the bathroom, Matthew discovered that both the shower and the sink had only one spigot – no hot water. The steamy weather combined with the shower's icy cold water was quite a shock for Matthew, who never took a cold shower before. He shivered through a very short shower, and never could plunge his whole body under the streaming cold water. Nevertheless, he felt much more comfortable for about fifteen minutes, until the heat and humidity overwhelmed him again.

As they ate dinner, Norma said, "We talked to Father Santiago, the priest at the church where Teresa used to go, and he will perform the marriage ceremony. You and Teresa need to go to the Dirección Ejecutiva de Ingresos tomorrow to get your marriage license."

Matthew asked, "What place is this where we get the marriage license?"

Pablo responded, "That would be the Executive Directorate of Revenues."

After dinner, they all watched the news on television, which reported in Spanish:

> *Señor Matthew Ward, a soccer star with the LA Galaxy team in Los Angeles, California, arrived at the Toncontín International Airport today to reunite with Señorita Teresa Amador, his fiancé. A couple of months ago, the United States deported Señorita Teresa, who lived in the country as an undocumented migrant. Crowds gathered around Señor Matthew seeking autographs, while Señorita Teresa made her way through the crowd to join the man she loves. The crowd cheered and applauded as Señor Matthew kissed and embraced Señorita Teresa, seen here, shedding tears of joy. When asked what his plans were, the news anchor translated Matthew's response into Spanish, "I'm here to marry my fiancé, Teresa, and take her back with me to Los Angeles."*

Of course, other than the mention of names and his own words, Matthew didn't understand anything, and he was surprised to see himself on television in Honduras.

Early in the morning, roosters throughout the neighborhood began their strident crows, another new experience that woke Matthew up much earlier than he cared for. Soon he heard the sounds of a radio broadcast, which he guessed was reporting the news. While listening to the Spanish broadcast, which he again didn't understand at all, he was surprised to hear his name. The newscaster reported that Matthew Ward, the soccer star, arrived in Tegucigalpa.

For breakfast, Norma prepared eggs, sausage, yuca, orange juice, and coffee.

Matthew kissed and hugged Teresa, and he sat down at the table with Teresa's family for breakfast. Pablo prayed in Spanish, "Dear God. I pray all will go well for the upcoming wedding and that Matthew and Teresa will be able to overcome any obstacles which might prevent them from returning to the United States together. May they know happiness in their marriage, and please bless them with children who will make them proud. Amen."

Teresa translated Pablo's prayer into English and gave Matthew his plate of food. When he saw the yuca, he asked, "What's this?"

Teresa smiled and explained, "It's yuca. It's a root vegetable. You'll find it's similar to a potato, but it's somewhat fibrous."

When he tasted his food, he commented, "I can't believe how much more tasty everything is. The eggs have more flavor. I've never tasted sausage like this before. It's much meatier than other sausages I've eaten. I like the yuca. But, best of all, is this coffee. It's stronger than I'm used to, but not bitter. I love it."

With a sense of pride, Teresa replied, "I'm glad you like everything. While there are many problems in Honduras, the food here tends to be more delicious because it's organically grown."

After breakfast, Matthew and Teresa caught a bus to make their way to the Dirección Ejecutiva de Ingresos so that they could get their marriage license. The morning temperatures were more comfortable and not so stifling. Matthew noted that city buses were all used school buses, imported from the United States, and Teresa explained that they were privately owned. The owners painted the picturesque buses' exteriors with unique color patterns, which, in most cases, incorporated red, white, and blue paint. It was customary for the emergency exit door at the back of the buses to portray a beautiful goddess of a woman, provocatively dressed in minimal clothing. Most of the buses had huge air horns mounted on top, which were in constant use.

The interior of the bus in which Matthew and Teresa rode displayed elaborate, tropical landscapes painted above the windows, separated by women's names, written in cursive scripts. Christmas lights strung throughout the bus's interior added a gaudy touch. The bus's sophisticated sound system blasted loud salsa, merengue, and mariachi music, which inspired the passengers to move to the beat of the music.

People occupied all the seats and stood in the bus's aisle. When Matthew and Teresa got on, it was all they could do to squeeze in. As people exited the bus, they had to dance around Matthew and Teresa and others. Matthew and Teresa soon were able to get seats, not together, but close enough so that they were able to converse.

Matthew asked, "Is every ride on a bus like going to a party here?"

Teresa's giggle was like a happy song. "Riding a bus here is much more fun than riding the boring buses in Los Angeles."

They got off the bus and ventured through the tumultuous, crowded streets. In addition to stores and restaurants, kiosks lined the sidewalks and sold a wide variety of products, services, and foods. Products and services included, among other items, watches, intimate clothing for women, cologne and perfume, electronics, cellular phones, lottery tickets, and barber services. The aroma from the food kiosks revealed the availability of grilled meats, caramel candies, coffee, and other delicious treats. Matthew decided he had to try the succulent grilled meat, which had a delicious smoky, spicy flavor.

The sidewalks, made narrow by the kiosks, were full of pedestrians, and Matthew felt somewhat intimidated as Teresa helped him squeeze through the crowd. Teresa warned him to beware of pickpockets. Matthew found he was like a magnet for all the beggars along the sidewalk, which saw this American as a potential wealthy donor. Vendors shouted out the products they sold, and their voices, amplified by megaphones, competed with the constant sounds of car horns and the many buses' air horns.

By the time they arrived at the Dirección Ejecutiva de Ingresos, the temperature climbed the thermometer, sweat formed wet patches on his shirt, and Matthew felt drops of sweat dripping down his back and chest. After they got their marriage license, they stopped at a restaurant for lunch. They sat at a table close to a fan, and Matthew felt some minor relief from the sweltering heat and humidity. He was the only American in the restaurant. Nervously looking around the restaurant, he was intimidated to find that he was also the only white guy – a minority of one. Having seen Teresa and Matthew, the soccer star, together on television during their embrace at the airport, many of the restaurant's patrons surrounded their table, struggling with outstretched arms, holding paper and pen, to get Mathew's autograph. After lunch, they repeated their expedition through the crowded streets. The party on another picturesque bus entertained them on their way home.

The day of the wedding arrived. Matthew put on a suit. Pablo took him to a local restaurant for breakfast, while Susana and Norma got Teresa ready for the wedding. Pablo and Matthew planned to arrive first at the church, followed by Susana, Norma, and Teresa. The wedding would occur at the same church in the *barrio* where Teresa used to live. The *barrio* was on the opposite side of the city from where Pablo and Norma lived, and Teresa had not visited the *barrio* since her deportation from the United States. She was anxious to see who from the *barrio* might attend her wedding. Among others, she hoped to see her friend, Leticia.

On the way to the restaurant, Pablo and Matthew snaked through heavy rush-hour traffic congestion. Matthew found the constant honking of horns to be an annoying torment, and he noted that traffic lights were almost nonexistent. He commented, "I've never seen such chaotic traffic before. How do you drive here?"

Pablo explained, "The secret is what we call aggressive accommodation. Driving in Honduras is nothing like driving in the United States, where the flow of traffic, for the most part, circulates in a very orderly fashion. Here, when you want to make a turn or cross an intersection, you must get a corner of your car in front of an approaching car on the adjacent street – that's the aggressive part. Once you get a corner in, the other driver must let you in – that's the accommodation part. Everyone understands this manner of driving, and no one can go very fast when driving in such traffic. Otherwise, aggressive accommodation would never work. You'd be surprised to know there are not so many car accidents, despite the way we drive."

After breakfast, Pablo and Matthew arrived at the church. Friends and family took their seats, along with several soccer fans and news reporters. Pablo accompanied Matthew to the church altar, where Father Santiago was waiting.

The organist played the wedding march. Teresa appeared in the doorway of the church wearing an elegant Spanish-style white wedding dress with a veil. She carried a bouquet of red flowers in her hands. The white dress and flowers enhanced the beauty of her cinnamon-colored skin and her long, silky black hair. Matthew was captivated by this enchanting, beautiful Latin American woman who would soon be his wife. Susana and Norma walked with her to the church's altar. When they arrived at the altar, Norma took the flowers from Teresa, and Susana and Norma sat down. Tears of joy flowed down their faces, which they dried with laced silk handkerchiefs.

Matthew took Teresa by the hands, and they faced each other. Her perfume was like air that one never tires of breathing in. Teresa looked up at Matthew with adoring eyes and a broad, happy smile.

Matthew looked at her with a nervous grin and said, "You look lovely, my love."

Teresa beamed with joy.

Father Santiago asked, "Who gives this woman to be married?"

Susana, Teresa's mother, stood with tears in her eyes and replied, "I do."

Father Santiago then asked Teresa to accept her wedding vows, and Teresa replied, "*Si. Acepto.*" (Yes. I accept.)

The only thing Matthew understood was Teresa's response when she said, "Si." The priest then asked Matthew to accept his wedding vows, which he didn't understand at all. But, when Father Santiago paused and looked at Matthew, he said, "Si. I do."

Father Santiago directed Matthew to put the wedding ring on Teresa's finger.

There was an uncomfortable silence, and Teresa looked at Matthew with a puzzled expression on her face. Pablo whispered to him in English, "You may now put the wedding ring on Teresa's finger." Which he did.

Father Santiago then announced that Matthew and Teresa were husband and wife, turned to Matthew, and said, "Señor Matthew, you may now kiss your bride."

Looking around, Matthew shrugged his shoulders. Teresa tilted her head with a playful smile and an expression of expectancy on her face. The people in the church broke out in subdued, subtle laughter.

Pablo again whispered in English, "You're now married, and you may kiss your bride." Which he did.

Matthew and Teresa turned to face the congregation. They all applauded, and Susana returned the flowers to Teresa. When they exited the church, Teresa turned and threw her bouquet of flowers over her head. When she turned back around, she was overjoyed to see that her friend, Leticia, caught it.

At the reception afterward, there was music and food, with much merriment. Many guests asked Matthew for his autograph. Matthew, who was bathed in sweat, removed his coat and tie. Teresa made arrangements with the church to change into her dance costume, which included the broad cobalt blue skirt, adorned with material gathered and sewn on the skirt, and accented by braided trimming in a zigzag pattern. It also included the embellished blouse, which matched the color of the skirt.

Matthew commented, "My. You look flamboyant."

The music played included a selection in which Teresa performed the jarabe yoreño colonial folkloric dance. Matthew had no idea how to do his part of the dance, which required him to try to get Teresa's attention and then act as if he gave up and lost interest. That didn't happen. Instead, he stood and watched his bride with surprised amazement. Teresa danced circles around Matthew with delight and flirted with him by spreading her full skirt, shaking it in a sensuous Latin way. And she rocked her shoulders from side to side, displayed a teasing, naughty smile, and looked at Matthew out of the corner of her eye.

Bewitched, Matthew watched with a smile that reached his eyes.

After the reception, Mr. and Mrs. Matthew Ward departed in a taxi to the Tegucigalpa Marriott Hotel, where they had reservations, and where they enjoyed the ecstasy of consummating their marriage.

~.~

On Monday, Matthew and Teresa went to the American embassy on *Avenida La Paz* (Peace Avenue). There, they met Roger, a consular officer, to inquire about getting an immigrant visa for Teresa.

An avid soccer fan, Roger recognized Matthew right away and said, "I'll do my best to help you." To confirm what he had heard on the news, he asked, "Where did you meet Teresa?"

"We met in Los Angeles."

Again, to confirm his understanding, Roger asked, "Teresa, were you in the United States with a legal visa?"

Afraid her answer might prevent her from getting an immigrant visa, she wiped tears from her eyes with a tissue and said with a deep frown on her face and a crying voice, "No."

"So, I understand you were deported. Is that true?"

Teresa now began to sob, and she nodded her head.

"Have you entered the United States without authorization more than once?"

With sobs that would not let her speak, Teresa shook her head, "No."

Turning to Matthew, Roger asked, "How do we know your marriage to Teresa is legitimate? What evidence exists to demonstrate that your marriage is more than just a means to help Teresa return to the United States as a legal resident?"

Matthew explained how he rescued Teresa when ICE took her brother, her aunt, and her uncle into custody, and he said, "Soon after that, we started dating, and we fell in love. ICE put her brother, Pepe, in a cage with other migrant children, and my parents agreed to become his foster parents. They brought him and Teresa into their home to live.

Teresa and I took her brother, Pepe, to Disneyland to celebrate his birthday, where I asked Teresa to marry me. A couple of months ago, as I think you know, ICE arrested and deported Teresa, and I came to Honduras to marry her. My parents and Teresa's family here can corroborate what I've told you. So, Teresa and I became engaged because we truly love each other, well before her deportation."

Roger explained, "Please understand I had to ask you these questions. You'll be happy to know, the first time a person enters the United States as an undocumented alien, it is deemed to be a misdemeanor, and therefore not a felony or a serious crime. So, Teresa is eligible to apply for an immigrant visa or green card as your wife. There's a five-step process to get a green card for family members. It is crucial to follow all the steps in this process to avoid any delays."

Teresa's face brightened as she heard this news.

Matthew leaned forward and asked, "Great. How do we proceed?"

"What documents did you bring with you?"

"We both have our passports, our marriage license, and our wedding certificate."

Roger directed them to complete a form I-130, *Petition for Alien Relative*, and he explained, "We must submit this application to the United States Citizen and Immigration Services. I must tell you. This application process can take several months."

Matthew and Teresa shook their heads with looks of despair and frustration on their faces. Matthew asked, "So, do I have to leave Honduras without my wife?"

"Maybe not. I'll also help you prepare another petition, which, if approved, will allow you to take Teresa to the United States while the form I-130 is being processed. We should be able to process this additional petition within a couple of weeks. In the meantime, Teresa needs to get a medical examination to confirm she has no infectious disease and no serious mental or physical disorder. Do you anticipate any such medical problems?"

Teresa replied, "No, señor."

Roger gave Teresa a list of required vaccinations and said, "You will also want to get a record of vaccinations, which confirms you have received the vaccinations on this list."

Matthew asked, "Do you anticipate any showstoppers?"

Roger replied, "In normal times, my answer would be no. But with today's political climate in the U.S., there are no certainties."

"I presume you'll contact us when you have pertinent news?"

"Of course."

"You know, Roger, I must tell you my family and I were born in Canada. We are Canadian citizens. And we faced no difficulties whatsoever to immigrate and become naturalized as U.S. citizens. I find it sad that Teresa, and others like her, must face so many obstacles to come to the United States."

"I must say and lament this has always been the case, and it is unfortunate. And it grieves me to say that it's even worse with the Trump administration."

After they left the embassy, they went to a nearby restaurant for lunch, and Teresa asked, "What do we do if our petition is denied?"

Matthew rubbed his chin and leaned forward. "Well, that will complicate things. However, I also brought my Canadian passport, and I coordinated with my Uncle Wilbur in Vancouver, British Columbia. So, my fall-back plan is to take you with me to Canada if necessary, and my uncle has agreed to provide you with a place to stay while I arrange to bring you into the United States from Canada."

Teresa tilted her head. "Will that work?"

Matthew shrugged his shoulders. "I have to confess, I don't know, and I hope we don't have to find out."

Both Matthew and Teresa felt uneasy due to the uncertainty of their situation. When the waitress brought the food, Matthew prayed, "Dear God. We thank you for this food you have blessed us with. You know how important it is for us to be together as husband and wife, and we pray that our efforts to get Teresa an immigrant visa will be successful. Please help us to honor you in all we do. Amen."

Over the next two weeks, Teresa took Matthew to many fascinating places. She said, "One of the first places I want to show you is the *barrio* where my family used to live. But we must go during the morning hours because that is the best time of day to avoid possible encounters with gang members. Gang members are not morning people."

Matthew was interested to see where Teresa used to live, but was nervous when she mentioned the threat of gang encounters. Teresa looked all around as the bus approached the *barrio*, hoping to see people and places that she remembered, but also to confirm that gang members were not present. Her family's shack was still there, now occupied by another family.

Shock prompted him to cover his mouth with his hand when Matthew saw the shack where Teresa used to live, and he asked, "So, you lived here with your parents and two brothers?"

"Yes. We did."

"Wow! I think this shack is smaller than my parent's bathroom!"

The stench of rotting garbage in the muddy street made Matthew wince his nose. He shook his head in disbelief when he saw the impoverished conditions in which the people in this *barrio* lived.

They stopped at a cafeteria in the area where Teresa's family used to sell their burritos and ordered coffee and tamales. While they ate, Teresa saw her friend, Leticia, and she called to her.

When she came over to the table, Teresa stood. With tears in their eyes, she and Leticia hugged each other.

Teresa said, "Leticia! I thank you for attending my wedding. I'm sorry we didn't have a chance to talk. How are you?"

"Yeah. I couldn't stay for the reception. I had to work. I'm fine. It's so good to see you again."

Teresa said to Matthew, "This is my best friend, Leticia. I haven't talked to her since before I migrated to the United States."

Matthew replied, "Hello, Leticia. Teresa has told me about your friendship. It's good to meet a friend who is so important to her."

Teresa translated Matthew's greeting for Leticia.

Leticia asked, "So, tell me about this man you married."

Teresa explained how Matthew rescued her when ICE captured Pepe and her aunt and uncle.

"Wow! What a story. I heard on the radio that Matthew is a soccer star."

Teresa swelled with pride. "That's right. You should have seen the crowd which gathered around him to get his autograph when his plane arrived in Tegucigalpa."

Leticia asked, "Will you be here long?"

Teresa replied, "We're doing the required paperwork so that I can return to the United States as a legal resident. I think you know I got deported not long ago. So, we're worried about whether or not the U.S. government will approve my resident visa."

"That sounds rather tenuous."

"Yeah. But that's what we're facing."

After they left the cafeteria, they picked some wildflowers on the way to the cemetery to visit her father's grave.

Teresa began to weep as she said to Matthew, "You'll remember I told you how gang members tortured and killed my father."

Matthew put his arm around Teresa while they visited the grave for about fifteen minutes.

They also made the risky decision to enter barrio 18 turf to visit Raúl's grave, Teresa's former boyfriend and dance partner.

Still waiting for the state department's approval, Teresa took Matthew to visit other points of interest in the area around Tegucigalpa, including the Parque Naciones Unidas El Picacho, where they enjoyed the park's walking trails and the 20-meter-high statue of Jesus Christ. They took a bus trip to visit the Mayan ruins of Copán. And they visited many of Tegucigalpa's better restaurants, including the Restaurante El Patio, where Matthew enjoyed their specialty, sausage and beef *pinchitos*, which included yuca fries. While there, they also enjoyed their featured live mariachi music.

Finally, Matthew received a call from Roger at the American embassy, and he said, "I'm happy to tell you your temporary petition to take Teresa to the United States is approved, while her immigration application is being processed. Can you come by today to pick up the paperwork you'll need, so that Teresa will be able to enter the United States legally?"

Matthew looked at Teresa, smiled, and mouthed the words, "We got the approval!"

Teresa jumped up and down, and tears of joy filled her eyes.

Matthew then said to Roger, "We're leaving for the embassy right now!"

After receiving the documentation Matthew and Teresa needed, Roger said, "Congratulations. So, all I need from you now is an autograph."

Back in the USA

At the Toncontín International Airport, Teresa said her emotional and tearful goodbyes to her mother and her aunt and uncle. Then she and Matthew boarded their flight back to Los Angeles, where Cynthia, Matthew's sister, waited alone for their arrival. When Matthew and Teresa emerged from the baggage claim area, Cynthia ran to Teresa with tears flowing down her cheeks.

Her impassioned embrace caused Teresa to drop her suitcase, and her eyes opened wide with surprise. She paused for a moment before she wrapped her arms around Cynthia, who cried out, "Teresa, forgive me for the hateful things I did to you. I'm so sorry. And I'm so happy to see you return as Matthew's wife."

Crying together now with Cynthia, Teresa tightened their embrace and responded, "It is my joy to forgive you. And I'm aware of, and I thank you for the close relationship that has developed between you and my brother, Pepe."

This tearful reunion also brought tears to Matthew's eyes. He put his arms around both Teresa and Cynthia and said, "I'm so happy to see that two of the most important women in my life are now friends."

From that point on, Teresa and Cynthia would be intimate friends.

When Teresa and Matthew arrived at his parent's home, the tearful reunion between Pepe and Teresa brought abundant tears to everybody's eyes.

Peter and Martha organized a wedding reception to occur at their church. Large numbers of church members attended, and Pastor Gilming officiated at a wedding ceremony where Matthew and Teresa repeated their wedding vows, which Matthew fully understood this time. Cynthia participated as a maid of honor, Pepe was the ring bearer, and Andrés, owner of the Resaurante El Potrillo, filled the role as best man.

After a couple of months, Teresa received her resident visa, and she applied for and received her Social Security card – a real one. She was now a legal resident of the United States.

Matthew and Teresa purchased a home. They took steps to adopt Pepe, and Teresa announced she was expecting a child. She gave birth to a daughter and named her Isabel. Teresa's life, which was once dominated by tears and tragedy, was now filled with tenderness and tranquility.

While Teresa had many sad memories of her life in Honduras, there were, nevertheless, many fond memories as well. As a legal resident, she could now leave and return to the United States as she desired. Matthew and Teresa traveled on occasion to Honduras, where they visited her mother, Susana, her Aunt Norma and Uncle Pablo, Leticia, and other family and friends.

After receiving her bachelor's degree, with a major in business administration and a minor in Spanish, Cynthia went to law school and became an immigration attorney. She helped obtain a visa to bring Susana, Teresa's mother, to the United States as a legal resident.

The time came for Matthew to end his soccer career, and he went into politics. Starting as a City Council member, he held several elected positions, which led to his election as a U.S. Senator. Legislation, which he introduced, provided legal residency for people, known as dreamers, who, as innocent children, came with family members to the United States illegally. Such dreamers had no say in the decision to become undocumented aliens. Before this legislation, dreamers lived in constant insecurity due to the threat of deportation.

Pepe, who arrived in the United States as a six-year-old boy, was one of the dreamers who benefited from Matthew's legislation, which allowed him to become a legal resident. He, Teresa, and Susana saw the day come when they celebrated their naturalization as U.S. citizens.

Pepe, Teresa, and their mother, Susana, opened a successful chain of fast-food restaurants called *Pepe's Pinchitos*, which featured Honduran cuisine. The most popular item on the menu was beef *pinchitos* with yuca fries.

After some years, Susana suffered a stroke, and, as she lay dying in the hospital, Teresa, Pepe, and Susana's grandchildren, along with Matthew, Cynthia, and their parents, gathered around Susana's bed. Teresa, with tears in her eyes, said to her mamá, "I'm so glad we could be together during these past few years. I love you, Mamá." As her mother slipped away, Teresa and everybody else, despite their sorrow, rejoiced to know that Susana was now reunited with Pedro, her husband, and José, her son.

Cynthia wrote a best-selling novel that told Teresa's tale, and the novel eventually became a movie.

www.ingramcontent.com/pod-product-compliance
Lightning Source LLC
Chambersburg PA
CBHW070922180626
46817CB00003B/1171